# SHERLOCK HOLMES AND THE SWEDISH ENIGMA

*The Sherlock Holmes Mysteries by Barry Grant*

THE STRANGE RETURN OF SHERLOCK HOLMES
SHERLOCK HOLMES AND THE SHAKESPEARE LETTER
SHERLOCK HOLMES AND THE SWEDISH ENIGMA

# SHERLOCK HOLMES AND THE SWEDISH ENIGMA

## Barry Grant

This first world edition published 2012
in Great Britain and in the USA by
SEVERN HOUSE PUBLISHERS LTD of
9–15 High Street, Sutton, Surrey, England, SM1 1DF.
Trade paperback edition first published
in Great Britain and the USA 2012 by
SEVERN HOUSE PUBLISHERS LTD.

British Library Cataloguing in Publication Data

Grant, Barry.
  Sherlock Holmes and the Swedish enigma.
  1. Holmes, Sherlock (Fictitious character) – Fiction.
  2. Wilson, James (Fictitious character) – Fiction.
  3. Cornwall (England: County) – Fiction. 4. Detective and
  mystery stories.
  I. Title
  823.9′2-dc23

ISBN-13:  978-0-7278-8128-1 (cased)
ISBN-13:  978-1-84751-411-0 (trade paper)

*All Severn House titles are printed on acid-free paper.*

Severn House Publishers support The Forest Stewardship Council [FSC],
the leading international forest certification organisation. All our titles that
are printed on Greenpeace-approved FSC-certified paper carry the FSC logo.

MIX
Paper from
responsible sources
FSC® C018575

Typeset by Palimpsest Book Production Ltd.,
Falkirk, Stirlingshire, Scotland.
Printed and bound in Great Britain by
MPG Books Ltd., Bodmin, Cornwall.

*For the Falköping Seven*

'I love my enemies, although not in a Christian sense: they amuse me, they quicken my pulses.'
Mihail Lermontov

# ONE
## Strange Visitor

We were just starting the fourth set when we were driven from the court by a passing thunderstorm. We kissed farewell in the downpour, ran for our cars, and I watched through rain-bleared windows as my fiancée drove away. By the time I returned to the flat that I shared with Sherlock Holmes, the torrential downpour had ceased and the sun was out.

'Well, Holmes,' I called, as I put my tennis racket in the hall closet, 'I lost again.'

His voice echoed from afar: 'What can you expect, my dear fellow, when you play with someone half your age?'

I stepped into the sitting room and saw the redheaded stranger.

'This gentleman has come to consult with me,' said Holmes.

I was delighted to hear it. Holmes had been refusing cases for months, and I was becoming a bit worried about him. I hoped this gentleman might have a problem that would suit Holmes's increasingly finicky tastes.

The redheaded stranger trembled uncontrollably as he shook my hand. 'I'm Bob Barrymore,' he said.

'James Wilson,' said I.

The man's eyes were very blue, glittering oddly. He was perhaps forty. Dishevelled. Brown sports jacket with elbow patches, corduroy trousers, running shoes. He had a Bluetooth receiver in his ear and he kept tapping it in the oddest way, as if he feared he was about to lose reception.

'If you cannot be frank with me, sir,' said Holmes, 'I'm afraid I cannot help you.'

The man walked to the fireplace, plucked his Irish flat cap off the back of our wingtip chair — surely an odd place to have hung it. He turned the cap round and round in his hands and said, 'I ask you bluntly, Mr Holmes: Will you help me?'

Holmes gazed at him intently. 'No, I don't believe I will.'

The man trembled violently, seemed about to explode. 'You will regret this day!' he shouted, then rushed by me and left our rooms in a seething cold rage. The door slammed behind him.

'Congratulations, Holmes!' said I. 'You may soon break the record for consecutive cases refused by a detective.'

Holmes laughed. 'He claimed his brother was murdered on the family estate by Bantry Bay, and asked me to go with him today to investigate. But I suspect there was no crime at all, for everything else he told me was a lie.'

'Lie once, lie twice,' said I. 'What sort of lies?'

'He said that he is Irish born and bred, that he flew in this morning from Limerick and arrived at our flat by taxi. He said that he trembles because he is suffering from Parkinson's disease, and that his name is Bob Barrymore. The truth is that he isn't Irish but cockney, came here not from Limerick but from somewhere no more than three miles distant, arrived not in a taxi but on a bicycle, suffers not from Parkinson's disease but from schizophrenia, and has a surname that begins with the letter "T", so it cannot be Barrymore.'

I slipped off my wet tennis shirt. 'You take my breath away, Holmes. But I suppose your deductions are, as usual, elementary – when properly understood.'

He flung himself into a chair. 'Yes, my dear Wilson – my flights of deductive virtuosity are impressive only at first glance – there is much less to them than meets the eye.'

'I wouldn't say *that*,' said I. 'But please . . . your train of thought?'

Holmes laughed. 'That he wasn't Irish was obvious because his accent was Cockney with only an Irish overlay, as you could hear yourself. That his trembling indicated schizophrenia, not Parkinson's disease, was clear because he held his hands twisted backwards, a side effect of medications for schizophrenia. That he came here not in a taxi but on a bicycle was obvious from his trouser legs, damp from splashing through puddles and wrinkled by the leg bands he had worn to keep his trousers out of the gears – not to mention that I saw a Velcro leg band dangling from his jacket pocket. That he came from no more than three miles distant was obvious since his sports coat was perfectly dry, yet the rain stopped only twelve minutes before he arrived at my door. So if we assume he could not have ridden faster than about fifteen miles an hour through London traffic, then . . .'

'All obvious, I admit,' said I. 'But the last name beginning with "T"?'

'I requested that he write his name in my client consultation book. He printed *Bob* very readily, but then wrote a capital "T" and, seeing his mistake, rounded the top of the "T" downward and turned it into a capital "B", after which he printed *Barrymore* carefully, as if fearing to misspell it. Conclusion? His Christian name is Bob, but his family name begins with "T".'

'Would you care for a beer?' I asked as I pulled on a dry shirt.

'Please, yes . . . but wait! Sir Launcelot has just announced the arrival of Detective Chief Inspector Lestrade.'

I looked at my devoted little mongrel, who was lying perfectly peacefully by the hearth. 'I didn't hear the dog say a word,' said I.

'Observe his nose is faintly twitching,' said Holmes. 'He does that only when Lestrade approaches.'

'I own the world's subtlest guard dog,' said I. 'He wiggles a nostril instead of barking.'

A moment later Lestrade wafted into the room like a quiet breeze. He gave Sir Launcelot a piece of chocolate. 'My heavens, Holmes,' said Lestrade. 'What business have you with Bob Tawp! I just met him on the stair.'

'Tawp, is it!' said Holmes.

'You know him, Lestrade?' said I.

'Too well. I recognized his red bicycle chained illegally to the railings on the far side of the square. Frankly, it occurred to me that he might be trying to work some scam on London's newest celebrity.'

'I hope I'm not a celebrity,' said Holmes.

'Hope what you like,' said Lestrade.

'Tawp seemed to be a very angry fellow,' said I.

'That is the least of his defects,' said Lestrade. 'He is a schizophrenic Cockney scam artist who lives in a cardboard box in an alley in South Kensington. Used to run guns for the IRA. A decade ago he came back to London and has been causing us problems ever since. Wish he had stayed in Limerick.'

'You phoned about two bizarre mysteries,' said Holmes.

'Now three,' said Lestrade.

'So much the better!' Holmes rubbed the palms of his hands together. 'I am hoping, Lestrade, that you will improve my mood by presenting me with a scuttle of crimes worth solving!'

I waved Lestrade towards a chair. 'May I get you an American martini?'

'Thank you, Wilson. You have converted me to that dreadful drink. And since I am off duty until six this evening . . .'

'I hope your burglaries are as bizarre as you promised,' said Holmes. 'I need a mental buzz – is that the modern term?'

'Good heavens, Holmes!' cried Lestrade. 'Will nothing satisfy you! You've tried cocaine. You've tried immersing yourself in murder and mayhem. Perhaps you should try grabbing hold of high tension wires – nothing seems enough for you.'

Holmes leapt up from his chair. 'You have developed a certain raffish – even outlandish – humour, Lestrade. It seems out of character!'

'It is the end of my career, old fellow, so I can afford to be a little outré. Frankly, I take you as my pattern and model of barely acceptable eccentricity. With lemon, Wilson, if you please.'

I mixed the martinis by the sideboard.

Lestrade, age sixty-four, slim and slight, reserved, his hair peppery with grey, sat with his usual calm and spoke in his always strangely reassuring voice. 'I believe, Holmes, you will find my offerings bizarre enough to suit even your exorbitant tastes.'

'I hope so.'

'The short of it is that we have had three thefts of Greek statues in five days. We assume the crimes are linked.'

Holmes seemed for a moment almost as agitated as Bob Tawp. He sat down again. He leaned forward, placed an index finger across his lips as if to hush himself, waiting eagerly for a fresh crime that might challenge him.

But now Lestrade deferred the anticipated moment. He reached into his leather case and said, 'Oh, by the way, I think I found what you wanted. I had no idea old Dr Watson had rescued so much stuff from your cottage in Sussex. We have a closet full of it at Scotland Yard.' He held up a small box. 'Is this it?'

'Exactly!' cried Holmes with delight. He took the box and opened it. 'A full ten!' he exclaimed. Then he drew out a metal and paper cartridge. It was about two inches long and a half-inch in diameter. He held it up. 'A Philpot Igniter,' said he.

'Never heard of such a thing!' said I.

Lestrade frowned.

'Made to my specifications in the year eighteen ninety-six by Professor Quigley Philpot-Smalls, who taught chemistry at the University of London.'

'But what is its purpose, Holmes?' asked Lestrade.

'The last time I used one was to distract a very corrupt MP. He ran out of his house when he saw fire break out on his carpet, and while he was gone I snatched from his desk a letter that put him into prison. Watson intended to chronicle that case, but he never did . . . and just as well.'

'Why *just as well*?' I asked.

'The case was not very instructive. I talked Watson out of doing it. He intended to call it *The Case of the Politician, the Lighthouse, and the Trained Cormorant*. Silly title.'

'Perhaps,' said Lestrade. 'But I've always wondered, where was the lighthouse?'

'Cornwall,' said Holmes, as he eagerly lifted another Philpot Igniter out of the box. 'Each igniter consists, as you can see, of a waxed cardboard bottom and metal top half. Pulling this pin out of the metal top releases chemicals inside. They mix, heat up, and cause the device to burst into flame. The number in red on each igniter indicates the time delay – "10" for a ten-second delay, "60" for a sixty-second delay . . . heavens, here's a "300" – five minutes! Didn't remember they went so high . . .'

'I wonder if they still work,' I said.

Lestrade examined one curiously. He seemed to have forgotten the purpose of his visit. I was in suspense, wondering if the mysteries he was about to present to Holmes would satisfy the great detective. Holmes had not had a case in weeks. And when Holmes is not on a case he is very hard to live with. He fidgets, falls into fits of gloom, holds conversations with himself, plays wild violin music far into the night, and occasionally fondles the desk drawer containing the cocaine syringe that Scotland Yard has authorized 'For Emergencies Only'.

In that memorable spring of 2010, Holmes should have had no trouble finding cases worthy of his mettle. But suddenly he had become strangely finicky about what cases he would accept. Everyone knew he was back in the game, and people were knocking on our door, demanding his services. *The Observer* had broken the news that it was Sherlock Holmes, not MI5, who had killed the Shakespeare-letter thief and ended his terrorist plot – a plot so bizarre that it had dominated headlines for weeks. In addition, bloggers had begun lighting up the Web with reports that it had been Sherlock Holmes, not detectives from Scotland Yard, who had solved the grisly Black Priest murder of sixteen months earlier – a case which was about to be published (I confess that I was the modest author) under the title *The Strange Return of Sherlock Holmes*. And now newspapers had begun publishing articles explaining how the renowned Dr Coleman, of St Bart's Hospital, had used advanced cell manipulation techniques to resuscitate Holmes after his ninety-year sleep in a Swiss glacier.

As a result of all this publicity, demand for Holmes's services ran high. Yet many a would-be client went away disappointed – and I simply could not deduce why. For more than a century Holmes had been able to find interesting features in even the simplest problems – so what had happened to him? For months he had been fretting that he had too little work to occupy his restless mind. Now people were flocking to his door, and still he seemed unable to find cases he regarded as sufficiently challenging. I remember the plumber from Eastcheap, for instance, whose toy poodle had left him a note (or so the deluded man said) warning him that his wife would be murdered – and an hour later the poor woman was found dead in her bathtub. Holmes refused the case. A day later a middle-aged lady from Lyme Regis turned up at our flat, sobbing, barely able to tell the tale of how her missing wedding ring had been discovered on the hand of a corpse in Pago Pago. Holmes – to my astonishment – recommended that she visit Scotland Yard. Most of all I remember the lovely young French woman I met one morning as she descended the staircase from our flat with two tears on her porcelain cheek. I guessed immediately what had happened. She told me the tale of how her fiancé, an Englishman, had taken her to visit Kew Gardens, had kissed her, had said 'I may be a while, ma chère,' then stepped behind a ginkgo biloba tree and vanished completely. She was desperate to find the young man, but Holmes had referred her to Scotland Yard. I tried to intervene with Holmes on her behalf – but *sans* success.

Holmes did eventually take on several cases that spring, though reluctantly. The case of the Transient Theatre Troupe, for instance, and the dilemma of Edgar Bacon. I pass over those two brief but brilliant bits of detective work in order to select, as more representative of Holmes's serious work in that early period in his new career, the curious adventure I have already begun to relate. It is a macabre and disturbing case. It began on that afternoon when a thunderstorm drove me from a tennis court. It is a tale that illustrates not only the quirky brilliance of Holmes's mind, but his deep concern for the least fortunate among us.

# TWO
## Three Missing Heads

'This past Saturday in Chelsea,' said Lestrade, 'a slightly larger-than-life-sized statue known as the Artemisium Aphrodite was stolen from the mews house of Richard Barrington, the well-known barrister. A neighbour discovered the crime. Barrington spends every weekend in the country and this neighbour feeds his macaw and his cat for him every Sunday morning. This past Sunday she found the bird decapitated and hanging upside down from its perch, dangling by its one chained leg. She couldn't find the bird's head. Then she noticed the Persian cat was gone. No sign of it. Only as she was leaving the house did she realize that the statue of Aphrodite was gone. She called the police. We interviewed the neighbours, one of whom, we learned, had seen an ambulance outside Barrington's house late the previous night. This elderly lady had noticed three people rolling someone towards the ambulance on a stretcher bed. She assumed Barrington had stayed in town this weekend and had taken ill. She said that one of the three medics struck her as odd, with arms too long and legs too short. His face also was odd, with a large jaw, narrow forehead, cheeks covered with black stubble, and rather large ears. She said he was a small, grotesque creature who reminded her of a distorted Leprechaun. She said she had seen the queer creature very plainly beneath the street lamp, but she was not able to describe the other two men, except to say that one of the others was a very big man. We think that the little fellow may be Wylie Blunt, a criminal well known to us. The last time we picked up Wylie he was carrying a knife with a blade a foot long. The ambulance was found abandoned on Blomfield Road. The Persian cat returned on Monday and was mewing at the door when Barrington arrived to appraise his loss. That is the essence of the matter.'

'I hardly think my talents are required to solve so commonplace a crime,' said Holmes.

Lestrade looked as if he'd been slapped.

I brought out the gin bottle again, and a glass, and I suppressed a sigh as I poured myself a drink.

The long-suffering Lestrade sipped his martini and ventured, 'I think you will find the second crime in my scuttle most pleasurably baffling, Holmes.'

Holmes slipped into that histrionic style that he so often employed to keep boredom at bay. He tossed his right hand in the air, 'Give me fuel for my creative fire, Lestrade – anthracite, Welsh boiler nuts or charcoal chunks! *Forsan et haec olim meminisse juvabit!*'

Lestrade had seen Holmes's fantastic behaviour too often to be much surprised by it. He calmly continued, 'Two days ago a Greek statue was stolen from the estate of Philip Corey, near Hemel Hempstead. His collection of ancient artefacts is displayed in a pavilion on his estate, and also in its surrounding gardens. The gardens and pavilion are some distance from the house and are surrounded by a formidable iron fence twelve feet high. The entry gate is locked at night. The centrepiece of Corey's collection is a head of Apollo, originally part of a now-headless marble statue in a museum in Athens. The Greeks say the head was stolen by Lord Anson in seventeen fifty-six and have repeatedly asked for it to be returned. But the Apollo has been in private hands in this country for two hundred and fifty years, so it is unlikely anyone will give it back to Greece. At any rate, Philip Corey commissioned a copy to be made of the headless statue in Athens, and on this copy he mounted his head – the original Greek-sculpted head. That head was stolen two days ago. The thieves expertly removed it from the replica torso. Philip Corey had gone to bed that night about midnight, so we believe the theft took place between midnight and six in the morning. The gardener arrived at six and noticed fifteen-foot ladders leaning on the fence, one inside, one outside.'

'Fairly ordinary burglary, then,' said Holmes.

'I wouldn't call it ordinary. A very large dead man was found lying in a sarcophagus near the decapitated statue.'

'Ah!' said Holmes, straightening up in his chair.

'Even more curious, the dead man was also decapitated,' said Lestrade.

'And the head!' cried Holmes. 'Did you find the man's head?'

I cringed a little at Holmes's seeming delight.

'We found no sign of the head.'

'No blood on the ladders?'

'No. They must have wrapped the head in something. No blood trail to anywhere. And one other curious point . . .'

'Yes?'

'The dead man was completely nude. No sign of his clothes.'

'Ah, it is all coming clear,' said Holmes, sighing.

'Clear?' said Lestrade.

'I presume,' said Holmes, 'that nothing was found in association with the corpse – no ring, no watch.'

'We were surprised to find nothing whatever.'

'I would have been surprised if you had.'

'Yet there was one thing,' said Lestrade. 'Clenched in his dead hand we found a nitroglycerine capsule.'

'Oh, that makes it altogether obvious,' said Holmes, wearily. The intense expression on his face had vanished. He stood up, put his hands into his pockets, wandered to the front windows and gazed out.

'It is not terribly obvious to me,' said Lestrade.

'Think back to Herodotus, *The Persian Wars*,' said Holmes.

'I'm afraid I've not read Herodotus.'

Holmes looked at him in surprise, quizzically, as if to discern if he were joking.

'A classical education is no longer *á la mode*,' said Lestrade.

'A pity.'

'Times change, Holmes, times change.'

'You would find the tale of Rhampsinitis most instructive.'

'I promise to look it up. Meanwhile . . .'

Holmes waved his arm through the air and cried, 'How strange, Lestrade! These things keep happening over and over, variations on a theme. That is the tedium of life, is it not? No wonder we weep with boredom and reach –' he pointed to Lestrade's martini glass – 'for drugs to keep us sane! Will nothing truly new ever happen to challenge us!'

'My heavens, Holmes!' said Lestrade, a bit of impatience in his tone. 'If you don't think these events are startling enough to suit your taste . . . well, then you are more easily bored than the rest of us mortals.'

'Any idea who is responsible?'

'A group of Greek extremists have recently been making demands for the return of the Elgin Marbles and other Greek artefacts held in this country. They call themselves – well, I can't say it in Greek, but the translation is *Athena's Revenge*.'

'Ah, yes, Αθηνα την εχδτχηση,' said Holmes.

'They have repeatedly promised to steal what we will not return,' said Lestrade. 'Maybe they have started their programme. Barrington's Artemesium Aphrodite is on their published list of works supposedly stolen from Greece. So is the Apollo.'

'Have you considered the possibility that a private collector may be responsible?'

'I suppose you mean Lars Lindblad, your old nemesis?'

'Possibly.'

'Lindblad taunts us with allusions to his Grotto of Art, which we suspect is located in either Sweden or Morocco. But I doubt he's involved in this caper, my dear Holmes. Lindblad, curiously enough, prefers to take a personal hand in his crimes – quite the opposite of the man who caused you and my grandfather so much angst, the notorious Doctor Moriarty.'

'Professor Moriarty. He had no degree,' said Holmes. He frowned, musing on something.

Lestrade paused and watched Holmes closely. 'Well, yes. Perhaps Lindblad bested us in that Shakespeare letter affair, since it is true he escaped . . .' Lestrade shrugged. 'But not to worry. It all turned out fairly well, didn't it?'

'Not particularly well, Lestrade.'

'The point is, Lindblad has money enough to last him several lifetimes. He is now sixty and continues his crimes merely for the pleasure of mocking the world, which means that if he were involved in this affair he would be here in England. But we happen to know he is in Turkey. He was interviewed live on radio yesterday in Istanbul. He even referred to you.'

'Me!' Holmes raised a brow.

'He seems to idolize you as the only opponent worthy of his steel.'

Holmes laughed. 'So he told me. The man is an enigma. I don't know what to make of him.'

'A strange and dangerous Swede,' said I.

'Yesterday in that radio interview,' said Lestrade, 'he modestly proclaimed that he had confidence, after forty years of watching the fumbling performance of European police, that the only detective who had even the slightest chance of catching him was one who had died in nineteen fourteen.'

'I must end his career one of these days,' mused Holmes.

Lestrade swirled his martini, took a sip. 'Many have tried.' He stood up, walked to the front windows. 'Recently we've been directing our efforts at finding the Falköping Seven, a notorious group of Swedes who make up his inner circle. But we've had no luck there, either.' Lestrade turned, held up his glass. 'The mere presence of Sherlock Holmes is supposed to be sufficient to part the mists of mystery. But I confess, old chap, you haven't been much help to me today.'

'Sorry, Lestrade. I will do my best to help. Your problem is far from solved, and I am far from solving it. But the first two segments of the problem appear under skies so clear that I fancy I can see almost to the end of the road, in each case, before taking a single step. Without mists to lend mystery to the landscape, life loses much of its charm.' Holmes sighed. 'I would pay money for a morning of fog.'

Lestrade walked to the fireplace and looked up curiously at the picture above the mantel. It was by Émile Jean-Horace Vernet, who lived from 1789 to 1864, and whom Holmes believed to be his great-uncle. It depicted fighters on a barricade in the streets of Paris during the revolution of 1848. 'It is unlikely,' Lestrade said to Holmes (without looking at him), 'that you'll be interested in the Cheddington burglary, for it does not include outré circumstances of any kind. No cormorants, no lighthouses, no decapitations. It is mere chance that the theft was discovered at all – so small a statue amidst the multitudinous objects in that huge house. And there was no sign of breaking and entering. Scarcely a whiff of a crime.'

'Small breezes announce great storms,' said I.

'Another Greek statue stolen?' asked Holmes.

'Cycladic statue – plus a small dog and two pieces of Black Forest gateau.'

'Aha!' cried Holmes in a voice so shrill it startled me. 'A promising start! May I have a beer, Wilson? I am trying to become sociable.'

I poured him one.

Lestrade had been examining the painting by Vernet with some care. He now turned away from the painting and looked blandly at Holmes. 'Perhaps you have heard the name Aloysius Branford?'

'I have not.'

'He is a Buckinghamshire historian and antiquary, locally famous. BBC did a piece on him last year. His house near Cheddington is stuffed to bursting with antiquarian items and *objets d'art* from all over the world. The statue that was taken yesterday is from the Cycladic Islands, early Spedos type, from the Keros-Syros culture, made about two thousand five hundred BC. Branford is of the opinion that if he had not given permission for a photograph of the statue to be published recently in an art magazine, it would not have been stolen. He said that hitherto it was a very well-kept secret.'

'What other details?' asked Holmes.

'At seven in the evening the Branfords went to their Wednesday night bridge party. They arrived back home at a little after midnight and were surprised when their dog did not emerge from the doggy door and greet them. They couldn't find the dog in his usual places, so decided he must be sleeping with their daughter, Cecelia, who was visiting. But the daughter's bedroom was empty – no sign of the dog. Branford then noticed, quite by chance, that the statue was missing. He called the local constabulary. Because of the apparent connection with the London theft, I sent Nigel Lyme to assist in the investigation. I went with him.'

'Has the daughter been found?'

'Daughter, statue, dog and cake are all still missing. But the daughter has a history of disappearing without telling anyone. We expect to locate her soon. She's thirty-some years old. A medium. Séances, that sort of thing.'

Holmes sprang to his feet, began to pace. 'After the two pieces of cake were taken, how many pieces were left?'

'I rather doubt that the cake has any bearing on the case,' said Lestrade.

'Then why did you mention it?'

'The wife demanded that we include the missing cake. Rancorous old woman, would not be quieted. So we wrote the cake into the report. Probably ate it herself and forgot.'

'I am surprised at you, Lestrade!' said Holmes.

'I am too,' said Lestrade, and he laughed, shook his head. 'Getting curmudgeonly in my old age.'

'There is certainly mist in this matter!' cried Holmes.

'You are interested?' asked Lestrade, a surprised note in his voice.

'Certainly the case has many curious features,' said Holmes.

'Excellent!' Lestrade darted towards the door, evidently not wishing to stay around and give Holmes the chance to change his mind. From the entry hallway he called, 'I'll send Nigel Lyme around with a car at six tomorrow morning, and you can drive out to Cheddington with him.'

Lestrade was gone.

Holmes sat for a long while, his long legs crossed, staring at the shadows of leaves flickering on the darkening windowpanes.

Sir Launcelot pushed Holmes's shoe (making his leg bounce slightly), then pursed his lips and made an *Oooo* sound that I have never heard another dog make.

'The dog talks,' said Holmes, jarred from his reverie. He handed him a biscuit. 'It strikes me that Sir Launcelot might prove useful at Cheddington tomorrow. Do you suppose he'd agree to go?'

'You'd have to ask him,' I said.


# THREE
## Branford House


In early morning light, Branford House looked dismal, decrepit, and in such a state of decay that I had the impression it might crumble at any moment. When we rang, the small, odd figure of Aloysius Branford appeared in the doorway. 'Mr Holmes, I presume?'

He led us inside to a room which had once been the main hall of the ancient farmhouse and which for hundreds of years must have been a splendid gathering place. But now it had been overwhelmed by the artefacts of Mr Branford's collection, including paintings by Hogarth, ancient maps, historical documents in frames, Chinese root carvings, a stuffed Kodiak bear, Zulu spears, Amazonian shrunken heads, Medieval armour, and dinosaur skulls. Even the gargantuan fireplace was filled with items from his collection, among them a stuffed flamingo and a bookcase filled with incunabula.

Branford planted himself squarely in front of all three of us. 'I thought I'd seen the last of you, Inspector Lyme.'

'So did I,' said Lyme, who was a tall young man of thirty-two, blond, lean, self-assured, with a rather guarded manner. He was not very likeable, but he was the sort of person one would like to have as a companion in a dangerous situation. He gave the impression that if you hit him with a poker he wouldn't even notice.

Branford whisked off his glasses and looked up at Holmes with bleary blue eyes, and with trembling hands he wiped his glasses with a tissue. 'I believe I have told the inspector all I know. But I am anxious to be of help.'

'Please be good enough to guide me through what happened the evening the statue went missing,' said Holmes. 'I beg you to omit no detail.'

'I've been warned you are thorough,' said Branford. 'Come, gentlemen. I will walk you through the evening of horrible discovery.'

He led us out the back door to a tall garage and slid open the garage door to reveal, gleaming in gloom, an antique Bentley convertible coupé. 'On Wednesday night we left the house of our card-playing friends in Leighton Buzzard and drove home in this Bentley – she's four point five litres but I don't drive her like James Bond. It was about half twelve when we rolled straight into the garage, which I had left open. I helped my wife into her wheelchair.'

Branford now closed the garage door.

'I pushed Rose – come along, gentlemen – down this garden path. Just at this place where we now stand I realized that Doolittle had not barked. I unlocked the back door of the house, as I am doing now, pushed Rose inside – come in, gentlemen – and still Doolittle did not greet us and was nowhere to be seen. I continued down this hallway alone – come along, and be careful not to stumble on the Chinese dragon. This is our daughter's old room. I thought the dog must be sleeping with her. But the door to the bedroom was open, just as it is now, and you can see that the bed has not been slept in.'

Holmes stepped into the bedroom. 'I don't see a suitcase,' said he.

'Cecelia keeps toiletries and clothes here at the house, for she visits every month. I decided she and Doolittle might have gone for a night walk across the fields. Cecelia is a very flighty and unpredictable girl, Mr Holmes, and likes to commune with stars and spirits. Also, she deals with dangerous men. Last year she got up from our lunch table and left for Brighton without saying a word. Had she not sent us a bawdy postcard from there we might never have known where she went. So I knew she might have gone anywhere. In which case it occurred to me that poor little Doolittle might be sleeping in his favourite eagle's nest.'

'Eagle's nest?' said Lyme. 'You mentioned no eagle's nest.'

'Come this way, gentlemen. Doolittle was so fond of the eagle's nest that finally I put a blanket in it for him. There it is, on the floor between those two Cretan pithoi – and it was as empty as it is now. Then I happened to look up at that high shelf and noticed that my Cycladic statue had vanished.'

'Was it in that empty space next to the marble Aphrodite?' asked Holmes.

'Precisely.'

'I am surprised they did not take the Aphrodite,' said Lyme.

'They were after Greek art only, apparently,' said Holmes.

Lyme laughed faintly between rigid lips. 'Aphrodite *is* Greek, Mr Holmes.'

'But the statue,' said Holmes, 'appears to be a Roman copy of a Greek original.'

'You are correct, Mr Holmes,' said Branford. 'It is a Roman copy of a much earlier Greek original, and it was carved in the first century AD. At all events, when I saw that Doolittle was not in his eagle's nest, and saw that the statue was gone, I became frightened and hurried back this way, into the living quarters – if you will just follow me, please . . .'

'Hello,' said Rose Branford, gazing up at us rather assertively from her wheelchair. The fingers of her thick hands drummed on the arms of the wheelchair. 'Mr Holmes, I presume?'

'At your service,' said Holmes.

'We are in such a mess,' she said, in a hoarse voice.

'We will try to set things right,' said Holmes. 'Never fear.'

She waved her arm to comprehend the whole vast room. 'When we were first married I had beautiful plants in this house, but now there is no room. We live among dead things.'

'Lead us to the kitchen, my dear,' said Branford.

'Dead things,' she repeated loudly. 'This is the House of the Dead.' Then she spun her chair with startling speed and thrust herself ahead. We followed her into a very large kitchen.

'Here,' said Aloysius Branford, pointing to the phone on the wall, 'I called Cecelia but she did not answer. She often leaves her phone off for fear it will interfere with spirit voices.'

'Spirit voices?' said Lyme.

'She is a medium, she speaks with the dead,' said Rose Branford.

'I should imagine she finds her conversations a trifle one-sided,' said Holmes.

'Pardon me?'

Holmes ignored her. He pointed to one of the figures in a large family photograph on the wall. 'I fancy that is Cecelia?'

'Yes,' said Rose, peering upward. 'That was taken ten years ago. She is the oldest, and next to her is Alice, then Kirk. Then Bertie, our baby. They are all one year apart in age.'

A little black dog sat in front of the family, head cocked. A patch of white around one eye made him look slightly comical.

'And that is Doolittle?' said Holmes.

'He was just a pup then,' said Branford.

'I have told the police that the gateau was missing, but they didn't seem terribly interested,' said Rose Branford, looking intently at Holmes. 'I feel the cake might be an important matter.'

'We have considered the matter of the gateau,' said Nigel Lyme, barely moving his lips.

'There might be DNA on the plate,' she said. 'There might be clues in the pantry.'

'I obtained the statue in nineteen seventy,' said Mr Branford. 'Last year I allowed a photograph of it to appear in an art publication, and I fear that was my mistake. Till then few knew of its existence in my house.'

'The boys adored the gateau,' she said. 'They sneaked to the gazebo to feed it to the dog. I warned them.'

'It would be difficult to sell that statue, now that it's known,' said Branford.

'Boys will be boys,' said Rose, 'but there are limits.'

Holmes gazed down at her with a cynical distance in his eyes. He took his unlit pipe out of his mouth and said, 'Where are the boys now?'

She shuddered, as if the thought were too much for her. She shook her head, she waved her hand dismissively. 'One dead, one gone. Gone with the flowers of my youth.'

'How long have they been gone?' asked Holmes.

'Bertie turned his brother in to the police, and my husband threw Bertie out of the house – and they were both gone in a gust of autumn wind, so to say. Ten years ago.'

'The gentlemen are trying to do their job, Rose!'

'Kirk was a criminal, there is no doubt. He stabbed cattle and stole a car, Mr Holmes.'

'We needn't go in to all this, Rose,' said her husband. 'He was a spirited youth. That is all there is to be said.'

Rose spun her chair and looked at him. 'A child who cuts off a cat's head is more than spirited!'

'We shouldn't be having this discussion now,' said her husband.

'Oh, you and your statues and dead things!' she cried. 'Look what they have wrought! We live in the House of the Dead!'

'How you talk! I don't understand you, Rose!'

'He hid the cat's head amidst this stuff, Mr Holmes –' she waved her hand – 'and he laughed when I shrieked, for it was I who found my pretty kitty's head—'

'Please, Rose!'

'It is easy to look at ancient truths,' she said.

'Please, Rose! Gentlemen, if you will come this . . .'

'Looking at today's truth is more difficult,' she cried.

'Why did he cut that cat's head off?' asked Holmes.

'A stage, Mr Holmes,' said Aloysius Branford. 'A childish stage.'

'He was sixteen,' said Rose.

'He said the cat was a demon,' said Mr Branford. 'I am sure he believed it. He was overwhelmed by thoughts of vampires and other horrific creatures, and all that sort of thing they show in films and on the telly. He believed in zombies and ghouls and whatnot. He was encouraged by his older sister, Cecelia, the two of them always talking about warding off evil – just a childish stage, really. Of that I am convinced.'

'And where is Kirk now?' asked Holmes.

'In jail in America,' said Mr Branford. 'He stabbed a man in a bar in Muscatine, Iowa.'

'He must be out by now,' said his wife.

Branford shrugged. 'Perhaps.'

'All we have now is the girls, Cecelia and Alice.'

'And what of Bertie?' asked Holmes.

'He turned his brother in to the police for stabbing cattle, and my husband ran him out of the house, Mr Holmes. Two years later we had word that Bertie had drowned in a ferry accident in Greece. He was only twenty.'

Holmes turned to Nigel Lyme. 'How do you think the thieves got into the house?'

'Evidently through the small window in the kitchen, which was unlocked. Only a very small person could get through that window, but Wylie Blunt is only a little bigger than a child. Here is his picture.' Lyme slipped a mug shot out of his pocket and showed us. Wylie Blunt was a very strange-looking creature, with big ears, narrow head, eyes close together. The witness's description of him as a 'distorted leprechaun' seemed rather apt.

'I put Kirk through that kitchen window when he was small, years ago,' said Mr Branford. 'We had locked ourselves out. That incident inspired me to hide an emergency key by the garden shed.'

'Is the emergency key still there?' asked Holmes.

'Yes, I checked,' said Lyme.

'I'd like to see the gazebo,' said Holmes.

Rose Branford whirled her chair round and opened the pantry door. 'Here is where the gateau and pies always sit. On that first plate you can see what's left of the Black Forest gateau in question, Mr Holmes. Would you care to examine it?'

'I don't think I would,' said Holmes.

# FOUR

## The Black Forest Track

Branford led us briskly through the garden, past the blue sheets blowing on the line, towards the old, vine-entwined gazebo. 'Haven't used it in years,' said he.

Rose Branford came rolling far behind us with desperate haste. 'Where is that girl! The sheets have been up for three days!'

Holmes darted ahead and warned us to stay back as he unlatched the door.

Nigel Lyme and I leaned into the open doorway. In the centre of a round room stood a round, white wicker table and two chairs. Sunlight streamed through the lattice on the far side, making a strange chessboard of light and shadow that seemed to slide over Sherlock Holmes's body as he crawled on hands and knees towards the table.

He held a magnifying glass in one hand. He looked back at us, face tense with anticipation. 'Please, gentlemen, do not come in!'

Even I, by the slant of light, could see faint footprints in the dust that Holmes was avoiding as he crawled. He closely examined the floor near each chair, inch by inch. He touched the tip of his index finger to his tongue, touched it to the floor, touched it to his tongue again. 'Ah!' he cried.

He rose slowly, like a man doing t'ai chi. In three bounds he darted out of the gazebo. He looked at Mr Branford and said, 'Bring me one of Doolittle's toys, please!'

'Toys?' said Branford. His thick lips hung open.

'I will try to get your dog back,' said Holmes.

'I'd rather have my statue back.'

'That may take a little longer,' said Holmes.

Branford stumped away towards the house.

Nigel Lyme gazed sceptically at Holmes and then slipped his hands into his pockets, as if he had decided to have nothing to do with the project in hand, whatever it was.

'I have formed a partial theory,' said Holmes. 'I would now be glad to hear the Scotland Yard theory.'

Lyme spoke with barely moving lips – it occurred to me he should have been a ventriloquist. 'Wylie Blunt was identified by a witness at the scene of the Chelsea burglary. It is likely he also participated in the theft at Hemel Hempstead, not only because the theft involved another Greek statue, but because we found blurred fingerprints on the ladders that seem to match his prints on file at Scotland Yard – yes, Mr Holmes, old-fashioned fingerprints! We travel every avenue to find the truth in these modern days. We simply have more avenues than were open to you in your day, which is why our results – I think most would agree – are generally better than what you could achieve in the old days.'

Holmes did not reply.

'It is my view,' said Lyme, 'that in all probability Blunt, a very short and slender man, slipped in through that window in the kitchen – narrow as it is – and let a confederate into the house through the front door. Together they located the statue, carried it out to a vehicle, and drove away with it. Simple as that. The circular drive is cement, so no tyre tracks were visible. No neighbours are near enough to have seen or heard anything.'

'And the missing dog?'

'The daughter took him with her someplace, undoubtedly. I expect, Mr Holmes, we will soon learn that they are both back in London.'

'I hope you are right!' said Mrs Branford. She put her hand to her mouth, as if in horror.

Holmes turned to me. 'You have always bragged, Wilson, about Sir Launcelot's tracking abilities. Shall we put him to the test?'

I walked to the car and soon returned with Sir Launcelot. His bent little brown ears were flopping as he trotted, his short tail swiping the air like a windscreen wiper.

'His eye is gone?' asked Aloysius Branford, as he handed me one of Doolittle's tugs.

'Someone flicked it out with a bullwhip,' I said. 'But he sees well enough.'

I gave Sir Launcelot a whiff of the other dog's tug, and said, 'Find!'

Sir Launcelot willingly danced off across the lawn, circling crazily round the gazebo. Then he began making passes across the open yard as if he were a fighter plane on strafing runs. On the third pass he gave a sharp yip, veered, and headed west along a path that passed through the trees and across the fields in the general direction of Cheddington.

'Come!' cried Holmes, striding away after the dog.

Lyme and I hurried after him.

'Good luck!' cried Rose Branford, waving a handkerchief from her wheelchair.

The spring fields were carpeted bright green with crops I couldn't yet recognize, and the land was flat around us, and in the distance rose the ridges of Buckinghamshire. We passed a black and white Shire horse in a white-fenced field; he looked as rare as a unicorn with his huge white feet and white-streaked mane and white-streaked tail. We passed somnolent sheep the colour of stones; they were scattered across a field that seemed to undulate with their *baaa*-ing. Lancy led us past a pasture where a Brahma bull stood motionless as a statue. Our course was generally along the edge of fields, but Sir Launcelot often veered into the fields, then came back, veered again, always trending westward along the hedge line. The footpath became a public bridleway. Sir Launcelot darted into the opening of a hedge and began to moan and yip, as if he were peculiarly interested in this place. I urged him out and he continued on.

We came to the Grand Union Canal and there Lancy turned right and led us about a hundred yards along the rough bank, no towpath. He stopped at the water's edge, sniffed the water nervously, backed up, circled, stopped again at the canal edge, barked at the water.

'The scent ends at the canal,' I said.

'Perhaps the dog we are following swam across,' suggested Lyme.

'Come!' said Holmes.

Holmes darted away to the south, and he came to a lock after a hundred yards, and he crossed over the canal on the lock gate. We followed.

Holmes seemed on the scent himself, his hawk nose high and his body almost trembling with anticipation as he darted away to the north along the towpath. He halted just opposite the place where the trail had ended on the other side of the canal. He called to Sir Launcelot, snapped his fingers at the ground. But Sir Launcelot could not pick up a scent. The earnest little dog sniffed the grass margin, walked in bewildered circles. We then continued walking north along the towpath. After about a hundred yards Sir Launcelot gave a yip and began sniffing the bank.

'On scent again!' cried Holmes.

Lancy trotted earnestly, ears bouncing, nose low, and we hurried to keep up. He led us along the towpath, past the pretty, white Seabrook Lock Cottage. We came to a bridge over the canal. We did not cross it, for here the dog turned left on to a little road that soon turned into a green bridleway closely hemmed in by shrubs. He stopped at a wide steel gate held closed by a loop of baler twine. Beyond was a road. As Sir Launcelot sniffed a heap of old baler twine by a fence post, I slipped the leash on him. I didn't want him to get hit in traffic. We opened the gate and walked out into the road and walked along it a little distance, then turned left into another road. Sir Launcelot now sniffed along a very straight scent trail, no veering right or left. He turned right on to a path that led us through a tunnel beneath the train tracks. Beyond the tunnel he turned left and sniffed along the edge of a green field.

'Dog seems headed for the train station,' said Nigel Lyme.

Lyme was right. The path veered left, rose up an embankment, and Sir Launcelot led us into the parking lot of the Cheddington train station.

Holmes walked to the ticket window and asked the agent, 'Were you on duty here yesterday morning?'

'From six till ten past ten in the morning, sir.' He pointed to the sign listing those hours of opening.

'I wonder,' said Holmes, 'if you recall a man who bought a ticket yesterday morning and was carrying a heavy package about two feet long wrapped in blue cloth.'

'No, sir, I don't.'

Nigel Lyme slipped the picture of Wylie Blunt out of his pocket and pushed it under the window cage. 'He might have looked like this.'

The ticket agent glanced at the picture. 'Never seen this gentleman before. Very distinctive, he is – I would have remembered.'

'But I suspect,' said Holmes, 'you may recall a chap of a very different sort – a blond young man about thirty-one, six foot two or three inches tall, blue eyes, with a small black dog on a leash, probably a leash made of twine.'

'Indeed, I do,' said the ticket agent. 'I thought it odd, the leash of twine. The gentleman looked a bit shabby. But he seemed a very decent chap, quite handsome features. He enquired about a ticket to Bodmin in Cornwall.'

'Bodmin!'

'I informed him of the fare, told him he must change stations in London. He would arrive at Euston and depart from Paddington. The young gentleman then enquired about bus schedules from Bodmin Parkway to Mortestow. I looked up the schedule for him on my computer.'

'He bought a ticket to Bodmin Parkway?'

'Only to Euston. And he paid with a fifty-pound note, which surprised me.'

'Why did it surprise you?'

'As I say, sir, he looked a bit shabby.'

'Did he take the dog on the train?'

'Yes, sir.'

'Was he carrying luggage?'

'I didn't notice.'

'No bundle?' asked Nigel Lyme, hopefully.

'I can't say, sir.'

We walked slowly through the parking lot and down to the road below and turned towards town.

'There used to be a pub not far away, just along the station road,' said Holmes. 'We should soon see it, if it still exists. It's called –' Holmes frowned – '*The Horse*, or . . .'

'When were you last here?' asked Lyme.

'Eighteen ninety,' said Holmes.

Lyme laughed. 'You have a good memory, Mr Holmes.'

'There it is,' said I. 'The Three Horseshoes.'

'I suggest, Inspector Lyme,' said Holmes, 'that we ask the local constable to meet us at The Three Horseshoes, and ferry us back to your car.'

Lyme's gangly strides had carried him a little ahead of us. His mobile flickered into his palm as he put in the call. He slipped the mobile back into his pocket. 'Well, Mr Holmes, it seems you bet on the right dog.'

It was only ten in the morning, the pub not open. We made ourselves comfortable at a table on the patio.

'I am curious,' said Lyme. 'What made you follow the dog?'

'Cake crumbs and dog prints in the dust of the gazebo,' said Holmes.

'It did seem unlikely,' said I, 'that a burglar would take time out from his task to investigate the pantry.'

'Unless the burglar happened to be a son whose memory of sweeter days led him there for old times' sake,' said Holmes.

'Where he found the famous Black Forest gateau,' said I.

'And the dog was glad to see him after ten years' absence, and the boy played out the rest of the memory, went to the gazebo with his dog, and they ate the Black Forest gateau together – I found a crumb or two on the gazebo floor, as well as dog prints and man prints. On the glass tabletop was the dust print of an object about two feet long. A bare statue would have touched the top only in certain places, but this object blurred the entire area, as it would if wrapped in cloth or paper.'

'And you surmised,' said I, 'that he had used one of the blue sheets from the clothes line . . .'

'Your powers of observation are becoming keener, Wilson! Kudos! I noticed a space on the line where a sheet would have fit between two others, and I saw that a clothes peg had fallen on the grass beneath.'

'And why would Kirk Branford steal his parents' dog?' asked Lyme.

'I suspect,' said Holmes, 'that Kirk tried to make Doolittle stay home, unsuccessfully. The dog kept following him.'

'So we were able to follow Doolittle,' said I.

'That seemed the easiest way,' said Holmes, 'since we had no object with Kirk's scent on it. The dog ranged far and wide through the fields all the way to the canal, where—'

'It swam across,' said Lyme.

'Evidently,' said Holmes, slowly. 'Perhaps Kirk wouldn't let it cross the lock, and the dog therefore followed him by running parallel to him on the far side. And then swam across, and caught up to him at the metal gate before the road.'

'Where you noticed the old baler twine in the weeds . . .'

'Yes,' said Holmes. 'A guess on my part. For from that point onward the dog did not range out from side to side as he had done before, but behaved as a dog must when leashed. Lancy pulled you straight along the roadway, and straight along the edge of the field to the station.'

'Will he dispose of the statue in London, Mr Holmes?' asked Lyme.

'It seems unlikely that he would take it to a remote town in Cornwall,' I said. 'I'm not even sure I know where Mortestow is.'

A strangely respectful tone crept into Inspector Lyme's voice as he said, 'Does it seem to you, Mr Holmes, that this case may be related to the burglaries in Chelsea and Hemel Hempstead? That has been Lestrade's theory.'

'I don't know,' said Holmes. 'The modus operandi is surely different.'

'No decapitations discovered so far,' said Lyme. 'But I worry about the girl. Where could she be?'

At that moment the local constable arrived and spirited us away to the House of the Dead.

By noon we were back in London.

I took leave of Holmes to spend a few hours at my club. That evening when I got back to our flat in Dorset Square, Holmes had news. He rose from his chair and brandished a computer printout in the air. 'The report on Kirk Branford has come through from Scotland Yard. It makes for very grim reading.'

'As bad as that?'

'He is a sadist, a thief, a psychotic and a brawler. As a child he stole sheep and cut off their ears, then turned them loose. He maimed cattle by sneaking up to them in fields at night and ramming a knife into their stomachs. When he was caught and sent for psychiatric examination he told the psychiatrists he was in league with the devil, who was his master. He next stole a car after beating its owner almost to death with a tyre iron. He spent time in prison for this at age twenty. He also cut off the ear of a man he brawled with in a pub in the United States. When he was released from prison for this last crime he vanished and he has not been heard of since. He is now thirty-two.'

'And just getting started in his career, evidently. Where will you begin searching for him?'

'London. I shall start by talking to the younger sister, Alice, and then will visit the flat of the missing girl, Cecelia. It may be Kirk has gone to one of them. And yet, he may have gone to Cornwall. A pity if I am making the wrong guess. If he went to Mortestow, taking with him the statue and the dog, the scent will be vanishing hour by hour . . . a bit of a dilemma.'

'Say no more, Holmes! The cavalry has arrived!'

'My good fellow!'

'Dear Rachel is out of town for the week, so there will be no more tennis for me for a while. And I have no obligations in London at the moment. I am free as air.'

'It would be a very great favour if you would go, Wilson – but, mind you, it will be dangerous.'

'You forget that I'm a karate expert,' I said. 'And very quick.'

'You forget that he's a knife expert, and very mad.'

'I haven't forgotten.'

'Stabbing creatures is his favourite sport, according to all reports. Just locate him, my dear Wilson. Do not approach him.'

'I shall use the utmost discretion.'

Holmes looked at me kindly, and gently reminded me that I was no longer young. 'I am not sure, dear fellow, that a brown belt in karate – earned forty years ago – qualifies you as an expert.'

'But it is a confidence builder,' said I. 'They used to call me the mongoose – that's my claim.' I glanced at my watch. 'I ought to be able to make Exeter by this evening. I'll drive the rest of the way in the morning.'

'Excellent! And tomorrow I will go see Alice Branford.'

I packed only essentials. When I returned to the sitting room with my kit I found Holmes leaning over the coffee table with a Collins road atlas open to plate six. His thin finger was tapping the map. 'Curious name – *Morte* is *death* en Francais, *stow* is *place* in Old English.'

'Farewell, Holmes. I'll be in touch.'

'Send me email reports, Wilson. We might as well be modern.'

'We can hardly help being so,' said I.

As I drove, the stars came twinkling out in grey dusk. It occurred to me that Kirk Branford must be in London. Why would he go to a remote coastal village in Cornwall? I think Holmes felt the same. Yet, Holmes being Holmes, no possibility could go unexplored, and the man *had* inquired about Mortestow. Anyway, it would be a journey. An amusement.

I reached Exeter about ten in the evening, found a pleasant inn, walked Lancy in spring mist, then left a request with the concierge that I should be awakened at six.

# FIVE

# The Admiral Hawke Inn

From: AfghanWilson@QuillNet.com
To: HellmeshCrooks@QuillNet.com

My Dear Holmes,
As I approached the North Cornwall coast the roads grew narrower and foggier, which made me feel as if I were entering some strange land unrelated to the rest of the world – perhaps the old Cornwall of legend, filled with pirates and mists and wreckers who made their living luring ships on to the rocks. Fog became so dense that I finally was forced to pull off the narrow and winding road and stop on a green open space that had appeared through a rent in the billowing damp. I switched off the engine. A few moments later a bus emerged out of grey mist and stopped, and the bus backed up on to the green grass and parked beside me. The door opened and an old woman stepped down, carrying a big bag. She hobbled off down the tiny road between hedges. She quickly vanished in mist. If a car came along that road she would, I thought, be in danger. The bus driver got out, walked towards the gate of a nearby field. There he leaned, staring into the fog at a small group of Shire horses who floated on the pasture like ghosts.

I got out and walked over to the driver and asked him where I was. He said this was the Mortestow bus stop. So I was in luck! He said he was the first bus of the day from Port Paul. I asked if he had recently carried a young blond man with a black dog to this stop. He stared like a zombie into the mist and replied, 'Yesterday afternoon.'

'Did he carry luggage?' I asked.

'No,' he said.

When I walked back to my car I noticed, attached to the tall post of the bus stop sign, a black ink drawing of a monster – a dragon with the head of a man. The monster clutched wicked knives in its four claws. A long black cape floated from its scaly back as it flew through the air on fantastic wings. I could not figure out what it was meant to advertise. I put Sir Launcelot on his leash and led him to the spot where the old woman had stepped off the bus, presuming that this must be close to the spot where Kirk Branford had stepped off the bus the previous day. No sooner had I given him a whiff of Doolittle's tug than Lancy lurched away across the green field, nose to the ground, tugging me. By and by a white building emerged from the mist. A signboard hung from a timber above the door: **Admiral Hawke Inn**. On a small white sign to the left of the door were printed the words *Dogs welcome!*

A wisp of fog crowded over my shoulder as I pressed through the doorway and into the gloom of a low-ceilinged room.

'Welcome aboard!' came a cheery voice.

'Good morning,' I replied, blinking.

Light gleamed from glasses hanging above the dark bar and from the brass of a cutlass mounted on a ceiling beam.

'Hello?' I said.

Stillness answered me.

Then I heard a sound . . . a shape stood up behind the bar, the shape of a young lad. 'Sorry, sir, didn't see you come in.'

'Pardon me? But you said *hello*.'

He laughed. 'That was the parrot.'

I felt in a hallucinatory state of mind, which I attributed to the strangeness of my journey – the narrow roads, the disorienting fog, the uncertainty as to exactly where I was, the isolation of the place, the sudden gloom of the inn.

'Welcome aboard!'

I looked about and finally saw the parrot.

'That's Ensign Squeers,' said the lad.

He was a huge and colourful parrot. He was standing on a perch to which one leg was shackled. Ensign Squeers gave me a sceptical eye, fluffled his wings, and cried, 'Attention on deck!'

'Is he in charge?' I asked.

'I am sir – I'm Jack Blankenship. Do you wish a room?'

'Perhaps. Yesterday, did a tall blond man of about thirty come in here with a little black dog?'

'I wasn't working yesterday,' said Jack, 'but my mother might know. She'll be back this evening.'

'Do you have any lodgers at the moment?'

'Billy is in room one. And I believe there may be someone in room three, but I'm not sure.' Jack bent down behind the bar, brought out a book. He was a handsome lad, maybe sixteen. A lock of brown hair fell lazily over his forehead above his blue eyes.

The shiny wooden bar had a base of stone, and all round gleamed bottles and glasses in stacks. Overhead a multitude of beer mugs hung from dark ceiling beams. On the wall to one side, by one of the fireplaces, a blackboard listed wines by the glass and various Cornish ales. Brass pots and pans hung in front of one fireplace. On the mantel of the other fireplace a flock of old metal teapots looked like ducks walking in a line. On one low ceiling beam hung an antique matchlock rifle, next to the cutlass.

Jack pointed to the two last names in the guest book. *Billy Baffin, Kyle Bartlett.* 'I haven't seen this person Bartlett,' said Jack. 'Ilsa left food by the door last night. Maybe he is ill.'

I walked outside. The fog had lifted a bit. The bus had vanished. Lancy tugged me towards a path through the hedge, then across the narrow tarmac lane where the old woman had vanished, and on to a footpath that meandered downhill through fields of sheep and cattle till it reached a small river running along the valley bottom. There the path veered left along the riverbank. Lancy was so full of enthusiasm that I was quite certain that Doolittle had passed this gloomy way. Huge trees, shadows almost black. A feeling of foreboding came upon me. For the first time it occurred to me I might not be entirely wise to be here alone following a sadist with a penchant for cutting heads off corpses, decapitating macaws, maiming livestock and stabbing people in bars. Scarcely had this cautionary thought fled through my mind than I glimpsed a ruined church off to my left amidst trees. Shrubs grew from its glassless arched windows, grass sprouted from the tops of its ruined and roofless walls. The whole crumbling hulk seemed about to collapse into the overgrown churchyard – a churchyard that once must have been beautiful but that now was a crazed helter-skelter of cockeyed gravestones being swallowed up by rampant weeds.

A wild and romantic picture it made, that church.

Ahead of me a white mill house appeared. A footbridge carried the path over the water. Sir Launcelot ignored the bridge and went straight to the mill house door, and suddenly there I stood. I had not quite decided what I was planning to do. So I knocked.

No answer.

All at once I seemed to have lost my appetite for this whole adventure – a fact I mention, my dear Holmes, merely to explain the atmosphere that seems to pervade this whole region. I can't think why *atmosphere* should have any bearing on the case. But you asked me to report all, and this is part of the 'all'. I have faced incoming rounds in Afghanistan and seen my share of bloodshed in recent years, not to mention that in my earlier days I served in Her Majesty's special forces with some distinction. I am familiar with feelings of fear. But I don't recall ever feeling the sort of *gloom of soul* that has come upon me from time to time today. I half imagined a monster of the sort drawn on that signpost would open the door. The most frightening thing about that monster on the post was its head, a man's head, thin-lipped and faintly fanged and evil-eyed. What could they have been advertising?

I was about to turn away when the door opened. A man appeared. 'Yes?'

That polite word revived me. Or perhaps it was just the effect of seeing a pleasing human face. This particular face wore an expression of pleasantly cautious surprise, curiosity. An Indian face. Fifty years old, perhaps. The man was slim, long arms, long hands. On the middle finger of his right hand he wore a stunning gold ring with a large ruby set in it. He wore neat but very worn clothes – grey slacks, a light-grey turtleneck sweater of waffle weave. Beneath the turtleneck was a bulge, as if he wore a neck brace.

He saw me looking at the huge ruby ring, and he held out his hand to show it, and said, 'I'd let you examine it, but I can't get it off any more. Too tight.'

'I am looking for a gentleman who I believe lost a watch,' I said. 'I met him at the Admiral Hawke Inn. He left the watch by his empty beer glass. He said he lived in this area –' I waved my hand vaguely at the surrounding woods. 'I have come to return it, if possible. He is a bit over six feet – about your height, a little more than half your age – blond hair, blue eyes. He had a black dog with him.'

'I may have seen him,' he said.

'Ah, then I am in luck!' I said.

'By all means come in . . . you must be exhausted!' he said. 'A long walk from Mortestow. I'll fix you a cup of tea.'

His invitation was so enthusiastic, so unexpected, that I almost accepted. 'Oh, I really must be getting on,' I said.

'Walking tour?' he asked.

'Exploring the coast path,' I said.

'What a fine adventure!' he replied. He had a knack for falling in with another person's mood. 'Have you come down from Minehead?' he asked.

'Oh, I'm just doing bits and pieces, not the whole Southwest Coast Path,' I said.

'You know why the path was built, don't you?'

'I'm not sure I do,' said I.

'Smugglers,' he said. 'In eighteen twenty-two His Majesty's Coastguard was formed to patrol the entire coast of Britain, and the path around Cornwall's coast was created so that foot patrols could peek into every cove and cranny.'

'Have you walked the coastal path?' I asked.

'Years ago.'

'Your accent sounds a bit Oxford,' I said.

'No, I'm from the other place,' he said. 'Sinjin Chitterlie.' He reached out his hand.

'James Wilson,' said I, and we shook.

'You aren't from the hospital, I think?'

'Hospital?'

'My apologies,' said he. 'You do not look like a doctor, after all.'

His hair was long, falling a little below his ears, mostly brown with streaks of grey. His nose and lips were thin, his eyes blue-grey.

'It is a strange area, this,' he said. 'Hawke's Moor behind and the cliffs ahead and the sea dancing madly in the distance like a dervish. A strange corner of the world, this.'

'Wrecker country,' I said.

'What terrible times those must have been, even for the wreckers themselves!' he said breathlessly. 'Don't you think? Watching ships smash up on the rocks and then waiting for sailors to drown so they could take their cargo and sell it to feed their starving families. A sickness that money could have cured. Money cures all ills, you know!'

He kept talking. I didn't quite understand all he said, but he said it all fluently, yet with little lacunae, as if a record needle had jumped and the river of his thought flowed smoothly on in another place, in what was essentially a monologue that was only occasionally diverted from its course by tiny questions I managed to insert. His style was warm. At first I found him amusing and intriguing. Later he began to strike me as odd. He said his mother was Irish, his father Sikh. The name Sinjin, he said, was a variation on St John, his mother's favourite saint. He said he subscribed to all religions nearly equally – name one, and he had studied it, he said – and he had been back to India many times. He was down here in Cornwall only for a brief holiday. There were several other cottages here at Kittle Mill, he said. Then he began to speak of drugs, how he had been an alcoholic for ten years. He said he was now a counsellor who helped others escape addictions of all kinds – sex, cocaine, booze – and his view was that some sensitive people, like Coleridge, should not be cured of their addictions, which made me think of you, my dear Holmes.

I kept waiting for him to return to the matter of the blond man with the black dog. He didn't. I felt as if a spell had frozen me to the spot. I wanted to get away, but couldn't. Then Lancy saw a butterfly, tugged at me, and broke the spell. 'Sir Launcelot is anxious,' said I with a laugh. 'I must be on my way.'

'I wish I had a Guinevere for him! Perhaps he might like a biscuit?'

'Don't want to make him fat,' said I, and I stepped off the porch. But I made one last try. 'The blond man with the black dog,' I said. 'You have any idea where I might find him?'

This question seemed to give him pause. I thought he might actually give me some information. 'I don't know where he went,' he said, finally.

'Thank you,' said I.

Sinjin Chitterlie stepped forward out of the doorway and stood at the edge of the stone porch. 'Farewell, sweet man!' he cried, and he gave a wave as I hurried away.

I had intended to go back the way I'd come but Sir Launcelot was determined to tug me towards the footbridge and over the water. He led me towards a white cottage peeking out of trees on the far side of the river. In for a penny, in for a pound, thinks I – and somewhat against my better judgement I approached the door. I heard voices inside. I knocked. No sound now but the cawing of a crow in a nearby tree. I walked quickly away from the cottage, glanced back. In the lower window I glimpsed the face of a black man.

Lancy tugged me along a two-track dirt road. I pulled out my ordnance survey map and it appeared to me that if I kept walking I must come to the Blytheland–Mortestow road. I had been surprised when Sinjin Chitterlie had mentioned a moor in the vicinity, for we were far from any of the large moors. But I now noticed, just east of Blytheland, a small patch labelled 'Hawke's Moor'.

At the road Sir Launcelot turned left, tugging hard. Kirk Branford had certainly done a lot of walking, but for what purpose? I leave the question to you, Holmes. You have admonished me to simply collect facts and leave the theorizing to you. This I am happy to do.

The high green hedges on either side of the narrow tarmac road were wild with bluebells and white flowers. I hurried. The narrow road was full of curves. I kept wondering whether I could flatten myself and dog against the hedge in time to keep from being hit if a car came upon us. After about a mile I passed by a grocery story containing a post office. Several cars were parked out front. I reached a scattering of old buildings around a green. One was the Blytheland Inn. A few paces later the wisp of a village was gone. I was beneath a massive canopy of trees on a narrow road betwixt two high stone walls. Lancy paused at a driveway marked by two large stone pillars. On one of the pillars PENLAVEN was inscribed in gold on a dark plaque. Beneath it, a small sign:

Bed and Breakfast
Self-catering Cottages.

We descended a broad black drive towards a sprawling medieval house. The drive forked. Sir Launcelot pulled me in the direction that the **SELF-CATERING** sign pointed, but I overruled him and went left towards the office. I entered a small courtyard, flagstones underfoot. Gardening tools. Various potted plants. A stone tank gurgled softly as water from a pipe ran into it continually. I pushed a button by a large door. The door yawned open and a slender woman about my age appeared. She smiled very widely. 'Yes, may I help?'

There was a nervousness about her, as one senses in a thorough-bred horse. A brittle edge of elegance. Or perhaps uncertainty.

'Do you have a room for tonight?' I asked.

'We rented our last single just yesterday,' she said. 'And I'm afraid we don't allow dogs.'

'Beautiful house,' I said, hoping to engage her in conversation and learn more. 'How old is it?'

'It is in the Domesday book.'

'Ten eighty-six? That *is* old.'

'Very.'

She was losing interest in me.

'May I look around?' I asked.

'Certainly,' she said. And she vanished into the house.

I walked around the perimeter of the building, across the huge lawn, and came finally to the self-catering wing of semi-detached cottages. Here the exterior walls were of ivory stucco, upon which thick-stemmed purple wisteria climbed everywhere. I thought I heard a dog yip. This, as you might imagine, gave me pause. I let Sir Launcelot off the leash to see what he might do. He ran to the door at the end of the wing. I heard again, distinctly, the bark of a small dog. I looked up and saw the face of a child in a window, and behind it the face of a woman. The shade came down.

We climbed the steep driveway and walked the gloomy road back to Blytheland.

I took lunch at the bar of the Blytheland Inn and afterward I walked out on to the road and started for Mortestow. A woman in a car slowed and asked if I would like a ride. I was glad of her hospitality. Soon Lancy and I were sliding along the narrow lane watching flowers flash by on either side. When this woman learned I was a tourist and had not yet walked on the cliff path, she advised I must do so instantly. She dropped us off at a spot near Flint Cove where a path led up to the cliffs, and she gave me directions. As I started upward she leaned out her window and called, 'You must be sure to see Swallow's Nest! The sign is small, so look closely.'

I had had quite enough walking to suit me, but when I reached the coastal path I was very glad I'd made this extra effort, for the view was spectacular. The gloom and mist of morning had vanished and the battering breeze of mid afternoon was brilliant with light.

Not a cloud in the sky. I was atop a coast of cliffs a hundred feet or more high that stretched as far as the eye could see, north and south. I edged through the lush grass until it turned into empty air, a sheer drop straight down to jagged black rocks and the swirling sea. To my left lay a little cove where waves swept in over the sand like long flat folds of white lace. Straight ahead I could see a black mound of rock surrounded by sea and laden with gulls that looked, from this height, like splats of their own droppings. The day had grown warmer, the breeze felt good. I walked north along the coast. To my right lay green fields sprinkled with white sheep and cattle, to my left the sea air sprinkled with white gulls. I climbed over a small rise and was surprised to see a stone cottage, much weathered. It stood very near the edge of the cliff. The roof looked new. The padlocked door was freshly painted green. I tried to peek in through the windows but the glare of the sun prevented me from seeing anything.

I now was on the lookout for the path which the woman had promised would take me away from the coast and down to the Admiral Hawke Inn. I like a good vigorous walk, but I'd had one, my dear Holmes, and I was ready for a bit of a sit-down. At last I saw a gap in the hedge, a wooden gate, and a sign announcing **Public Footpath**. I passed through the gate and had just started down the path when cold uneasiness ran up my spine. This had been happening all morning, as I have said. I looked back and saw – you may not credit this – a huge wolf-like creature streaking along the top of the cliffs. In an instant he was gone. It happened so quickly that fear did not leap into my veins until well after the event. But I was shaken, almost trembling, as I made my way down the path. At last I found myself on the green patch of land where buses stop and where my car was parked. I pulled my travelling bag out of the boot, walked towards the Admiral Hawke Inn, and as I reached the door, and pushed it open, I heard hearty laughter, and a loud voice.

'Innkeeper – more wine for me and my friends!'

The speaker sat at a round table in the far corner of the pub, beneath the porthole window. He was a heavy man. He wore a grey sweatshirt with SORBONNE written across the front, a blue navy cap, a red bandanna knotted loosely round his neck. His big fist was wrapped round his nearly empty wine glass. 'More wine!' he cried. His big left fist slammed the table.

'Welcome aboard! *Bawk bawk bawk!*' cried the parrot.

'Yes, sir!' said Jack Blankenship.

'Bring me the rest of the bottle, Jack, and put it on the tab!' cried the other. 'And bring a glass for this gentleman.' He waved a thick hand towards me. 'Sit down, sir! Sit down! You are welcome to Billy's ship!'

'Thank you,' I said.

'Bring your father to me, young Jack – I have news for him!' cried Billy.

'My father is not feeling well, sir,' said Jack.

I sat down at the table across from the big man. He reached into a leather packet that hung from a leather strap round his neck. He fumbled, and pulled out a thick wad of fifty-pound notes. He plunked them on the table. 'Take these to your father, Jack. And let me know when I've run through them!'

Jack gazed in astonishment at the clump of banknotes.

'Take them, my lad!' cried the other. 'I have come into money! I have owed your poor father and mother all these weeks, but now all is square.'

Jack took the money and walked slowly away, looking at it in amazement, as if he thought it might explode. Soon he came back with a bottle and my glass. He poured the two glasses full. 'Anything else, Billy?'

'Not at the moment, lad – but stay on deck!'

'My name's James Wilson,' I said. 'Thank you so much for the wine.'

'Billy Baffin,' said he, reaching his hand across the table – a thick, strong hand, nails ragged and two of them black, as if he'd hit them with a hammer.

'Have you been here long?' I asked.

'A snug berth it is, mate! Fine food, choice booze, and sea views from my crow's nest quarters!'

'And where was your berth before this?'

'The street and the sea,' said he.

I sipped my wine.

Billy tilted a glassful down his throat, then pulled a small book out of his leather wallet, majestically, and he held it up as a preacher might hold a bible. 'Tell me, James Wilson, have you ever had to beg on the street?'

'Fortunately not,' I said.

'You will never know what a snug berth means until you've begged on the street, lad!' said he.

'I can imagine,' said I.

'You know Jim Swallow, of course!' he cried.

'Never heard of the man,' said I.

'Ye gods!' cried Billy. 'He was a poet, and he doesn't always rhyme – but he has reason in his music.'

'Reason and music are excellent things,' said I.

Billy Baffin tapped the book with a thick black finger. 'It says here that Swallow was born in Liverpool, and was on the street three years in San Francisco, which is where he wrote these poems – and then he came here and built the Swallow's Nest.'

'Where is the Swallow's Nest?' I asked. 'I tried to find it but missed it.'

With thick thumbs Billy Baffin moved the edges of the pages, finally managed to open the book to the page he wanted, and he read in a raspy voice:

'Laney at last went mad – she lost it –
Screamed from the street at an upper storey –
Was harried away, was carried away
By cops in all her glory.

The snot that dangled from her lip
Was full of light, like gin or beer,
She stared, quite mad, and cursed her dad,
And never shed a tear.

Her hair all rope, her clothes all torn,
Her flaccid flesh, like fish, was melting:
Now at last she's far beyond
The realm of rape and welting.

They hauled her to the psycho ward
And drugged her, slugged her (so I've heard)
To cure her of her crazy flight
They caged her like a bird.

No longer will she dart and dive
Deep into garbage like a gull
Let's hope the madhouse haute cuisine
At last will keep her full.

She's flying out (I hope) by now
Toward inner space, toward realms of stars,
Where she'll no longer be aware
Of slobber, doors and bars:

She's flapping now into the dark
On crazy wings as frail as cloth,
Toward fires she hopes are Christmas candles
Meant to warm a moth.

Oh, Laney, Laney, best of luck
The street's a cold, uncaring place
Perhaps you'll find a fiery suck
Of joy in inner space.'

Billy snapped the book closed, poured another glass of wine. 'I have an extra copy,' he said, pulling a small book out of his satchel. 'You read it.' He handed it to me. 'But you must give it back.'

I took it and thanked him.

He looked at me with one eye wide and one eye half closed. He waved his hand vaguely, drank off his wine, poured himself another glass. He lifted the glass towards me. I raised my glass, clinked his, and we drank.

'No rum!' cried Billy. 'Bring me no rum, Jack! Not yet.'

'No, sir,' said Jack, polishing a glass.

'I never drink rum until five o'clock,' said Billy Baffin. 'Bad for the liver, mate – and I don't want mine replaced. I've seen enough of that.'

'Best to keep your liver intact,' I said. 'But booze, you know . . .'

'Jack, Jack!' cried Billy. He cupped his hand to his ear, as if listening. He began to tremble.

'Yes, sir.'

'I hear something! The vampire is coming!'

'No one is coming,' said Jack.

'Please look and see, Jack. Be a good boy, just look and see.'

Jack went to the door of the inn, opened it, looked out. He came back inside. 'No sign of him, Billy.'

Billy grabbed Jack's arm, hard. He held a long thick finger in the boy's face. 'You must never lie to old Billy . . . if you see him . . .'

'I wouldn't lie to you,' said Jack.

Billy, trembling, his eyes wide in horror, released him. And took a swig.

'I see your suitcase, sir,' said Jack, leaning down to me. 'You wish a room?'

'Whole rooms full of livers!' cried Billy.

'Yes, I would like a room,' I said. 'For me and my dog.'

'Dogs are welcome,' said Jack.

I followed him to the bar, produced my credit card. 'Have you many guests staying tonight?' I asked.

'Just Captain Billy in number one, and the sick person still in room three.'

'Do you have a room with a sea view?'

'Room four,' said Jack.

'Then four let it be,' said I.

'More wine for me and my friends!' cried Billy, slamming his glass so hard on to the table that Jack lurched and looked nervous.

'Welcome aboard!' cried Ensign Squeers.

The boy showed me upstairs. My room was fresh and pleasant, with a fat bed, beamed ceiling, dresser, desk. As I sit typing I can see a slice of distant sea through the window.

This evening I shall try to learn from Mrs Blankenship about Kirk Branford's arrival here yesterday afternoon. I have no doubt that he arrived by bus, that he walked to this inn, that he then walked to Kittle Mill, and that he then walked to Penlaven Manor House. I suspect he is at Penlaven at this moment, though I cannot be sure. The mysterious lodger in room three worries me a little. It strikes me that Branford may have left the dog with a confederate at Penlaven, and come back here to the inn. The register lists the name Kyle Bartlett in room three – but, of course, he would not have used his real name. Why he has come to this desolate part of Cornwall, or how his movements relate to the theft of the Cycladic statue from his father, I have no notion as yet. You would be happy here, Holmes, for all is shrouded in mystery.

In any event, I remind myself that my task is to provide you with facts and to leave the theorizing to you. This I am happy to do.

Please let me know that you have received this email. I shall send another after supper if the evening provides me with further information.

All best wishes,

*Wilson*

# SIX

# The Tale of a Poet

From:AfghanWilson@QuillNet.com
To: HellmeshCrooks@QuillNet.com

My Dear Holmes,

Scarcely had I sent you my last email when there came a knock at my door. It was Jack Blankenship. He asked me if I could come downstairs and help him with Billy Baffin. I accompanied him to the bar where Billy had fallen off his chair and wedged himself in the corner in such a way that, drunk as he was, he couldn't get up. He could only howl orders. Jack and I finally managed to get Billy back on to his chair.

'Now, there's a good lad!' cried Billy, clasping Jack's arm. 'And thank you, Mr Wilson.'

'Quite all right.'

'Now, Jack, you get old Billy a double rum, on the double, for old Billy needs something to keep him steady.'

Jack hesitated and looked at me – whereupon Billy slammed the table with his fist and cried, 'Rum, by god!' with such fury, and with such a horrid look, that I thought he might be acting a part. Jack got the rum. Then I asked Jack if I might have a word with his mother, for I hoped to learn what she knew about a tall blond man with a black dog. Jack informed me that his mother had just called and said she must stay at her sister's in Port Paul for another day. She would not be back until tomorrow afternoon. I broke away from the bibulous Billy and went outside to take Sir Launcelot for a walk and to ponder this disappointing news.

I intended to walk down the road and over the hill to investigate

Flint Cove, which Jack has informed me is the only place within miles where a boat can safely land. He says some people call it Smuggler's Cove, referring to rum-smuggling activities famously carried out there by one Samuel Shake in the nineteenth century. But the proper name, he says, is Flint Cove, and that is the name on all the maps. I thought I'd like to see the rock where Samuel Shake was shot by a revenue agent. Apparently a plaque marks the spot. My plan was thwarted, however, by rabbits. Sir Launcelot saw two rabbits in a field, could not control himself, and by the time he had returned from his chase the air was turning cool and the sun was sliding pell-mell towards the sea. I headed back to the Admiral Hawke Inn without seeing Smuggler's Cove. It was eight o'clock when we reached the inn door. Inside, Lancy was delighted to find he had company awaiting him in the form of a Border Collie, a Brittany Spaniel, a Labrador Retriever and a Cairn Terrier, whose owners were enjoying large beers.

I took my place at a table in one of the alcoves, well away from Billy Baffin. I ordered supper. Jack was the waiter. I saw a middle-aged woman appear in the kitchen door, apparently the cook. A lovely young woman named Ilsa was behind the bar briskly serving and talking cheerful banter in a way that suggested she knew everyone. 'Is number three not having dinner tonight?' she asked Jack.

'Not come out of the room all day,' said Jack.

Ilsa gave a facial shrug as if to say 'La-Dee-Da!' Then she darted back to her beer levers and pulled one. A little later I saw the cook going up the stairs with a tray of food.

As I enjoyed my excellent meal, a man with a Jack Russell terrier came in and, looking about, asked if he might share my table. He was perhaps sixty, white hair, average height. A slim and wiry old gent he was, with a pleasant smile and easy manners. He introduced himself as Dr Livesey.

Blonde and bouncy Ilsa came over and greeted him and set down his glass of Scotch with ice. Then a slim, pale man in a wheelchair appeared beside our table. It was James Blankenship, Jack's father. The doctor asked how he was doing and Mr Blankenship answered frankly, but without self-pity, that he was not doing very well.

At this point a rather odd-looking man entered the bar and stood near Ensign Squeers. He began fiddling with the parrot's leg shackle.

'Here, don't do that, Davy!' said Ilsa.

Too late. The bird flew – the queer fellow who had evidently unleashed him held up his arm and ducked, awkwardly. The parrot flailed across the room at head level in a great whuffle of air and feathers.

People ducked.

The bird made an orbit and returned to its perch.

'Come away from there, Davy!' scolded Ilsa. She pushed the fellow away and gave him a light swat. Davy was blank-faced, his blue eyes empty. He looked to be about thirty. He wore sea boots and a Royal Navy cap. His hand twitched occasionally. There seemed something amiss with Davy.

'Hay for the horses, wine and cheese for all my women – and you, the sultry one, come with me!' cried Billy.

But no, it wasn't Billy! It was Ensign Squeers using Billy's voice!

After this long speech the bird got very excited and cried *bawk bawk* and fluffed his wings and danced about on his perch.

'Did he really say all that?' I said.

'A very talkative bird,' said Dr Livesey. He sighed the resigned sigh of one who was at one time amused by all this uproar, but is amused no more.

Billy Baffin rose to his feet in the low-ceilinged room. The lights cast odd shadows. 'Silence!' he thundered, and the murmur of voices died away. An uneasy silence fell. I couldn't tell if people were frightened or amused. 'Now we shall have the evening's gospel reading from the poetry of Reverend Swallow,' said Billy.

'Here, here!' said someone, feebly.

Billy pulled the little book out of his pocket, held it up to his face. 'Tonight's reading is *The Man In The Bubble*,' said he. And then he read as follows, in a booming preacher's voice:

> 'Maybe he wants to help us, buy us
> a meal and a cup – I think he does –
>
> but I reckon even he can't do
> what he wants, or he'd at least step
>
> on to the street and say *Hi*
> and hand us a fiver, but the poor

bastard is frozen in his cosmic café
with fork of food halfway to lip,

and before he could spot us and decide to help,
and stand up and leave his meal

cooling on the table, and step out
on to the tilting street, we'd be long gone.

Fat cats are trapped behind glass
eating gaily, and we're on the street,

and god himself is floating in the huge
bubble of everyone's imagination,

clutching at the side like a kid suffocating
in a plastic bag, sobbing soundlessly,

gasping – we don't hear a thing . . .
poor bastard, we'd help him if we could.

Here endeth the gospel for the day.'
    Billy sat down and poured a glass of rum.
    The crowd in the bar applauded lightly – whether in appreciation
or in fear I could not tell.
    I leaned to Dr Livesey and asked what he could tell me about
Reverend Swallow, whose name I had heard mentioned so very
often since I had arrived. The doctor kindly gave me a brief history
of the man. Swallow, he said, had arrived here in the 1980s and
become vicar of St Anne's church in Mortestow, a position he held
for twenty years until he killed himself. He was born in Liverpool.
As a young man he had made a name for himself as a wild surfer,
but he soon tired of Britain's feeble surf and moved to Hawaii to
catch the big waves. He eventually ended up in Southern California
where he got a job as a waiter and caught the California surfing
scene in the sixties. In California he tuned in to LSD, marijuana
and God, and there it was he became horrified by the plight of
homeless people, in part because he became one himself. He lived
for two years in a cardboard box in the Tenderloin area of San
Francisco. Finally, he got counselling and financial help and returned

to England in the seventies. There he took a degree in theology, was admitted to the priesthood, and was assigned to the small parish of Mortestow in the north of Cornwall. Here, it is generally recognized, he did much to help the poor and the ill, but he had not forgotten his early attraction to marijuana and poetry. He spent months building a little wooden shack embedded under the cliff edge, which was completely invisible from up above. And in that little hideaway, invisible to walkers above him while it afforded him a view of the sea far below, he sat and smoked weed and wrote poems; and there he also devised the sermons that stirred people to great heights, but also eventually stirred some of the community to discontent. He was regarded as an eccentric, and he became more and more eccentric as years went by. He married Sara Timmons from Bodmin, and the year after their marriage he fell out with several people in Mortestow who claimed he had links with the devil. All the children of the community, however, found him enchanting, and the children attended his 'special church meetings', which were celebrations of all religions – Druidism, Hinduism, pantheism, and so on. He told the children, on one occasion, that more and more he was drawn to pantheism, the oldest religion of all. He said there were spirits in the streams and the trees and the fishes and the birds.

'And what did you think of him, Dr Livesey?' I asked.

'I thought him eccentric – we English often are, aren't we? I also found him to be most interesting and intelligent company. Many's the drink Jim and I enjoyed together in this very inn. And I thought him harmless – until the end, when I began to have doubts.'

'And what was the end?' I asked.

'One day,' said Livesey, 'he told his young charges that their catechism was complete and that all that remained was the final celebrational ceremony. The three girls and two boys met with Reverend Swallow at Kittle Mill, which was then owned by the church – it has since been bought by foreign investors, the same who founded the new private hospital, taking over the old Cornwall Hospital for Sailors. At the Mill they discussed some religious texts and Jim gave them each a copy of the King James version of the Bible. Each Bible was inscribed with this note: *This is your chosen path to God, though there are others. Let us journey towards higher ground and make the leap of faith together.* Swallow, with his acolytes following behind, then climbed to the cliffs, intending to end their meeting in the Swallow's Nest, where the Reverend promised to give them each, as a parting gift, a symbol of love and sacrifice. He had arranged for his wife to light candles and place them on the path that led down over the cliff edge to his hidden hut, Swallow's Nest.

'It was a dark and moonless night. They hiked up from the River Neep, crossed the Mortestow road, and continued up the cliff path towards Swallow's Nest. Jim walked ahead and the children followed behind him, all of them singing – one of the boys later said they never stopped singing. Even when Swallow warned them to avoid stumbling into the stone water tank in the dark, Swallow artfully inserted the warning words, "Be careful of the water tank!" right into the song as they went along – to the delight of the young people. When they reached the cliff Swallow said, "Follow me," and stepped over the edge. The first two girls followed him, and the second screamed as she went over. Her scream warned the third girl and the two boys behind, who held back and so lived. His wife, Sara, said she had lit the candles and then descended by the Admiral Hawke Inn path, for her husband wished his ceremony with the young ones to be his and theirs only. She waited for him at this inn, intending to meet him and the young people here when the ceremony was complete. But Swallow never returned. The villagers believed that he had intended to die and to take the children with him. As proof they cited the inscription in their Bibles, which certainly may be interpreted that way – though I have never felt that the inscriptions are such absolute proof as others claim. He was a strange man, Jim Swallow, and the sort of man about whom strange things are easily suspected. Many in this village have never forgiven him . . . or his poor wife. She moved away for a few years. But his grave in the churchyard called her back. She has now come to live out her years in Mortestow. She is scorned by many, but she suffers the opprobrium meekly. She is tolerated. But I think she will never be comfortable here.' He took a sip of Scotch. 'Too many withered hearts and nasty tongues.'

As Dr Livesey finished this tale he looked suddenly towards the door – a woman was just stepping into the pub. She was followed by a huge hound, whose head was considerably higher than the tabletops. 'Good evening, Sara,' said he. He introduced me to Sara Timmons-Swallow. She sat down at our table. She was a quiet-spoken old woman with bright blue eyes and round cheeks that still retained a little of the sensual plumpness of her youth. The dog was as mild-mannered as his mistress. His scruffy-haired face was on a level with mine as he stood beside me and looked around and did his best to find a place where he could lie down without blocking traffic. And suddenly I realized this must be the huge creature I had seen bounding along on top of the cliffs. 'Did you walk your dog on the cliffs this afternoon, Mrs Swallow?' I asked.

'Yes,' she said. 'He loves to run there.'

'I say, Sara,' said the doctor, 'did your husband write these poems when he lived in San Francisco, or here?' He drew from his pocket the same little volume that Billy Baffin was so fond of, *Street Song*.

'I believe he started most of them in San Francisco,' she replied, 'and when he came here he revised many and added more. He finished the book right here, on the cliffs.'

Billy Baffin roared, 'Rum, Jack! Rum! Slam them down, boy! Be no timid soul!'

Jack set down a bottle and glass. He was about to hurry away when Billy grabbed his arm and raised his thick hand as if to admonish the boy. 'I've done terrible things, lad, terrible things to people! *The Phantom* rises and flies, and it's old Billy at the helm, taking poor souls to Hell! Take your lesson from old Billy and avoid crime. Look what I've become, lad!'

'Scalpel! Scalpel!' cried Ensign Squeers in a strange, pinched voice.

'Not this again,' groaned the doctor, sighing in exasperation. 'It's the same old routine.'

Billy was on his feet, lumbering towards us with a drink in his hand. 'He'll not have my gizzard!' he cried. 'The thin man will stay away from Billy Baffin or I'll split him crown to toe!'

'Who is this thin man you always rant about?' asked the doctor, firmly.

'The Devil himself!' cried Ensign Squeers, and he began to jump up and down on his perch. Getting himself all worked up again.

Billy bowed to old Sara. 'I have come into money,' said he. 'I like this berth, and I'll not leave it for fear of any man or vampire or devil!'

'Excellent policy, Billy,' said Sara, smiling.

'And when I run out of money, I'll take the dive!' said Billy.

'What nonsense,' said the doctor.

'Drown, sir. Drown in the deeps,' cried Billy. 'I shall fill my pockets with nothing and sink into the deeps, and drown. For death is a treasure to a man without gold.'

'You'll drown in liquor, that's what will do you in, my old lad,' said the doctor. 'Mark my words, Billy Baffin. Lay off the liquor or you'll end yourself.'

'Your husband was a true poet,' said Billy, nodding down and pointing at Mrs Swallow. 'I am but a rhymester.' Whereupon he put his hand over his heart and said, in an impressively rum-rough voice,

> 'I've had a good run, so switch off the sun
> And wish me a soft goodnight.
> I'll not complain of wind or rain
> Or quit while still it's light.'

'Were you once an actor, Billy?' I ventured. 'You declaim impressively.'

'I have been many things,' said Billy, 'but I grew old.'

Billy wandered back to his accustomed table.

'He's a drunk who's been in one too many ports,' said the doctor. 'I pity him. But many fear him and stay away from this inn for that reason. Yet poor Mr Blankenship cannot afford to throw him out.'

'He does not frighten me,' said Sara Timmons-Swallow.

'I suppose not,' said the doctor.

The locals drifted away, dogs vanishing from beneath the tables. Billy Baffin still sat and drank. He motioned to me and I sat down with him, hoping to learn something about the lodger in room three. 'Must give my dog a walk soon,' I said.

'Have a care, lad!' he said. 'Mortestow is a dark region.'

'There is a sliver of moon to light my way,' I said.

'Ahh, you are not wise in the world!' he whispered.

'You might have a point,' I said.

He waggled his thick finger. 'Beware the phantom ship that rises and flies and brings lost souls. You can see her from the cliff at high night tide.' He swallowed rum and rambled on, unstoppable – making less and less sense. I could see I'd get no information from him tonight. 'Beware the Mouse Hole Cottage – I've seen many enter but few return,' he whispered. 'Ghouls hunker in the old church graveyard. Beware the thin man in a bat costume who stands at cliff's edge. He is the devil himself.'

'Scalpel! Scalpel!' cried Ensign Squeers in a strangled voice.

'Phantom lights in the tide – stay away on those nights and you will be quite safe,' said Billy, raising his thick finger at me, in admonition.

Evidently poor Billy has a serious mental problem. I left him sitting almost alone in the bar, and I took Sir Launcelot for his last walk of the day. As we returned up the quiet stairs to my room I saw a tray of dirty dishes outside of room three. I paused and listened at the door. For a long while I heard nothing. Then I heard a tiny sound. I couldn't place it. Soft scraping as if someone were sharpening a knife on a whetstone.

It has occurred to me that Billy may not be quite as mad as he seems. Could he be involved with the smuggling ring? His drunken talk about phantom ships makes me wonder. And his attempt to scare me makes me suspect him. I will try to look in his room and see what I can learn. He keeps his door locked, however. Several times I have tried his door handle when I knew he was down in the bar. But always it has been locked.

No theorizing. That is your department, Holmes. I abstain. But a chilling thought has crossed my mind: the name on the register for room three is Kyle Bartlett. The number of letters in each name matches the number in the name Kirk Branford. Is it possible he left the dog with his friend at Penlaven House, walked back here, and has been hiding in his room?

*Wilson*

# SEVEN

## Here Be Dragons

From: AfghanWilson@QuillNet.com
To: HellmeshCrooks@QuillNet.com

Dear Holmes,
This has been a day of discovery, confusion and (I suspect) hallucinations. I will try to write it all down concisely. I am, at this point, very glad that you are the theorizer, I the mere gatherer of facts and images.

I arose early. As I left my room I saw that the door to number three was half open. I glanced in, saw no one, cautiously entered to investigate. I found a rumpled bed. No luggage, no clothes. The only thing I detected of the mysterious lodger was a faint scent of lilac. The individual appeared to have vanished without a trace. I thought he might be downstairs, but I found the public rooms deserted. Breakfast would not be served for an hour. Having seen where Jack had put the guest register behind the bar, I decided to have another furtive look at it. Under yesterday's date I found the name *Kyle Bartlett* printed in a stylish hand in blue ink, on the line for room 3. Place of residence, *Liverpool*.

I stepped out into the fresh gloom of morning. The first light of the day seemed to rise out of the damp grass. I let Sir Launcelot off his leash. He scampered away across the field and beat me to the car. I drove (with hedges nearly brushing me on either side) the narrow jig-jag roads to the village of Blytheland, about two miles. An eighth of a mile beyond the Blytheland green I turned into the driveway of Penlaven. As that huge medieval hulk floated up towards me, I turned at the fork towards the wing containing the self-catering units, where purple wisteria climbed cream-coloured walls. I knocked on the door of the end apartment. Inside a dog barked. I knocked again – and the door opened a crack.

'Good morning,' I said. 'Can you tell me where the proprietor is located? I'm a bit lost.'

The face in the dark opening was young and quite beautiful. She was a woman of perhaps twenty-five. She appeared to be Indian, and when she spoke I was convinced this was so. Her voice was silky and she spoke in the clipped Indian accent always so intriguing to me. She said, 'I am afraid you should have turned left at the branching road.' She pointed. Her slender arm wore a thin gold bracelet. 'Just drive to the other side and you will see a little court-yard. Go in there.'

She seemed nervous. But whether this was because she feared me, or feared something in the room with her, I could not be sure. She began to close the door. I heard a dog yip. I said, 'They allow dogs, then?'

'I don't really know,' she said.

As she closed the door I heard a child cry 'Mama'.

I drove back to the Admiral Hawke Inn, had breakfast, then strolled for the first time all the way down the little lane (between high hedges) to the village of Mortestow. I emerged from the lane by the church of St Anne's Parish. The village lay mostly far below me, in a folded green landscape of hills. I had a crow's view: roofs peered out of trees, tiny cattle were placed on far fields that swelled up out of the valley like a wave. I walked round and went inside the church. Light fell through the windows upon an open Bible on the lectern, a huge new bible with pages freshly white, startling in so ancient a church. Here Reverend Jim Swallow, poet, weed smoker and ex-surfer, had given his famously inspiring sermons in the days before his parishioners had turned against him. I walked outside into the tumbled graveyard and after much searching found his stone in a far corner, a flat marble stone, oddly modern amidst the ancient, lichen-grey, broken and mostly indecipherable tomb-stones sprouting cockeyed out of uneven ground everywhere around me; ground so heaving and mouldy that one might almost imagine an army of the dead were trying to push up into the air. On his stone a small bouquet of wild flowers had been placed. I presumed I knew who had put them there.

I must tell you, Holmes, I'm a little puzzled. I called your mobile phone twice late this morning, but was shunted each time to voice-mail. I have tried to reach you all day and have almost concluded that either you have lost your phone or I should be worried about you. Please respond to this email the moment you get it, my dear fellow. Humour me.

I ate lunch out back of the inn on a lawn dotted with wooden picnic tables. Then I noticed young Jack bent over at a far table, working industriously. He was so intent upon his work that he was unaware of me until I was standing behind him. The paper beneath his quick-moving hands was filled with monsters of the most bizarre sort.

He looked up. 'Oh, hello!'

'I didn't know you were an artist,' I said.

'I like to draw creatures,' said Jack.

'I think I've seen your work, on the sign by the bus stop.'

'Sometimes the urge comes upon me,' he said, and he drew back so I could see his work: a huge creature, half bat and half lion, was flying over the small figure of a man on the cliffs below – a man evidently unaware he was about to run over the cliff edge. He was looking up in horror at blood dripping from the creature's teeth, and at the knife held in its right claw. The sense of perspective was dramatic, and it was all boldly drawn.

'I'm off to see Flint Cove,' I said. 'Which is the shortest way?'

'I'll take you,' he said, quickly folding up his large drawing pad. 'I like to draw there.'

We set off together along the road towards Port Paul but soon turned and followed a footpath to the sea. The tide was in, Flint Cove brimming with blue. Jack told me it is the only cove for miles where a craft can safely land. It is perhaps a quarter of a mile across where it meets the open sea, and a quarter mile deep from beach to sea. To the north, the high rocky cliffs taper down to the valley by which we had entered the cove.

'People drive over to the far side, usually,' said Jack. 'It's pretty good swimming over there. There's a little patch of sand.'

'I don't see a road,' I said.

'It's behind those trees. It comes pretty close to the beach.'

Jack opened his huge sketchbook and showed me a few of his ink drawings. They were quite good, though not to my taste. Several involved monsters decapitating people, or slicing out their hearts – very graphic pictures of monsters with knives and victims screaming. I asked Jack what prompted these, and he laughed and said he got his ideas from bad dreams and Billy Baffin. He said poor Billy was always ranting about having his gizzard cut out, or his heart sucked dry by a vampire.

'How long has Billy been at the inn?' I asked.

'A month,' said Jack.

'I suppose the legends of Mortestow provided plenty of inspiration before Billy turned up,' I said.

'Strange goings on, Mr Wilson.'

'Like?'

'Ever since the days of Reverend Swallow, and before that back into ancient history, when giant bats flew overhead.'

'Come now, Jack!' said I.

He laughed. 'Who knows?'

'Billy seems a bit on the edge,' I said.

'He's scary when he's drunk, when he's threatening to kill people,' said Jack. 'But Billy is the one who is scared.'

'Of what?'

'Scared of the thin man.'

'Who is this famous thin man?' said I. 'Does he exist?'

'Maybe it's just a demon from a dream.'

'You never saw him?'

'Once. I saw his face looking in at Billy through the porthole window.'

'Maybe it's a tall blond fellow with a black dog?' I said.

'No, not him. I've never seen that person. My mother might know. She's visiting her sister in Port Paul. She needs a little rest. She works too hard now that my father is ill. Dad had two heart attacks. He's been to hospital many times, the one in Bodmin. He may go up to London to a specialist.'

'What of Dr Livesey? Does he have a surgery here in Mortestow?'

'Retired. But he lives nearby and that is a comfort to Mum. We ask his advice. They've started a new hospital near here, but Dad's doctor is in Bodmin.'

Knowing your habit, Holmes, of considering everyone a suspect, I shall paint a brief sketch of young Jack – whose eccentricities and enthusiasms are the natural ones (I believe) of a healthy and curious youth. He is a slender and earnest young man of sixteen, with a handsome head flowing with brown hair, and blue eyes, and a quiet manner. The way he dutifully waits upon his ill father and does his chores at the inn is a heart-warming sight. He seems a model son. But I confess his pictures make me shudder a bit. He has a strange fascination with the cruel and the weird. Perhaps we all do. Maybe that is why horror tales sell better than serious novels. He also seems taken with the idea that a supernatural world exists parallel with this one. I can't be sure whether this is just a game with him, or a belief. As we enjoyed the wild isolation of Flint Cove, young Jack suddenly flipped a page of his sketchpad, and sketched another strange creature.

'What is it, Jack?' said I.

'The Mortestow Conflagrator,' said he. 'He's a ghoul who ate many dead bodies in the old cemetery.'

'The cemetery in the valley of the River Neep, by the ruined church?'

'That's it,' said Jack.

'I've never heard of a Conflagrator,' I said.

'He can look at something and make it burst in to flames.'

'Handy when camping,' I said.

'It's true – the Conflagrator ghoul makes graves burst into flames. Lichens and moss will burn,' said Jack. 'And the old graves are covered with growing things.'

'Have you ever seen it happen?'

'I might have,' said Jack – and he suddenly pointed out to sea. 'It's Davy Deeps.'

On the sparkling blue a lumbering old dory danced in deep distance, grew larger, and soon I could see the figure holding on to the outboard motor. By his faded blue cap I recognized him as the little fellow who had released Ensign Squeers from his perch the previous night. He stepped out into the sea and waded ashore with a rope, hauling the front end of his craft on to the shingle. We walked towards him.

'I hope you weren't towing trash, Davy,' said Jack.

Davy Deeps was a queer little man, only thirty or so but bent and weathered. He hodged and bobbed on the shore as if dancing in embarrassment. He smiled a broken-toothed smile and shook his head.

'The beach looks very clean,' said Jack. 'You have done a good job, Davy.'

Davy waved a hand and walked away towards the far side of the cove, sort of rolling side to side when he went, looking right and left.

'My father pays him to keep the beach clean,' said Jack. 'We tell him to haul the trash he finds to the bins behind the inn, but many times Davy has towed it out to sea in bags, and tried to sink it with rocks, but the rubbish washes ashore eventually.' Jack laughed, frowned. 'I can't tell if poor Davy really does not understand. Or if he is fooling us.'

'He might be a little sly,' said I. 'What is that jetty used for?' I pointed to a stone jetty far down the beach to the north.

'Used to be part of the mining works,' said Jack. 'Mouse Hole Cottage is just above it – you can't see it from here.'

'Does the cottage have a green door?' I asked.

'That's it,' said Jack. 'You can't get to the jetty from here at high tide, but you can walk there now.'

While Jack sat drawing, I walked far down the beach to the old stone jetty, and then out on to it. I returned to the shingle, wended my way amongst black boulders, and I noticed a steel door in the rocky cliff face. I walked close to investigate. Barely visible words had been stencilled on the door in black paint: **Danger, Mine Works**. I nonetheless tried the door handle. Wouldn't budge.

When we returned to the inn I sat on the lawn and cogitated, read my map, laid plans. I ate supper rather late. Few people were about on a Sunday evening. No Billy Baffin. I went to my room, fed Sir Lancy, studied my maps some more, and devised a plan.

Though I strive, as you advised, to avoid theorizing, I must tell you that if some sort of smuggling operation is going on in this area, it is very likely centred at Kittle Mill. Consider these facts: when Kirk Branford arrived here he visited the Admiral Hawke Inn, but perhaps only to use the facilities or to have a drink, and then he went directly to Kittle Mill, where he visited two cottages. Second, consider that Sinjin Chitterlie obviously had seen Branford, but was secretive about this. Third, Kittle Mill is isolated. Fourth, a track leads from the mill to the Mortestow–Blytheland Road – a dirt track that even heavy lorries could travel. And it is not far from there to the shingle beach at Flint Cove which young Jack has advised me is the only decent place for miles around for landing a boat. I am certain that a craft of forty or fifty feet, a light cabin cruiser or a fishing boat, for instance, could quite comfortably anchor in Flint Cove at high tide, and could serve as a lighter to ferry stolen goods out to that 'Phantom' ship that Billy Baffin spoke of. In my letter yesterday I described Billy as a rather amusing blowhard, perhaps slightly mad. To my astonishment, and horror, I have learned this evening that much of what Billy says is far from mad.

You will find a map attached as a .jpeg file to help you understand this area. I drew it this afternoon using my ordnance survey map as a guide, eliminating irrelevant detail and adding certain items such as the Admiral Hawke Inn, the ruined church, the dirt track to the mill house. Mr Blankenship corrected a few points. He added Swallow's Nest and something I never heard of, Death Drop – according to him this is the spot where Reverend Swallow led two girls over the cliff to their deaths. I think the map is pretty nearly correct.

This evening at dusk I left Lancy in the room and set off walking along the road towards Blytheland. I wore dark clothing, for I intended to do a little breaking and entering if occasion allowed. I listened intently for the sound of any approaching vehicle, and I made ready to flatten myself against the nearest hedge to avoid being killed in the dark. No vehicles appeared. When I reached the break in the hedge I turned left on to the dirt track that led to Kittle Mill. Very soon I saw headlamps ahead, a vehicle coming towards me. I plunged off the track and scarcely had I obscured myself behind a bush when the vehicle's lights blazed near, bathing the

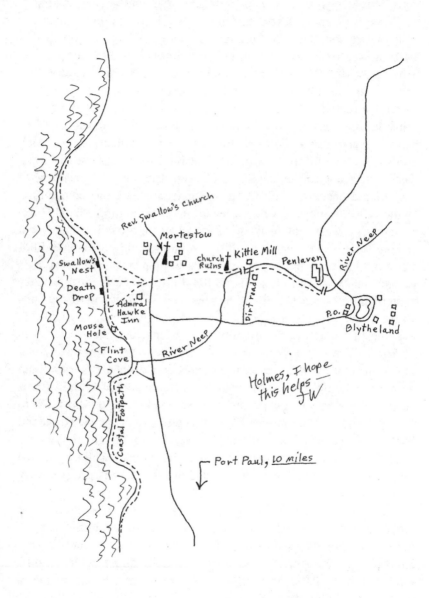

Rev. Swallow's Church

Mortestow

Swallow's Nest

Death Drop

Admiral Hawke Inn

Mouse Hole

Flint Cove

Church Ruins

Kittle Mill

Penlaven

River Neep

Dirt road

P.O.

Blytheland

River Neep

Coastal Footpath

Holmes, I hope this helps
JW

Port Paul, 10 miles

area in light. It was a silver-coloured van. At the road it turned right towards Mortestow and Port Paul, and the sound of it faded away.

I walked on, feeling much the same sort of queasy fear I felt when I went on night patrol with our troops in Afghanistan. My eyes grew accustomed to the gloom. I did not use my pocket torch. The moon had not yet risen. The starlight sifted down and lit the white wall of the south cottage. I walked past that cottage and towards the mill ahead. I looked in a window at the back of the mill, shone my light in it. A kitchen. I tried the back door. It was locked. It seemed to me that if statues were being smuggled out of the country, Kittle Mill must be the staging point. I walked back towards the south cottage, which was utterly dark. I had resolved to break in if I could. As I made my way through the dense dark, suddenly the door of the cottage flew open, light flowed out, and I was caught in the glare. A short burly man appeared in the lit doorway. 'They're back!' he cried, and he plunged out the door towards me, waving a bar or stick over his head as he came. Another man appeared in the doorway behind him. I felt discussion would be fruitless.

I turned and ran. As you know, even at my age I am rather fleet of foot, at least for short distances – tennis court distances, you might say. I ran over the footbridge and headed north along the river path towards Mortestow. I heard my pursuer's feet on the boards of the bridge. When I glanced back I saw him coming towards me. Then an odd thing happened: he fell. And as he fell he cried out, 'Oh, god! Get this thing off me!'

The man just coming behind him opened his arms as if to lean down and lift him, but then he lurched backward with a cry of pain and shrieked, 'I can't get any closer, Eddy!'

The moon slid out from behind a cloud. I saw the man lying on the ground on his back and clutching at his throat in a frenzy. I heard a fluffing sound as a swirl of darkness seemed to ascend from the fallen man. In that instant the sudden sliver of moon vanished behind cloud. A cold shiver shot down my spine. I hurried along the path as fast as I was able.

I think it my duty to report to you not only precisely what happened *as I perceived it*, but to report my own psychological state, for psychological states not only are induced by perceptions, but colour perceptions. I blush to say, Holmes, that I was afraid.

And perhaps *imagining things*. The thought of vampires occurred to me.

I hurried up the path, stumbling occasionally in the dark, running slower and slower as weariness overtook me. The moon rode out into a gap between clouds, threw a shaft of silvery light on to the ruined church and its graveyard – I was just passing the gap in the trees when I saw a white creature floating in the graveyard. I can assure you it was a fact, this white blur rubbing through shadows. I stopped running and watched. My heart was pounding, but perhaps more from exertion than terror. I realized that the man in white – if man it was – was kneeling by a grave. Indeed, he was, in fact, leaning *into* the grave. This seems implausible when written in an email. But that is what I saw. I could not help but think of Jack's Conflagrator Ghoul. I half expected the grave to burst into flames. Then came a howl from the direction of the mill, and this seemed to startle the creature. It rose, merged with shadow, vanished. The moon disappeared behind clouds. Utter blackness enveloped me. Overhead, shivering trees seemed to signal the approach of a storm. I could feel the change of atmosphere tingling my skin. I hurried away along the river path. Then the path bent to the right, leading up towards the cliffs.

It is with some reluctance, my dear Holmes, that I relate the rest of what happened this evening. You are likely to suspect that I have been hallucinating. I have wondered myself. It is late, I am tired. I can only endeavour to report the facts as I know them, as succinctly as possible. I leave it to you to judge whether they are facts indeed, or mere figments of a mind deluded by the Cornwall moon.

Till now the evening had been calm, but suddenly the forest grew restless. As I ascended the path out of the river bottom, I could hear branches tossing overhead, and leaves thrashing. When I emerged into fields a brisk breeze pressed my cheek. Ragged herds of dragon-clouds galloped past the moon. I reached the narrow blacktopped road that ran between the inn and Mortestow. Suddenly a compulsion came upon me, despite the wildness of the night, to continue up on to the cliffs. Partly I wanted to dare the dark, and mock it for having scared me. Mostly I was just curious. Billy's tale of a phantom ship that rose and flew at night was doubtless no more than a muddle of Billy's fantasies, yet it fascinated me. I'm here to find facts. I thought I should have a look. I did not take the road back a few hundred yards to the inn, but crossed it and passed through the hedge and continued up the path.

Now, if you look on the map I am attaching to this email, you will see that the path rising from the Neep Valley crosses the road and then very quickly branches into three paths, all three leading up to the cliffs: the Inn path to the left, the middle path straight ahead, the Mortestow path to the right. All three end on the sea cliffs, but about a quarter mile apart. The Mortestow path is farthest to the north. But as is usually true in this world, what looks plain on a map is far from clear on the ground. I decided to take the middle path, which is a little shorter than the other two, and I started up it. But after a few yards I saw a fork bearing to the right, a small path, and I realized it was the path to the village. Somehow I had gotten on to the Mortestow path. Uncertain what to do, I continued upward. I hadn't gone far when the moon vanished again and I was in utter blackness. I scarcely dared move. Then again the clouds parted and I could see pretty well. I hurried up the path, which ran along a hedge at the edge of a field. Suddenly the moon went out again, like a blown match. A moment later I banged my leg on something and crumpled to the sod. It was a stone watering trough. I sat down on the edge of it, rubbing my knee. Then I continued, limping slightly, till eventually I emerged from the grip of the shadows and came out on to the top of the cliffs where the air was faintly lighter.

Breeze was blowing briskly. Clouds scudded past the waning moon. I stayed well away from the cliff edge. The eastern half of the sky was still sprinkled with stars, the western half mostly cloud. I turned and walked south along the undulating grass. I had not walked far when I saw a man standing by the cliff edge, facing out to sea. I was not entirely surprised that someone might have come out for a night stroll on the cliffs. Yet there was something in this creature's attitude, his stillness, that arrested me. He wore a long black coat that whipped in the wind. He extended both his arms – and he vanished!

I can describe the phenomenon in no other way. He was standing there, tall and slim and black in the starlight. And a moment later he was gone. Vanished completely.

A sick feeling ran through me. I knew I had just seen suicide committed. Or else – I confess this mad thought occurred to me – I had just seen the vampire mentioned by Billy Baffin. You know,

Holmes, that I have been accustomed to seeing horrors, real horrors – seeing soldiers maimed, seeing men die on all sides of me. I am no stranger to real horrors. But I cannot deny that at this instant I felt a different kind of horror.

I walked towards the cliff edge, looked over. I could see nothing. I soon lost my appetite for gazing over edges. The sea was lashing below, throwing up little white flashes of waves in the moonlight. I walked on, squeezing my mobile phone in the bottom of my right front pocket, as if I were going to take it out and use it. I thought perhaps I should report what I had seen to the police. A little later I began to wonder if I had seen anything at all but shadows and moonglow. I found myself walking faster, absorbed in a whirl of thought that stirred my stomach.

The moon vanished under a fast-moving ceiling of cloud. In black space off to my left lights moved. Vehicle lights. They moved slowly up through a sheep field. Near the cliff tops the vehicles halted. I crouched down.

Six men emerged from the first silver van. I could see them in the headlights, blurs. They marched upward towards the cliffs. When they reached the end of the field they emerged through the hedge on to the grassy cliff tops. They walked oddly, and then I realized why: they were carrying a long box, three men on each side. They carried the box to Mouse Hole Cottage, opened the door, hefted their burden inside. Light appeared in the window of the cottage. They came out again, returned to the vehicle, brought up another box. They repeated this procedure a third time. Three heavy boxes they put into the cottage, each just the size that could contain a life-size statue.

Both vans had only their parking lights on now. The men gathered round the second van. By and by all six again marched up through the sheep field, single file, on to the cliff top, and now each was carrying a box about the shape of a medium-size ice chest, and the boxes were blinking like fireflies. They carried the boxes into the cottage. I realized the vans in the sheep field were turning around. They jiggled away, downward towards the Mortestow road. In an instant their tail lights vanished. The light in the cottage window went out. I was alone in darkness.

The weather was growing wilder, lightning flickering over the sea. Breeze had become wind. Above its moaning I could hear faint booms of thunder in the far distance. I rose from the swale where

I crouched and walked straight to Mouse Hole Cottage. I shone my pocket torch through the window. The cottage was empty. Utterly empty. Bare dirt floor. Nothing more could I see.

The first tiny pin-pricks of rain were touching my forehead. I looked over the cliff edge at Flint Cove below, and I saw a boat making its way seaward through heaving surf. The lights were unmistakable, green on the right, red on the left. How large a craft she might be I could not tell, but the lights moved inexorably towards the sea. Then a crack of lightning illuminated the black world for an instant, and afar off in the dark I saw a sleek white ship appear – evidently riding at anchor a half-mile out. She vanished when the world went black. As if she had never been.

Rain peppered me. I found the path – to my own amazement – as if I had known where it was. Down and down I rushed. I reached the door of the inn just as the downpour began.

'Hello, Billy!' said I, for he had raised his glass to me as I entered.

'Man the lifeboats!' cried Ensign Squeers.

I was grateful that there were some people in the bar. I sat down with Billy and Dr Livesey, and as I did so Jack rushed by me to the porthole window and closed it, for rain now was rushing down in sheets, blowing in and wetting the floor. Booms of thunder resonated, more felt than heard.

'It's a boomer,' said Billy.

'Relax, just relax!' said Ensign Squeers in a strangled, odd accent, but in a soothing tone.

Billy's head was cockeyed on his shoulders. He lifted his glass. 'I should have been a pirate,' he said. 'I'm weak with age and drink, but I'll pilot no boat for a vampire!'

Mr Blankenship rolled up to us in his wheelchair, raised a hand to silence Billy. He looked very grey. 'Please, Billy.'

'Sorry, guvnor. Meant no harm.'

'That's OK, Billy.' He rolled away and vanished behind bottles. He did not look good to me.

'You go to bed, Dad,' said Jack.

'Your mother home?' I asked the boy.

'The storm has kept her in Bodmin for another day,' said Jack.

A boom of thunder rocked the room, and another lash of rain hit the windows.

'I'm glad I'm snug and not on the street,' said Billy. He fumbled in his shirt, pulled out his gospel, opened to a page. He held up a

hand and scowled at everyone in the room, silencing them. Then
he read, in rum-hoarse voice:

> 'If you're breathing it's your lucky day:
> the sun burgeoning out of the Bay
> and coffee bursting hot on lip,
> strangers talking exciting nonsense
>
> and all the world fat with the strength
> of your bulging hope, brain, balls.
> Sure, yes, I'll sing you sad
> stories of starving streets, but not
>
> today, not now, not in the
> sunny kitchen of morning when a gingham
> sky is blowing. In every condo
> in North Beach the toast is about
>
> to pop like a prayer, and I'm hungry,
> so let's linger and never blow
> home, gulp the sun like a grapefruit.
> For always overhead I hear
>
> a wave of darkness rumbling near
> through fleets of stars all winking, sinking.
> Soon the wind will blast my cup,
> the Bay go black, and time run up.'

'You should have been an actor, Billy,' I said.

'I should have been a pirate!' cried Billy, and he pounded the
table with his fist, and two glasses jumped.

'Come now, Billy – none of that!' said the doctor, sternly.

'The thin man likes to cut, but he is nothing to a man like me!
I can cut a man six ways from Sunday, cutlass or carving knife!'

'Scalpel!' cried Ensign Squeers, getting excited again.

'Pumpkins,' said Billy.

'You will drink yourself to death,' said Dr Livesey.

'My grandfather was a bag of pumpkins,' proclaimed Billy.

Dr Livesey shook his head as the thunder boomed. 'Nobody will
be going home soon, not until this lets up,' he said.

'Forty years ago,' said Billy, 'a bigger storm than this blew up in Bristol Bay, a boomer. A bully of a storm.'

'No doubt, no doubt,' said the doctor.

'My grandfather's boat capsized. The pilothouse roof came off and floated, the boat sank. Men were a'clinging to the pilothouse roof, and they shouted they must swim for shore. My grandfather clung to a bag of pumpkins and he told them to cling to the pilot-house and not to swim. But they wouldn't hear him. Off they went, swimming into waves as high as a house. Grandfather clung to that bag of pumpkins all the stormy night, and next morning on flat seas a ship picked him up.'

'Yes?' said the doctor, impatiently.

'Yes, what?' said Billy.

'My heavens, Billy, you don't know how to tell a story. What happened to the men who swam for shore?'

Billy's eyes grew wide, and he shook his head. 'They haven't arrived yet!'

Another crack of lightning and thunder punctuated this remark. I departed for my room. And here I've been this last hour, my dear Holmes, typing up this report. I hope you will find it, in regard to details included or omitted, neither too long nor too short. In looking back on it I fear I may have wandered. I think of the apology Pascal appended to one of his letters – *I am sorry this letter is so long; if I'd had more time I'd have made it shorter.*

I am copying this email to Lestrade, since you seem to be incommunicado recently. If for some reason your computer is down, I trust he will be able to get you a hard copy. Please do send me a reply the moment you receive this report. Send an email or send a text message to my mobile. I am beginning to worry about you.

With all best wishes,

Wilson

# EIGHT
## A Message From Lestrade

From: Lestrade@met.police.uk
To: AfghanWilson@QuillNet.com

Hello, Wilson,

I received your phone message about the white ship and the apparent smuggling operation. We have taken what measures we could. I am very glad you sent me a copy of your last letter to Holmes, and I hope you have had a response from him. I haven't heard from him in several days. Holmes seems to have vanished completely. I have begun, frankly, to worry.

The day you left for Cornwall, Holmes finally managed to contact Alice Branford, who for some reason keeps her phone off most of the time. From her he learned that her sister, Cecelia, was quite safe. The truth is that Cecelia Branford was in a trance in Wapping, communicating with spirits, when the crime was being committed near Cheddington. The story is that on Wednesday one of Cecelia's older friends died, and the friend's son wished to get in touch with his mother's departing spirit immediately. So Alice Branford drove from London to collect Cecelia in Buckinghamshire, then drove her back to Wapping where Cecelia held a séance at the residence of the bereaved young gentleman. Holmes was rather put out at all this nonsense, in quite a state. At all events, he wanted me to go with him that very evening to interview Cecelia Branford on Primrose Hill. So I went. As it happened, her sister Alice was there, the two of them just preparing to hold a séance to contact their brother Bertie. According to both sisters, Bertie drowned ten years ago in Greece when the ferry on which he was a passenger sank in a storm near Santorini. The story they gave us was the same that we heard earlier, that Bertie had been thrown out of the house by their father, who was angered when Bertie and his friend, Daniel Ma, went to the police and told them that Kirk was maiming cattle. Kirk went to prison as a result. According to

Alice, Bertie was always a cheerful sort and decided to take this opportunity to travel around the world. He got only as far as Greece.

Holmes asked if we could stay for the séance, and perhaps talk to Bertie. Both women urged us to stay. During the séance Holmes had a nice chat with the dead Bertie. In the course of that conversation he asked questions that seemed to trap Cecelia, and to reveal that Bertie was, in fact, still alive – or else that Cecelia was a charlatan. I was recording the whole session. Here is the relevant section. Cecelia did the talking for dead Bertie, in a strange low voice.

HOLMES:  Do you miss any of your old friends from Buckinghamshire?

BERTIE:  Daniel Ma.

HOLMES:  What is Daniel Ma doing now?

BERTIE:  He is a stockbroker in the city.

HOLMES:  How is he doing?

BERTIE:  Very well.

HOLMES:  How do you know?

BERTIE:  He told me.

HOLMES:  Who else do you miss?

BERTIE:  Only Doolittle.

HOLMES:  Why?

BERTIE:  We are very alike.

HOLMES:  In what way?

BERTIE:  Neither of us can swim. I should have followed his example. He won't go near water.

Holmes then asked several other questions, mostly about Bertie's dog, Doolittle, and his last days in Greece. Then came the final question.

HOLMES:  Have you ever communicated with Mr Ma at a séance?

BERTIE:  No.

HOLMES:  Then how did he tell you he was doing well?

At that point Cecelia seemed confused. She closed her eyes, began shaking her head, and finally she threw up her hands in exasperation and said, 'He's gone. Bertie has vanished.'

Holmes took my arm, thanked the two sisters, and we abruptly left the séance. You know how Holmes can be. On the way out to the street he said, 'It may be worthwhile to meet this man Daniel

Ma. If we don't learn something about Bertie, we may learn something about Kirk. Evidently Ma has known the family for years. See if your smartphone can find his number.'

I found it, and Holmes phoned Ma, who agreed to talk with him at his club in an hour and a half. Holmes asked me to go with him and I did.

Ma was a very genial, bright and easy-going chap of Chinese descent. He had known Bertie at school, had known for years that he had never drowned. Bertie had in fact swum ashore on Santorini and made his way back to England, working jobs wherever he could get them. Bertie had decided it was convenient, from the point of view of avoiding his family, to remain drowned.

As we stood in the National Liberal Club talking with Ma at the bar, and later on the terrace overlooking the Thames, Holmes was the terrier he has always been, barely on the edge of politeness as he demanded details. And Daniel Ma, when he realized he was really speaking to Sherlock Holmes, was willing to give details. Ma told us that five years ago Bertie Branford had gone back to university to become a nurse, but that some scandal caused him to leave. Ma did not know what the scandal was all about; Bertie would not tell him. Ma lost track of Bertie for a while, then one day saw him at the British Museum, looking rather seedy. They had lunch together at the restaurant in the British Museum, and Bertie informed Ma that on the street he was known as 'Bad Dog' – for reasons unexplained. That was a year or so ago. Daniel Ma did not see Bertie Branford again until last month when he saw him on the street selling *The Big Issue*, the newspaper sold by homeless people. Ma was on a bus at the time, got only a glimpse, but he was certain it was Bertie. He hasn't seen Bertie since.

It was late as Holmes and I strolled out of the National Liberal Club. Just as we turned into Northumberland Avenue we passed an old man hobbling along towards the Embankment, and I saw Holmes eyeing him. A few paces later Holmes flung his arm at the darkness and proclaimed that he had a plan. He intended to descend into London's nether world, become a street person, and fish up Bertie Branford from the depths – for old Rose Branford's sake. I asked him what on earth he meant. He replied with words to the effect, 'There is something very strange going on, Lestrade, and I mean to find it out.'

'But have you time for good deeds?' I asked.

He laughed and said that you, James Wilson, were a long-time warrior, courageous to a fault, and that you were on the case in

Cornwall, and that he trusted you to find Kirk Branford if the man could be found at all. Meanwhile he would fish up Bertie.

The next day while doing my Saturday shopping I found myself in the area where Daniel Ma had spotted Bertie Branford. Something prompted me to make a little detour and have a look. On the corner I saw a man selling *The Big Issue*, but it wasn't Holmes. I then noticed, not far off, a man sitting on the kerb sorting through soda cans he had collected, pouring the last drops from the bottoms of the various soda cans all into one soda can – presumably to create a swallow or two for himself to drink. He was a tall, thin individual, and he seemed to keep giving me the eye in the oddest way. I soon recognized Holmes beneath the ragged and greasy garb. I stared in disbelief, and he bobbed his head and winked at me and kept at his task. I walked away and left him to his strange devices. Since then I have not heard from him. That was two days ago.

If you should hear from Holmes I would appreciate your letting me know immediately. Also, if you should need assistance of any kind, Wilson, you know my number. I am always at your immediate service.

*Lestrade*


# NINE
## Three From the Sea


I have somehow deleted the next two emails I sent to Holmes, so at this point I am compelled to rely on memory, and on the notes I made in my journal.

I received Lestrade's email in early morning and replied to it immediately, informing him that I would instantly pass on any news of Holmes that came my way, and I requested that he do likewise for me. I assured him that meanwhile I would continue my efforts to locate Kirk Branford.

After breakfast I walked with Sir Launcelot along the grassy and undulating tops of the sea cliffs. In Flint Cove I saw no boats, only white seabirds soaring far below me. The phantom craft which last night had appeared briefly far out to sea in the lightning flash, was gone.

I gazed out over the gauzy blue, and pondered the events of the last few days. I began to worry about the young Indian woman at Penlaven. When I had spoken to her she had been very afraid of something – I had no doubt of that. At the time I had assumed that she was afraid I would discover she was sheltering Kirk Branford and his black dog, Doolittle. Now I began to wonder if I had made a mistake. Could she have been afraid of Kirk Branford, who was perhaps threatening her in some way? So little of what I had seen made sense to me that this new theory seemed as plausible as any. The more I thought about it, the more worried I became. I began to form a plan to learn what was happening at Penlaven.

At that moment another cliff walker caught my eye, a young woman. Her blonde hair blew in the breeze as she stood by a cliff edge, looking over. She turned and smiled as I approached with Sir Launcelot.

'Good morning,' she said.

'Good morning,' I said.

She petted Sir Launcelot. 'Isn't it amazing?' she said, pointing to something. 'He sat here and wrote his poems. I'm going down to have a look.' She edged near the cliff.

'A look at what?' I asked.

'Swallow's Nest. This is where Jim Swallow, the poet, sat and wrote.' She pointed to a stone post some twenty feet away, half hidden behind a clump of bushes.

I hadn't noticed it. *Swallow's Nest* it said, in fading small letters.

'According to my guidebook,' said the girl, 'the easiest way to find the path is to simply look for this white stone.' She pointed to the white slab she stood on. It was smooth and wavy as if worn by ages of water. Yet it was embedded in turf atop the cliff. 'See, here's the path.' She pointed. She took off her backpack, laid it in grass. Then she stepped over the cliff edge and down on to the path, and walked down to my left, seeming to shrink as she descended and as the bottom part of her body vanished below the cliff edge.

I kept Sir Launcelot on a short leash and followed her. The path was not quite as dangerous as it appeared from above. If a person fell, there were bushes to grab as one slid down the steeply sloping ground below us – before the sheer drop. Swallow's Nest was a small shack built into the cliff just beneath the grassy sod above. The girl opened its Dutch door to reveal a small room about six feet by six feet, with benches built along the two side walls and the back wall. Inside was enough room for the young hiker, me, Sir Launcelot, and perhaps one or two others if they didn't mind squeezing. We sat looking out through the open Dutch door . . . a spectacular view.

'When he sat in here and wrote,' she said, 'no one above would know it. He had complete solitude.'

'Are you a fan of his poems?' I asked.

'Oh, I rather like them – especially the *Street Song* collection,' she said. She smiled the exuberant smile of youth, reached out her hand. 'I'm Kyle Bartlett.'

'James Wilson,' I said. 'I believe you stayed at the Admiral Hawke Inn two nights ago?'

'Yes . . . I was ill.'

'I was in the room next to yours.'

'Oh, I hope I did not disturb you!'

'Not at all.'

'Terrible night. I was sick for a day. But I'm recovered now. I walked up to Clovelly yesterday, and now I'm heading back down the coast to Tintagel. I may go on down to Lizard. I don't know yet.'

'Travelling alone.'

'I got rid of my boyfriend one week ago today.'

'That's too bad.'

'Oh, no! This journey is my celebration. I feel so wonderful! At last I am free.'

'Good for you,' I said.

She pointed to our left with one hand, holding her guidebook in the other. 'Look, there is the Venus Pool. It is a natural catchment of rock that fills up with water when the tide is in, and holds it when the tide goes out.'

The Venus pool was trapezoidal and shining bright, the water still as a mirror amidst the sharp black rocks uncovered by low tide.

We made our way back up to the cliff top where Kyle Bartlett shouldered her backpack, and strode away to the south. She turned back towards me once – preening with youth, her blonde hair blowing – and she gave a final wave.

Something prompted me to pull out my mobile and call my fiancée in London. I told her I missed her. She asked if I'd be back to London by the weekend and I said I hoped so. But I explained that Holmes seemed to have gone missing, so all was quite uncertain.

When I got back to the Admiral Hawke Inn, Mrs Blankenship

had just returned from several days at her sister's house in Bodmin. She was a slender woman with greying hair, perhaps fifty, with red hands and kind but worried eyes. I asked her whether a tall young man with blond hair and a small black dog had come to the inn on Thursday afternoon. She remembered him well. He had demanded that Billy Baffin be roused from his room where he was sleeping. He and Billy then took their beers to the far end of the garden and sat at a picnic table and talked for a long while. Afterwards, she said, Billy was strangely quiet.

'Frightened, perhaps?' I suggested.

'Not frightened,' she said. 'Just subdued. Which is strange for Billy. As if he'd seen a miracle. I thought it quite strange.'

'Did you happen to hear the man's name?' I asked. 'Or the black dog's?'

'The gentleman kept saying, "Sit, Doolittle." So that was the dog's name. But I did not hear his name. Billy would know.'

'Do you know where he went when he left here?'

'I was in the kitchen, and next time I looked he was gone. He didn't have a car.' She shrugged. 'The last bus had gone. So I suppose he walked somewhere.'

After lunch I phoned Holmes. My call bounced instantly to his voicemail. I was beginning to worry. Descending into the depths of London in disguise was one of his favourite tricks in the old days, but that was years ago – a hundred and twenty years ago, in fact – and whether doing it now, after all his body had been through, was courageous or crazy one could easily wonder. Then again, perhaps sleeping a couple of nights on the street was no great trial after having spent nearly a century sleeping in a glacier.

I drove to Blytheland, parked my car by the green, made myself comfortable in the public bar of the Blytheland Inn and stayed for the whole afternoon. It occurred to me that if Kirk Branford were lodging at Penlaven, he might frequent this place. So I sat in the pub as locals came, locals went. I managed to chat with nearly all of them. But none had seen a tall blond stranger with blue eyes and a black dog. I learned no more than what I already knew – namely, that Penlaven was a luxury B&B with rooms and self-catering units, and that people often stayed at Penlaven while exploring Hawke's Moor. Towards suppertime I drove back to the Admiral Hawke and looked at my maps for an hour. It seemed to me that I should go to Penlaven and do whatever was necessary to learn whether Kirk

Branford was staying there with the Indian woman. As soon as I was sure of Branford's location, I would notify Holmes or Lestrade. From then on it would be the job of the official police to intercept any stolen goods that had not yet been moved out of the country through Flint Cove, and to make arrests.

At supper I enlisted the help of young Jack. 'Monster hunting,' I told him. 'Are you a pretty good climber?'

'I've climbed Wimbley Oak at night,' said he, 'when the world was full of witches and the wolves were on the howl.'

'Jack, Jack!' said I.

'It's true,' said he.

'I didn't know there were wolves around here,' I said.

'Used to be,' said Jack.

It was already getting dark as we left on our mission. We drove to Blytheland, parked by the green, then walked a few hundred yards down the dark and narrow road, turned left into the wide driveway of Penlaven. The night was windless and moonless. Below us we could see a few windows lit in different parts of the huge and sprawling medieval house. We took the right fork of the driveway, passed under the overhanging trees, and I could see that the two windows of the end unit were lit, as I had hoped. We walked quickly through the parking lot and on to the lawn beyond the house, and we hid ourselves in the huge black gloom-shadow of an oak tree. I had already told Jack that I wished to know if a tall blond man of thirty or so was in the apartment, possibly with a little black dog.

'What has this man done?' asked Jack. 'Is he a pirate?'

'You should write novels, Jack,' I said. 'Do you think you can climb the wisteria and look in that window to the right of the doorway?'

'No problem,' said Jack, and before I could warn him to be careful, he was gone, floating away towards the house through the starlight shadows on the lawn. I wondered whether it was right of me to have risked a young lad in this venture. But the window wasn't terribly high, perhaps eight feet from the ground, and already Jack was on the thick wisteria trunk, climbing like a bug. In a moment his head was at window level. He hung with legs wrapped around the trunk and hands holding on to the window ledge. He watched for perhaps half a minute. Then he dropped straight down and landed on grass. He brushed himself off and came running back

to me through a rain of starlight that made the whole scene seem
unreal. I felt as if I'd been watching a cartoon. The world that lay
before me – the oak shadow and the star rain on a rolling lawn,
and the ancient white-walled house hung with thick-branched
wisteria – was so hallucinatory and strange that I seemed to be
gazing at a fairyland.

'He's there all right,' gasped Jack. 'Tall blond chap with a black
dog on his lap – and a black patch over his eye.'

'Come now, Jack.'

'No black patch.'

'What was he doing?'

'Sitting in a chair. He was talking to a woman who sat on a couch
across from him. She was holding a child.'

'Excellent!' I whispered, and patted his shoulder.

We were about to step out of the oak shadow and on to the starlit
lawn when headlights appeared floating down the long drive. The
vehicle turned towards us and parked just under the very window
Jack had looked into. Three men got out of a silver van. Two were
big and wore white trousers and shirts, seemed to float in the dark.
The third was tall and thin, wore a long black overcoat, carried what
appeared to be a heavy walking stick. They walked briskly to the
door just under and to the left of the window Jack had peered into.
They knocked several times. We could see the east side of the building
where they stood, and we could also see the north end where now
someone was emerging into starlight from a door I had not noticed
before: it was the woman. She held a child. She hastened around the
west side of the building and vanished on to the front lawn. Meanwhile,
the door on the east side opened, a man appeared in it, there was a
stifled cry, and the two big men in white grabbed the fellow. They
hustled him to the silver van, while the man in the black coat stood
watching. The cut of the coat and the high collar and the thick black
hair made me think he was must be a young man. The walking stick
drooped casually from his hand. He looked like a figure out of the
eighteenth century – a road agent, or aristocrat.

All of them folded themselves into the van, and the van glided
swiftly away up the tree-gloomed drive, turned at the entrance . . .
its tail lights vanished.

'I need to get that dog,' I said to Jack.

A small dog had emerged from the side door and now was running
towards the front lawn.

Jack sprinted away in starlight, I followed. We circled the house and found the little creature at last. He was in the little courtyard where two days earlier I had first entered Penlaven. The courtyard was dimly lit by two yellow coach lamps on either side of the main door. The water was still running from the pipe into the stone trough. Potted plants still sat on the pavement. I grabbed a piece of twine that was hanging from a hook, intending to use it as a leash. But the little dog darted ahead, dodged Jack's reaching arms, and scampered out of the courtyard on to the front lawn. We followed.

As I emerged from the courtyard, one of the parked cars lit up, roared to life, and I saw the head of the young woman in the driver's window. The car backed, lurched ahead, shot up the driveway, and at the main gate it turned left, north. Towards Devon.

The little dog, meanwhile, was headed down the star-drenched lawn towards the river. He stopped to sniff. But as Jack drew near him, the little creature sprinted on through the inky shadows.

'He acts like he knows where he's going,' said Jack.

The dog reached the stream, turned right on a path. We followed him for a mile or so. Finally I asked, 'Do you know where we are headed, Jack?'

'We'll soon be at Kittle Mill,' said he. 'From there this path crosses the river on a footbridge and goes up towards our inn.'

'Yes, I've walked that section,' I said.

The little dog must have gotten tired. Suddenly he just sat down on the path. We walked up to him and he wagged his tail. I tied the twine to his collar. A fragment of moon had now lifted above the horizon and I could see the white of the south cottage amidst trees ahead. Jack informed me that we were closer to the Admiral Hawke Inn than to Penlaven, so we decided to walk on. He said his mother could take me to get my car in the morning.

I was glad to get the opportunity to have another look at the Kittle Mill settlement. I knew the dog had been here before and half expected him to tug me towards the cottage or the mill house, but he bounced merrily along and showed no inclination to do anything but walk beside me. I cautioned Jack to silence as we passed by the cottage and over the bridge. Having once been chased by two angry men here, I was not inclined to repeat the adventure. There were no lights on in either the cottage or the mill house. I supposed Sinjin Chitterlie was still in residence, wearing his neck brace or whatever it was, and still oddly anxious for company to talk to. For a moment I thought perhaps I should knock on the door and see if I could rouse him and learn anything. But another moment's thought convinced me this would be futile and foolish.

Jack seemed to know the path well. In places where I would have hesitated he struck on through the gloom. The moon slice overhead was appearing and vanishing behind fast-moving clouds, though the air where we walked seemed still. I glimpsed the ruined church tower off to my right. As we reached the path leading to the grave-yard, Jack whispered, 'Look!'

Far down the avenue of graves leading to the church stood a slim figure in a long black coat. He knelt by a flat gravestone, and lifted it.

'It's a ghoul!' said Jack. 'Should we get him?'

'Let's think about it,' I said, grabbing his shoulder to prevent him from rushing away.

The creature stood up from the grave.

'It looks like the black-coated man we just saw at Penlaven,' I said.

'But how did he get *here*!' asked Jack.

'Let's walk towards him,' I said.

We started up the gloomy path. The creature stood staring at us from shadow. Then it darted away towards the hulk of the ruined church, a black mass in the uncertain moonlight.

'It went into the church,' said Jack.

We hurried. I was anxious to query this man.

As we neared the blackness of the church door, a flame shot up just ahead of us, on the top of a gravestone.

'Oh, no!' cried Jack – and for the first time he sounded scared.

'It can't be that, Jack,' I said. 'He must have thrown a match into the dead weeds overhanging that grave.'

As if in answer to my words a missile of flame shot up, to a crackling sound, then died.

'A corpse is burning!' said Jack.

Jack seemed to be right. When I looked into the smoky fire I saw a man afire . . . but it was only a burning bush over a body carved in relief on the flat gravestone.

Jack had reached the church door. I hurried after him. We went in cautiously – the scene before us was like a moonlit garden: the weeds, trees, broken walls, rotten pews, an altar with a huge book on it.

'I can't see anyone, but he must be in here, Jack,' said I.

'Maybe we should go,' said Jack.

I was not, however, inclined to be frightened by shadows and match tricks. We stood, listening, motioning each other to silence. As we listened I heard a tiny hiss – and then the Bible on the altar burst into flames and began to burn like a torch – and somewhere in the shadows I heard the sound of something moving.

'We might as well go,' said Jack.

I realized I was responsible for the boy's safety, so I agreed. We left the ruined church and made our way down to the river path, and soon were on the path up towards our inn. Before I quite realized how far we had walked, I saw the lit windows of the Admiral Hawke beckoning in the distant dark.

'Was your impression that they took that man by force, Jack?' I asked.

'I could not tell for sure,' said Jack. 'He seemed to go with them very easily. But they were pushing him, I think.'

'Yes,' I agreed. 'That was my impression also.'

'I think he did not want to go,' said Jack.

The barroom was half full. Ilsa was dispensing beers. Jack hurried to help her. His mother was also behind the bar. It struck me as curious how when Jack was at the inn he was the most dutiful and courteous and mature of good sons, doing his work, attending to customers, helping his father move his wheelchair occasionally. Yet when he was outside the inn and on his own free time, he seemed to become suddenly free and easy and childish and fantastical, as if he lived half in the real world of work and family, half in the darker world of myth, superstition and strange horrors. I sat down at the corner table across from Billy Baffin, who was out cold, lying sprawled forward, drunk, on the tabletop. Doolittle was happy to lie down by my chair. He paid little attention to Patrick the wolfhound or to Ben the beagle or to any of the other dogs sprawled about the barroom.

Ilsa brought me a beer. I sipped, puzzling over what I should do, if anything, about reporting the possible abduction at Penlaven. As we had followed the dog across the dark lawn I had tried to call the police on my mobile, but in the sunken depths of the valley I had not been able to make a call. Now, after all this time had passed, I wasn't sure it was a police matter.

'In the dark many things seem possible,' said Jack, setting a plate of chips down by me. 'Could it have been a ghoul, you think?'

'At the moment, Jack,' said I, 'that seems as good a guess as any – but I doubt it is a correct guess.'

'I guess not,' said Jack.

I ate my chips, drank my beer, and finally I called the police and told them what had happened at Penlaven. The gentleman I spoke with assured me the matter would be looked into.

Sara Timmons-Swallow sat alone in a far corner drinking a small glass of wine. Mrs Blankenship spoke with her a short while, then hastened back to her work, delivering beers that foamed on small round trays.

'Just relax! Just relax!' said Ensign Squeers, in the same odd voice that he often said, 'Scalpel!'

'I'll not relax!' cried Billy, raising his head from the table. 'Get away from me or I'll dismantle you! Back! Back, damned creature!' Billy flung out an arm and almost hit me. His eyes were wild and confused.

Mr Blankenship rolled his wheelchair near and said soothingly, 'Billy, Billy, please. Please, my friend. These people want calm.' He waved his hand at the people in the room.

'Sorry.' Billy squinched up his face as if trying to get a grip on reality.

'Did Kirk Branford give you money, Billy?' I asked, springing the question on him, but in the friendliest tone I could manage. I thought I might catch him off guard in his slightly confused state.

'Maybe, maybe not,' said Billy, and winked at me drunkenly. 'I know no Kirk.' Billy sat himself back in his chair, rubbed his thumbs down the front of his Sorbonne sweatshirt, made himself tall, sucked in air. He raised his chin and roared, 'Hay for the horses, wine and cheese for all my women – and you, the sultry one, come with me!' He pointed at Ilsa.

Mrs Blankenship was upon him in an instant, transformed from her usual sweet self to the very picture of an angry landlord. 'Enough of that, Billy Baffin, or I'll have you out of here – whatever my husband says! You understand me?'

'Now, Elizabeth . . .' said Mr Blankenship, raising a feeble hand.

Billy was indignant, though penitent. He protested, 'You have allowed Ensign Squeers to say the same thing, and you have not chastised him!'

'But Squeers is a parrot and you are not!'

'No,' said Billy, meditatively. 'No, I am not.'

'Don't bandy words with me, Billy Baffin. No more of it!'

Billy raised a hand. 'No more of it, mum. No more of it!'

She went away.

Jack's father rolled his wheelchair over to our round table in the corner, beneath the porthole, and Jack brought his father what was evidently his nightly sip of sherry. 'You sure it is good for you tonight?' asked Jack, for his father looked rather weary and grey in the face, not at all good.

'My heavens, Jack,' said Mr Blankenship. 'A man must keep to his habits.' He set the glass on the table edge and looked at it kindly, as if savouring it before even touching it. 'Habits are good medicine,' he said quietly.

Jack grabbed his small sketchpad from under the bar, and a pencil, and sat down and began sketching. He turned Billy Baffin into a monster with big bat wings for arms.

'What are you drawing there, boy!' cried Billy in mock anger.

At that moment the door opened behind us and Dr Livesey appeared. He came directly to our table and said good evening, and sat down, and began drumming his fingers nervously on the table. 'I'll have the usual, Ilsa,' said he.

She brought Scotch on ice.

Mr Blankenship looked at the doctor. 'You seem anxious this evening, Selwyn,' said he, as his nervous hand set down the sherry.

'Perhaps I am, a little,' said the doctor. 'Have you heard what happened in the cove?'

Mr Blankenship shook his head no, and formed the word with his lips.

'Three bodies washed up on the beach.'

'Did a boat founder?' asked Mr Blankenship.

'None were reported,' said the doctor. 'Harold Davis saw something suspicious going on and called the police. When the policeman arrived at the beach he found Davy Deeps tying ropes around the bodies, about to tow them out to sea.'

'Poor witless Davy!' gasped Mrs Blankenship, who had come up and was standing behind her husband.

'My heavens!' said Mr Blankenship.

'The dead were two middle-aged men and a younger man,' said the doctor, and he took a sip of the Scotch. 'One man was black, and all three were nude.'

'Nude!' said Jack.

'Had been in the water for a day or so, according to what I've been told. And the strangest point of all,' said the doctor, pausing to take another sip, 'is that all were missing hearts, kidneys and livers. And one man had the third finger of his left hand cut off.'

Billy flung himself back in his chair, and his face was horror-struck. 'My god, it's that black-heart Cluj!' he cried.

'Ghouls!' cried Jack in a delirium of delight, and he began scribbling on his pad.

'Oh, Jack, please!' said his father, with an untypical burst of energy. He looked at the doctor. 'Do they know who the dead men were?'

'Strangers,' said the doctor.

A ghoul suddenly appeared on Jack's pad. He was plucking a sailor off a ship and raising a knife to plunge into his hapless victim. 'Some ghouls kill their own meat,' said Jack.

'Not much to go on to identify them,' said the doctor. 'They have taken the bodies away to be autopsied. I expect we shall learn more tomorrow.'

# TEN

## Cornwall Hospital for Sailors

The following morning I awoke early and walked with the two dogs, Lancy and Doolittle, down the lane to the Mortestow church. Its well-kept churchyard seemed in the morning sun to be just waking. Humble bees were humming huge in the bluebells, swallows darting about the belfry, butterflies just getting dry enough to flutter. A crow who sat atop the cross on the steeple jumped into the air and flapped away as if on urgent business, squawking.

A huge hound arose from behind a gravestone.

I jumped in surprise.

'Good morning,' said Sara Timmons-Swallow. 'I didn't mean to frighten you.'

I turned around and saw her standing by her husband's small flat stone.

'I like to keep the flowers fresh,' she said. 'Now I must go inside and light a candle for those who blame him unjustly.'

'Perhaps they will be changed by your forgiveness,' I said.

'I fear their opinions can never be changed, after all these years. There is no proof – it is a matter of faith, now.'

'I have a friend who would argue that proofs are always available, if one is but clever enough to find them.'

'It would take a deal of cleverness, in this case,' she said.

She was a quiet-spoken creature, perhaps a few years younger than I. We chatted a while longer. When she realized I was intending to walk to Blytheland where my car was parked, she offered to drive me. She hurried into the church and lit her candle, and met me on the road. Her car was small and I doubted we could all fit into it. But the Irish wolfhound had a style of sitting almost like a person on the rear seat, which left space for my two mutts. Sara drove me to the Blytheland green. I thanked her, drove back to the Admiral Hawke Inn, and as I arrived there so did Dr Livesey. He got out of his old Morris Minor and banged the door closed and looked across the gravel at me. 'Trouble,' he said. 'Blankenship had a bad night.' And he ducked inside.

Dr Livesey examined Mr Blankenship and quickly determined he must go to the hospital immediately. We put the sick man carefully into my car, which was large enough to accommodate five of us – Jack, the doctor, me, Mrs Blankenship and the patient. I drove fast along narrow, hedge-bordered roads, taking a few more risks than I might ordinarily have done. As we neared the turn-off that would take us to Port Paul and then Bodmin, Blankenship seemed to get worse. 'We haven't time,' said Dr Livesey. 'Turn left at the next roundabout, and we'll head for the new Cornwall Hospital for Sailors. Dr Savin should be there this morning – I knew him years ago in London.'

Three miles later the hospital hove into view – a strange place in a desolate locale, yet impressive. The architecture, like young Jack's monster drawings, was hybrid, both ancient and new. The half-ruined old monastery where the sick were cared for in the Middle Ages was one wing of the edifice. The other wing was a modern structure with such aerodynamic lines that it looked like it might be about to take off. The old half was what we saw on our left when approaching; the old monastery church was across the road from it, on our right. One could picture, in this unspoiled landscape, monks walking the path from the monastery to the church and back. We curved around to the left and the new portion of the hospital hove into view. Above the canopy over the front unloading area were the words **Cornwall Hospital for Sailors**. We got Mr Blankenship's wheelchair out of the boot and wheeled him inside. Very quickly he was taken away, and the others went with him. I moved the car to the parking lot, then sat down in the waiting room and took from my pocket the small book of verse that Billy Baffin had lent me, *Street Song* by Jim Swallow. The volume was dedicated simply *To Sara*. The frontispiece was a small picture of Swallow, and he looked like a very genial and easy sort, faint smile, eyes bright, hair combed but not too carefully combed, shirt open at the collar. He might have been a pop singer or a parson. I became absorbed in his poems for about a half-hour, and as I read them I could not but think of Billy Baffin reading them with gusto in the bar of the Admiral Hawke. It kept occurring to me that Billy must be deeply involved with the mysteries of Mortestow – but how? He had been on the street, he had been at sea, he had seen Kirk Branford four days ago, he had come into money recently, he had laid down a chunk of cash and apparently intended to stay at the Admiral Hawke indefinitely, he had dark fears of a certain thin individual, he was a drunkard, he wished he had been a pirate or a desert sheik. A fantastical individual was Billy, and hard to categorize. I doubted that even Sherlock Holmes's rational eye could discern the central thread that held Billy Baffin together – or that *once* held him together. For the poor man now seemed to be going to pieces. For such a man to be interested in the poems of Reverend Swallow was another surprise – though obviously his interest in part arose because he saw in Swallow a fellow spirit, a man homeless and fearful and alone and despised in San Francisco just as Billy had been homeless in Southampton. I thought Holmes might find the collection of interest, since he was himself (according to Lestrade) now homeless on the street in London. So in my next email to Holmes I took the trouble to type out and send him the last poem in the book, a poem called *Birthday*:

Laney brought out her blanket
And we sat in a circle of sun
And said sad things
We meant, and wept for sweetness.
Food, filth and fairly good
Wine felt wonderful,
But laughter it was that made us
Merry—and all we lacked
Was mercy. Tommy made
Many grammatical mistakes,
And Eddy seemed dumbfounded,
And Laney licked her cold sore
And told us mad tales.
But I said she wasn't
Mad, was a moth among friends.
*Blow out the candle quickly.*
We four kept
Company at the corner of Death
And Kindergarten, scratching and singing
As bravely as children, laughing
Back to the green and graceful
Days of mother and garden.
Nothing lasts long, she said.
But long enough for laughter.
*Blow out the candle quickly.*

I inquired at the desk and learned Mr Blankenship had been taken
to intensive care. I occupied myself watching the curious mix of
people wandering through the halls. I saw three or four rabbis
escorting individuals in wheelchairs and speaking Yiddish. I overheard several groups of people speaking a language I did not
understand or even recognize. I was surprised so many foreigners
had turned up here, at a hospital in this relatively remote location.
I grabbed a hospital brochure from the side table and read about
the history of the place, how it had been a monastery for centuries,
then for several hundred years a hospital for sailors, and most
recently had been purchased by a European Syndicate dedicated
to offering private hospital services in Great Britain, Poland,
Romania, Greece and various other countries. Mention was made
of a stained glass window that had once been part of the monastery

chapel and that could be viewed. I wandered around till I found it at the back of the hospital, on the ground floor. It marked the beginning of the old monastery building. As I viewed the old window I overheard a conversation taking place in a nearby echoey corridor, though I could not see the speakers.

A voice spoke sharply. 'Fritz, have you seen any sign of Mr Coombes?'

Fritz replied, in the perfect and slightly thick English of a Dutchman, 'No, I'm sorry, Doctor. He was missing from his bed last evening, and we've seen no sign of him.'

'We should have put a monitor on him,' said the other, and the voice seemed vaguely familiar, good English but with an odd accent.

'He seemed so civilized,' said Fritz.

'I'm sure!' said the doctor, and I heard his sharp footsteps as he walked away down the corridor. Fritz followed him. Their clicking footsteps grew fainter.

I found my way to the intensive-care unit nursing station where a very pretty young woman sat. She was strikingly beautiful, with warm lips, but a cheek that looked cold as marble. A glint in her blue eyes. Something was odd, as well as beautiful, about the shape of her entrancing face, the cheekbones so high as to be almost a caricature of sophisticated beauty. She was the ageless sort, and I couldn't be sure whether she was twenty-five or forty. This creature was querying Mrs Blankenship rather sharply. 'Perhaps he will sign it when he is able. Donating organs is something many people wish to do.'

'I don't think he will,' said Mrs Blankenship.

The girl ignored her, almost pointedly, and kept writing.

Dr Livesey, Jack and I went out for lunch in the nearby village. When we returned I noticed a long black hearse leaving the front of the old church across from the monastery, and I remarked that I thought it odd that if the graveyard was next to the church a hearse would be required. Dr Livesey explained that burial in the churchyard was no longer possible. The land was used up. Burials took place elsewhere; he wasn't sure where.

Mr Blankenship had to stay in hospital, as we expected. We left late in the afternoon and drove back to the inn. Mrs Blankenship was exhausted, very worried, but she had a night's work ahead of her, and the admirable woman bustled away and plunged into her duties at the inn. Jack helped her with his usual intent and earnest demeanour.

I hurried to my room and logged on to my computer: nothing. No word from Holmes or Lestrade. I sent Holmes an email report (one of the two emails deleted accidentally) of the day's activities. I hoped that, amidst his delvings into the depths of London, he occasionally would go back to our flat to have a bath and read his mail.

I was beginning to worry. I hadn't heard from him since I'd left London four days ago. Holmes is quirky, but this was unusual even for him.

I took the two dogs out for a last walk in moonlight, and I tried to make some sense of all the fragments of information I had encountered here in Cornwall, tried to discern some pattern that might lead to Kirk Branford or a Cycladic statue. I decided that the time had nearly come when I must give up trying to find a gang in Cornwall. I must go back to London to try to find Holmes. I would give it one more day. If I hadn't heard from Holmes by tomorrow evening, I would leave for London.

As I returned to the inn the light streaming from its windows was barely a glimmer in the immense blackness of the world. I was glad to climb to my room, shut the door behind me, give each dog a night-time biscuit, and go to bed. I must have fallen to sleep almost instantly. But I was disturbed by dreams of monsters flying at the edges of huge cliffs, like pterodactyls of old. They all wore black capes and top hats.

# ELEVEN
## Scalpel! Scalpel!

From: AfghanWilson@QuillNet.com
To: HellmeshCrooks@QuillNet.com

My Dear Holmes,
Yesterday I decided to send you no more email reports until I was certain you were receiving them. Events have taken such a drastic turn, however, that I feel compelled to send you the latest facts in this case – though I feel rather like I'm putting a note in a bottle and flinging it into a cybersea. I beg you, my dear fellow, if this letter comes before your eyes, please let me know *quam primum* that you have received it.

Knowing your penchant for excruciating detail, I have tried to err on the side of including too many facts rather than risking too few. I recall the mystery that you told me you encountered back in 1878, the solution to which depended entirely on the fact that you noticed how someone had pronounced the word *imprimatur*, which some pronounce emphasizing the third syllable, and some the second. So although I cannot imagine what most of the tavern tittle-tattle I am about to report can have to do with this case – particularly the amusing but irrelevant squawkings and mockings of the parrot – I have included all that I can recall, in hopes you may find some of it useful.

It was nearly eleven o'clock before I entered the bar of the Admiral Hawke this morning.

'Welcome aboard!' someone cried, in the voice of Billy Baffin.

'Relax, just relax!' said someone else, in a somewhat strangled voice with a faint foreign accent.

Ensign Squeers has so many voices that he is sometimes disconcerting.

Jack was sweeping the floor, Ilsa polishing glasses behind the bar, Billy Baffin brandishing a pint of lager in one hand and Reverend

Swallow's *Street Song* in the other. 'A murderer perhaps, but a poet true!' cried Billy.

'Dr Livesey says he was no murderer,' said Jack.

'Be that as it may!' cried Billy. He stared at the liquor, he stared at the book.

'You are drinking very early today, Billy' said I. 'The doctor has warned you.'

'Balvenie DoubleWood,' said Billy. He laughed. 'Purely medicinal.' Took another swig. Then he pointed a big arm at Jack. 'Stay away from liquor, lad. Far away! Let old Billy be a lesson to you.'

Jack tossed his hair back out of his eyes, smiled faintly, as if he wanted to be polite and avoid trouble. He kept sweeping.

Billy brandished the book. 'I've been on the street myself, lad! And liquor it was that put me there!'

'Is that so?' I said.

'Captain, was I. Condor line. And then a small incident at St Malo, slight miscalculation – the first of my career, mind! A passenger drowned. They measured my breath.' Billy held up thumb and forefinger and made a gap to indicate a quarter inch. 'I was toppled by half of one per cent.'

'Welcome aboard!'

An Irish wolfhound entered the room, looking huge as a horse. He sniffed the air, made his way to Sara Timmons-Swallow's customary table. He mildly surveyed the scene, his head well above the tabletop. Then he let his long legs slide in the most discrete manner as he lay down in his usual spot, out of traffic. Sara and a friend, an older woman, sat down by him. Sir Launcelot was very interested in the wolfhound, and so was Doolittle, but I told them both to sit back down and they did. A man with a basset hound took a chair in the nook round the corner from where I sat. He ordered a ploughman's lunch from Ilsa.

'Let me be a lesson to you, lad!' cried Billy. 'Stay away from liquor. Look what it has done to me! I've been on the street myself, lad, so I know the truth of it. I've slept cold and dangerous on hard pavements in Southampton three long years, and God forbid that you must ever do the same, Jack! But it is a close thing. Misery is very close to every man – at his shoulder, like. You have a job, lad. People look at you with respect. But men are fragile, Jack, and it takes but the touch of a feather to knock you into the gutter!' He reached out his thick hand and grabbed Jack's slender arm, and pulled him roughly towards him. 'Have you ever had to beg, Jack?'

'No, sir.'

'I have begged, lad! I have squatted like a coolie and begged by my bowl, and I have felt the coldness of my fellow men, and their warmth, too. I have begged pedestrians to look at me, or give me a coin. Even a mere look from a passerby was nourishment for the heart. And a ten-pence piece was a biscuit. And this man Swallow begged in another town, but always it is the same.'

Billy let go of Jack. Billy started to stand up, but fell back into his chair. He took a sip. He opened the book, apparently randomly, started to read:

> 'Street level's about the right
> Level, when you think about it. Sit
> In a Porsche and you can't really hear,
> Sit in a gutter and it's tough to utter
> A greeting except to sparrows. But street
> Level sings the human song.
> Even squatting you can look a man
> In the face and trace his flickering disgust,
> The thrust and parry of his glance,
> See his fugitive eyes go wild
> And leap like lightning into an alley.
> At striding, shuffling, stumbling street
> Level – the level of hydrants and shops
> And Saturday crowds – you can say a civil
> Word and look a man in the face
> And sometimes glimpse, behind his fencing
> Smile, his heart.'

In the corner I saw Sara Timmons-Swallow looking at Billy Baffin in mild amazement – and also in pride, or so I imagined – as he finished his performance. He ended in a whisky-rough voice that whispered the final words in an astonishingly sensitive cadence.

A moment later thudding and laughter announced that a tour bus had arrived and I could see through the window a crowd of people flooding towards the picnic tables on the lawn. Jack and Mrs Blankenship and Ilsa and another young woman were madly busy carrying out food and pulling beers and greeting the customers with cheery haste.

'You, the sultry one, come with me!' cried Billy, whereupon several women looked around hopefully, or maybe just in surprise.

'I was a castaway on the streets of Southampton,' said Billy. 'I was cold in winter and hungry all year, and then I fell from the kerb to the gutter, and from the gutter to Hell, Jack! Listen to old Billy and take heed, my Jack! Beware Romanians bearing gifts! I was rescued from the street and thrown into Hell by Dr Cluj!'

Billy paused. He seemed shaken at the mere remembrance of whatever it was he was remembering. Sweat broke out on his forehead. 'Rum, Jack!' he cried. 'Time for Billy's rum! I am a pirate!'

'Man the lifeboats!' cried Ensign Squeers, in a strange voice.

Several people from the bus looked at Billy in surprise and moved towards the other side of the room. Mrs Blankenship hastened over to our table and took a stern line with Billy. 'Mr Baffin – you must not frighten the other guests.'

'No. Sorry.'

She bustled away.

Jack got down the bottle and poured Billy a glass, somewhat reluctantly.

'Now, Jack, I know you are busy . . .' said Billy.

'I am, rather,' said Jack. He was holding a round tray of beers in his left hand.

'But I ask you a favour, as one man to another.'

'What is it?' asked Jack.

'Draw me a vampire, Jack! A sucker of blood!'

Jack delivered his beers, came back with a pen and drawing pad, and began to draw. With amazing rapidity a bat with a cape and a man's head appeared on the white paper, and Jack scribbled some trees beneath this flying, long-fanged beast. 'That should do, Billy,' said Jack, tearing out the sheet. 'You finish it.'

'I will add the details,' asserted Billy.

His big hands, with their broken and blackened nails, did not seem well suited to the task. But he took up the black felt pen and did surprisingly well. He sketched a few running victims far below the bat. He wrote Transylvania Express on the cape flowing out behind the creature.

All was murmur and pleasure in the quiet bar, people talking in low tones, dogs resigned to being good beneath the tables, the musical *clink* of glassware adding a cheery background music. Then, suddenly, something came over Billy. He froze. His eye rolled. He tilted his head, held up his finger, and said, 'Listen!'

A tapping sound. The window was open, and the sound evidently came from the stone walk leading up to the inn. Billy wiped his hand across his mouth nervously. He looked towards Jack, who had just drifted near with a tray of food for the man with the basset hound. Billy looked at the boy, and motioned to him. 'Jesus, there's a man coming, Jack – send him away. Don't let him in!'

'I can't very well turn people away,' said Jack.

'The devil himself!' cried Ensign Squeers, and he *bawked* and fluffed his wings.

'That's the truth of it!' gasped Billy.

'Man the lifeboats!'

As if heeding the parrot's order, Billy lurched up from his chair, holding on to the table, and lunged towards the staircase leading up to the bedrooms. He almost made it but not quite. A man appeared in the front door, cut him off. The man walked straight towards Billy, blocked him. He tapped his black cane twice hard on the wooden floor. He backed Billy up. Billy stumbled backward and almost knocked down the brass pot hanging on a peg by the fireplace. Billy sat down at the little round table by the hearth. Instantly the newcomer sat down opposite him, on the other side of the table, with his back to me. This newcomer struck me as oddly elegant, and strange. As if from a foreign realm or another age. And yet he was perfectly modern. He wore a long black overcoat. He carried a long black cane. I wondered if he could be the same slender man I had seen hustle Kirk Branford away from Penlaven, the same slender figure I had later seen fleeing into the graveyard of the ruined church.

Terror and anger clouded Billy's face. The Irish wolfhound was suddenly stiff and on his feet, growling menacingly, his whole body rigid. Sara Timmons-Swallow hastily put a leash on the dog. She nervously wrapped the leash around the table leg. She reprimanded him. But still Patrick the wolfhound seemed ready to attack. I half expected to see the table fly across the room as he lurched. The cocker spaniel was also on his feet, growling as he pulled on his leash – then fear seemed to overpower the little cocker and he put his tail between his legs, backed up, growling softly.

The newcomer faced away from me but I could clearly hear every word that he and Billy said to each other. Occasionally the stranger rapped his black cane on the floor to emphasize his points. 'You've signed a contract, Billy Baffin. You have taken the money. Now you must fulfil your bargain.'

'I do no deals with the devil,' said Billy.

'Fair is fair, Billy,' said the other, genially, and his pronunciation was excruciatingly correct, but his voice slightly strangled and strange, with a hint of foreign.

'And foul is foul,' said Billy.

'Come now, Billy Baffin! Be a reasonable man . . . and all will be well.'

Billy's face, which had turned almost white, now reddened. 'Damn you, Cluj – you'll not have my gizzard!'

'You must keep your promise, Billy!' cried the other. 'My client is depending on you at eleven tomorrow morning, depending on you for his life – for his very life, Billy! Depending on your promise. We must not disappoint him. One way or the other, Billy Baffin, I must not disappoint my client! Do you understand?' He tapped the cane on the hearthstones.

Billy seemed to shrink. Heavy old stones of the fireplace rose behind him and a huge brass pot hung next to his head, and he looked very small, like a scared child. A defensive and startled look had crept into his eyes. I felt sorry for the old reprobate, seeing him shrink so.

'Afterward, Billy,' said the man in black, in a cajoling and reasonable tone, 'after this is over you must agree to be my captain once more. Fly my *Phantom*, and you shall be well paid. My replacement captain is not satisfactory. You are the best that ever I had.'

Someone dropped a glass. The man in black turned his head sharply at the sound, and in that instant I glimpsed his profile, and it startled me – shocked me. Such a lean and sharply shaped and cruel face I have seldom seen. It was a face such as one might expect to see in a horror film, with eyes almost black, with nose as crooked as the beak of a bird of prey and as sharp as a knife, and with thin lips round a mouth so small one might almost wonder how the man got sufficient nourishment. He was, in fact, almost such a caricature of evil as Jack might draw in black ink. Yet his voice, though strangled, was strangely silky and appealing. I couldn't be sure. I guessed he must be a foreigner who had gone to university in England – perhaps to a public school, too.

And then I remembered where I had seen that face before: on the dragon flying by the bus stop sign.

'No Death Ship duty for me!' cried Billy.

'Welcome aboard!' cried Ensign Squeers.

Two people came into the bar, nodded to me, sat down at my table beneath the porthole.

'You are not being reasonable,' said the man in black, his tone hardening.

'You speak of reason, but deal in madness!' cried Billy, and he pounded the table with his fist. 'Speak not of reasonableness to me!'

The two people at my table gazed at this hearthside conversation in surprise.

The man in black rapped his cane hard on the flagstone hearth. Whether this was a threat or merely a nervous habit could hardly be guessed. Clearly, he was agitated. His voice had changed. 'You know what has happened to others, Billy Baffin. We have been partners, you and I, and I would not wish . . .'

'Not I!' cried Billy. 'I have not been your partner, only your pawn – easily sacrificed.'

The other laughed a nasty laugh. 'If you play chess, or any other game, with me, Billy Baffin, you will lose.'

They stared at each other. Billy's face looked like a mask of startled anger.

'I will have you, Billy Baffin. As agreed. One way or the other,' said the man in black.

Billy now stiffened, a faint tremor shook him, he glowed redder – and he exploded, 'You'll not cut me! I'll see you in Hell first, Dr Cluj!'

Billy put his hands under his side of the table and heaved it upward, toppling it, and Dr Cluj leapt up to avoid being crushed. Billy looked around, seemed about to grab the heavy brass pan. Instead, Billy lunged forward, reached up, grabbed the cutlass off the ceiling beam.

Cluj whirled about and made a dash for the door, skirts of his black coat floating as he whirled. Billy charged close behind, cutlass uplifted, and he slashed, and a slit appeared in the fabric of the black overcoat's arm, and red blood appeared. Cluj pulled open the door. He would have been caught, but Billy stumbled on the cocker spaniel. The dog yelped. Billy regained balance and rushed through the open front door and took a tremendous cut at the fleeing Cluj – his blow would have split Cluj from skull to hip bone – but the hanging wooden sign over the door intervened, and Billy's mighty blow was deflected . . . and a chunk of the swinging sign was gone.

I ran outside shouting for Billy to desist. The sign was creaking as it swung.

Billy stumbled across the green, waving his cutlass. But the sprightly figure in black was far ahead. A furry streak brushed my legs – the wolfhound bounded across the green like a strange rocket – but Cluj had nearly reached the silver van. He leapt into it, slammed the door. The huge dog circled the vehicle, barking. Now the cocker spaniel leapt in little bounds across the green to join him. The vehicle rolled backwards, then moved slowly off into the hedge-lined road and vanished towards Port Paul, pursued by two dogs.

Billy Baffin swaggered back inside and sat down in his old place. I thought he might serve us a rant while waving his weapon like a pirate. Instead he laid the cutlass on the table, folded his big broken hands on the tabletop, and looked about.

'Need a drink, Billy?' asked Mrs Blankenship.

'No, no,' said Billy. 'I've had enough.'

Mrs Blankenship walked away shaking her head.

Jack lifted the cutlass and put it back on its mounts on the ceiling timber.

'There is a bit of blood on the blade,' I said.

'I suppose we should leave it there,' said Jack.

'I suppose we should,' I agreed, thinking the police would wish the weapon untouched.

'Won't hurt a thing,' said Billy.

'Scalpel! Scalpel!' cried Ensign Squeers, in a voice very like Cluj's.

I asked Mrs Blankenship whether she had heard from the hospital. She said they were keeping Mr Blankenship another day, and that she would drive down in the afternoon to see him.

As I left the bar to come upstairs and write this report, Billy was in command, rising from his table and stomping across the poop deck, holding his arm in the air for some obscure purpose, and meanwhile the startled bus tourists were deserting the ship in droves. Many had seen the attack and were trying to avoid Billy.

'Man overboard! Man overboard!' cried Ensign Squeers.

For the last hour I have been writing this report in my room. From my window I see empty picnic tables on the back lawn, littered with empty bottles and glasses. The busload of tourists has vanished.

All is quiet. More uproar doubtless will ensue when the police arrive, which I expect them to do at any moment.

Please, Holmes, be good enough to let me know when you have received this report. On Monday Lestrade informed me you were descending 'into London's netherworld' to find Bertie Branford. I hate to picture you sleeping in a doorway. Sleeping in a glacier was at least clean and safe.

Yours,
*Wilson*


# TWELVE
## Strange Encounter

After sending my letter off to Holmes I descended to the bar where Ilsa was singing to herself and looking unusually bright as she polished glasses. Billy sat at his usual table with two middle-aged men whom I had not seen before. Everyone seemed most genial and unconcerned, which struck me as odd. I had no doubt that Dr Cluj, wounded and bleeding, had contacted the authorities by now, and that the police would arrive momentarily.

In this I was quite wrong.

I ordered a small lunch at the bar and asked Ilsa if the police had been called. Her musical 'Why?' almost convinced me that there was no need of police. 'Billy is a long-term customer,' she explained, shrugging happily.

'He attacked a man with a cutlass,' I said.

She laughed. 'People have their moods.'

I could not tell if Ilsa was peculiarly obtuse, or just a cheerful spirit who liked to put the best spin on things in this troubled and uncertain life of ours. She was certainly pretty. For some reason, looking at her, I was moved to call my fiancée in London. But Rachel wasn't answering, and her mailbox was full, so I was left feeling for a moment a bit stranded and lonely here in the strange gloom and sun of Cornwall.

'A fine woman she was!' cried Billy, his voice roaring suddenly from the nook. 'But she left me when I fell from grace and no longer had money.'

'It is hard to keep a woman without money or a horse,' said one of the men.

'Why a horse?' asked the other man.

'You, the sultry one, come with me!' cried Ensign Squeers, in Billy's voice.

I went out with the two dogs and we walked up the path. Flowers bloomed white and yellow and blue in the high green hedges, white sheep drifted in emerald fields, and then we broke out into the high ground and I could see, far below, the sea all wrinkled with wind and shattered with light. I walked north, past Death Drop and the middle Cliff Path. Just beyond Swallow's Nest I turned right into the Mortestow path and began descending. The dogs sniffed and chased each other between field and hedge. At the stone water tank Sir Launcelot rose up on his hind legs and drank as if he hadn't drunk in a week. At that moment my mobile phone made its noise.

I held the phone in the shadow of a hedge and read a new text message: *Kirk Branford gaoled for murder last month in Fargo, North Dakota. No sign of Holmes. Lestrade.*

I whistled to the dogs, walked down to where the three cliff paths met near the road, and so back to the Admiral Hawke. In the soft gloom and gleam of the pub Ensign Squeers ruffled his feathers, cocked his head, and looked me sceptically in the eye . . . and said nothing. Billy Baffin nodded to me as he picked up his pint and walked outside.

I ordered a pint and followed Billy on to the lawn. He sat at a distant table and read a newspaper. I sat at the umbrella table next to the inn. I am generally of a fairly steady temperament, but suddenly I felt done in. I was worried about Holmes, and utterly confounded as to my own purpose in being here. What could be the meaning, if any, of all I had discovered? I had not been following Kirk Branford, after all. Holmes had vanished. And the sundry mysteries of Mortestow seemed random, chaotic, unrelated – phantom ships, strange sightings in graveyards, maimed bodies by the sea, tales of a minister who died strangely with two of his female disciples, not to mention an aging seaman who roistered and roared at the Admiral Hawke Inn like some character out of a sea novel.

Holmes had admonished me to simply make observations and

collect facts, and leave the synthesizing and theorizing to him. This I attempted to do. But as a practical matter it was necessary to concoct temporary theories in order to decide what to investigate next, or where to direct my efforts. My present theory, though sketchy and full of empty patches, was that two of the men found dead on the shore were Sinjin Chitterlie, whom I had spoken with at the Kittle Mill House, and the black man whom I had glimpsed through a window pane in the South Cottage at Kittle Mill. The fact that the middle finger of the one dead man was cut off, and that Chitterlie wore a ruby ring on that finger, suggested this possibility. The third dead man, I theorized, might be the same who had tried to attack me, and who had fallen while clutching his neck and crying, 'Get it off me!' If these three were members of the gang smuggling art out of the country, it seemed probable that they were among those figures I had seen hauling crates of goods into Mouse Hole Cottage. Presumably they were, a short time later, aboard the lighter churning out of Flint Cove into black and stormy seas, presumably ferrying the booty to the waiting craft at anchor offshore, which might well be the hydrofoil that Billy once had piloted, the one he called *The Phantom*. Such was my theory of the moment. But who had killed the three men, and why their bodies were nude and maimed, were mysteries utterly beyond me. Perhaps these three were gang members who had somehow fallen out with their fellow thieves, and had been knifed, and their dead bodies stripped to make identification more difficult, and thrown overboard. Chitterlie had complained to me that the ring was so tightly into his flesh that he could no longer take it off, and evidently neither could those who killed him.

After supper, I checked my computer one last time. Still no word. About seven in the evening I walked out into fading light and picked up a short length of pipe from a pile of scrap iron by the shed. I smiled to think how Holmes's companion in the old days, Dr John Watson, often carried a revolver on dangerous assignments, as Holmes did himself. And here came I with nothing but a lead pipe in hand. I would have preferred a revolver. Already this case was strewn with dead bodies – headless and maimed corpses had been turning up with astonishing regularity. I intended to learn whether Sinjin Chitterlie and the black man were still at Kittle Mill. If they were, that was information for Holmes. If they weren't, I intended to enter the Mill House and see what could be found. If statuary had been stored in one of the rooms, I might see some sign of it.

I tied up the two dogs on the lawn behind the inn, gave them each a biscuit, and set off down the path with a swinging step, lead pipe in hand. I wore running shoes, tan safari trousers and a matching short-sleeved safari shirt with lots of pockets – in one of which was the mobile phone Holmes never called. As I swung along, lead pipe in hand, I felt rather jaunty. In my mind was jiggling another fragment of my present theory, a fragment that had to do with Billy Baffin. His odd conversation with the curious Dr Cluj seemed to suggest that Billy had once been part of the smuggling operation, as captain of the hydrofoil named *The Phantom*. But evidently Billy had fallen afoul of Cluj, refused to work, and now Cluj was threatening him, telling him he must return to work. All this might explain why Cluj had not filed a complaint with the police. If the police were brought in, Billy might expose the operation.

I reached the River Neep and followed the bank east towards Kittle Mill. To my left, above the greening massive trees, I saw the top of the ruined church protruding. The top edges of the old church tower were fractured and broken in such a way that they resembled the crenellated top of a castle – just such a ruined castle as one of young Jack's vampires might inhabit.

I stopped dead. Scarcely able to believe my eyes. Amidst the tumbled graves I saw a slim figure in a black coat. He was stomping on a grave. He looked pretty lively for a man just recently struck with a cutlass. I was stunned. My very thought had conjured him into existence, apparently. I couldn't help wondering whether I was imagining this whole scene. The light was very dim. The phantom figure vanished and I was relieved. An *ignis fatuus*, I thought. Nothing more than grave gas, perhaps. But a moment later he reappeared, moving swiftly. I quickened pace, hurried after him in almost a run. I gained on him as he floated swiftly above the graves. Beneath the gnarled limbs of a tree he stopped and began stomping on another grave. I cried out, 'I say, may I have a word, sir!'

He stopped stomping. But he did not turn to look at me. He was standing in shadow and I could not see him clearly.

I approached at a walk. A chill passed over my body. To see him standing there unmoving, frozen, seemed a threat of a most ominous kind. I strode forward purposefully and gripped the pipe more firmly. 'Sorry to intrude, sir,' said I.

He turned swiftly, face in shadow. 'Oh, do put that down, Wilson – someone will mistake you for a thug!'

I was dumbfounded to hear that familiar voice.

'Holmes!' I gasped. 'Is it you?'

'In the flesh,' said he.

'But what are you doing here!'

He raised an eyebrow. 'Solving crimes, Wilson. Solving crimes!'

# THIRTEEN
## Up From London's Depths

S herlock Holmes stepped off the grave mound on which he had been standing. He extended his slender hand. I shook it – amazed, as always, at the sinewy strength of it.

'You cannot imagine how glad I am to see you,' said I. 'I have written report after report, made call after call, and you have responded with silence. Thank god you are all right.'

'I hit a streak of bad luck, Wilson – my apologies. I lost my mobile phone in a storm sewer in Tottenham Court Road four days ago.' He flung his hand in the air, in impatience. 'Carelessness, pure careless! I was improvising a streetside drama involving soft-drink cans. I became overzealous, carried away – I confess it – by my own histrionics. I heard a beep. And the little silvery thing winked away into the gloom, not even touching the grate . . . and was gone.'

'So for the last four days I've been texting the sewer,' I said.

'Alas,' said Holmes, 'that is true. And I was nowhere near a computer until late Sunday evening. Only then did I read your reports.'

A crow squawked raucously in a tree high overhead.

Another crow answered. The dusk was thick.

'But why this masquerade, Holmes? That looks like the coat of Dr Cluj.'

'It is,' said he. 'I have had some adventures, Wilson. Curious adventures.'

'Stomping on a grave seems an adventure in itself.'

'Come have a look.'

He led me to the grave where I had first seen him. The lichen-covered headstone, once doubtless the pride of a stonecutter, was now so misshapen by time and weather that it looked like something crudely hacked from granite with a flint chisel. The grave plot itself was outlined with a rectangular frame of moss-covered stone. Lying flat on the top of the mounded rectangle was a large cross of stone, also encrusted with moss. Holmes kicked at the cross.

'Good heavens, Holmes!' I cried.

His behaviour seemed a bit outré, even for him. I knew he was a sceptic with regard to religion, of course. But there are limits.

'Never fear, Wilson!' said he. 'The gods will not be offended.'

'You should say God, Holmes. This is not a Greek temple.'

'It's stuck.' He kicked again. He stooped, pushed the small arm of the cross. He slipped his fingers under the edge, he lifted with both hands . . . a trap door in the top of the grave opened up. 'Come look,' he said.

I stepped forward with a feeling of revulsion, reluctant to look upon whatever loathsome sight awaited.

'What do you think of that!' cried Holmes.

I peered into the dim cavity. I couldn't get a grip. I had trouble believing. 'I'm stunned,' I said.

'You should be,' he said.

'Electrical switches?' I said.

'Precisely,' he replied. 'Instruments of torture, Wilson. They control the flow of electricity through the buried wire that encircles the hamlet. This is how Cluj keeps his victims at Kittle Mill with no likelihood of their slipping away. He fits them each with a collar which he assures them is a medical device to monitor their vital functions. In fact, it is a restraining device that will shock repeatedly, and with increasing power, as the wearer nears the perimeter of the hamlet. The collar cannot be removed without a key. If a patient attempts to remove it, electrical shocks are administered automatically.'

'Like an invisible dog fence?'

'Precisely. And thus are all the livestock of Kittle Mill kept here in the hamlet until needed at the hospital.'

'You have lost me, Holmes. Livestock?'

'That is how Dr Cluj refers to them in his private papers. I believe the livestock are already departed, but let us tear down the fence anyway.' He picked up a broken chunk of headstone from a nearby grave and began smashing the electrical connections in the grave at our feet. Sparks leapt and sizzled. A thread of smoke seeped into the air. He dropped the stone chunk into the hole. He hefted the door and let it thud closed, then stood up and wiped his palms on the long black coat he wore. He waved a hand towards the ruined church. 'Must have been an electrical line run down here years ago from Mortestow, for the old church has electric lamps. Evidently Cluj and company tapped into that line, ran a wire to this switch box, which they placed where no one would stumble upon it and meddle with it. Astonishing. Someone has spent a great deal of ingenuity on this operation, Wilson!'

'I can hardly believe you are really here, Holmes. You seem less likely than vampires or ghosts. I half fear I'm hallucinating. How did you get here? And tell me, why are you dressed in this fantastic way?'

He wore blue jeans beneath the coat, and flare-topped black boots that came up to his calf and that might have been worn by one of the three musketeers.

'Come,' he said. 'On our way up to the cliffs I will tell you a tale. But we must hasten to learn if *The Phantom* has returned.'

'You know about the hydrofoil?' I asked.

'I have been aboard her, Wilson! I have been aboard her!'

He floated away like a witch through the gravestones, headed for the main path by the river. I hurried after him.

'How long have you been here?' I gasped.

'Three days.'

'I am astonished.'

'Since Sunday afternoon. But let me go back a little and tell you how strangely fortunate I have been in this investigation.'

'I've been worried, Holmes.'

Holmes stopped suddenly in the path, turned to me, and astonished me again. He clapped my shoulders with both of his hands, and smiled, and said, 'You look good to me, Wilson. Very good indeed!'

We continued walking.

'The same afternoon you left for Cornwall,' said Holmes, 'I met Lestrade and we went together to visit Cecelia Branford on Primrose Hill. The other sister, Alice, was there, and the two sisters were preparing to hold a séance to contact their dead brother, Bertie.'

'I received an email from Lestrade,' I said, 'in which he told me how during the séance you deduced, or at least had good reason to suspect, that Bertie was alive, and that Cecelia Branford knew it.'

'Then I can omit that part of my tale. I suspect Cecelia is the only Branford that suspects Bertie is alive. For Alice was the one who demanded the séance, and Cecelia, it seemed to me, merely did her best to oblige her. At the séance I learned that Bertie's old friend, Daniel Ma, knew Bertie was alive in London. Afterward Lestrade and I visited Ma at the National Liberal Club and there Ma told me Bertie was on the street, and was known as "Bad Dog" amongst the street people.'

'Lestrade mentioned this. And how you determined to go on to the street in disguise to find him.'

'Yes. The following day I descended into the street in my oldest clothes, and wandered about the area where Bertie had last been seen. I did my drink-can drama, to demonstrate that I was slightly mad. As I performed I saw a middle-aged man sitting in a doorway, watching me. When I finished, I crawled out of the gutter and staggered towards him. He stared at me, slouched against his wall.

'"Where's Bad Dog?" I asked, and I held up the can I had half filled. "I owe him a drink."

'"Bad Dog gone," he said.

'So quickly was I lucky, Wilson! The very first street person I talked to knew Bad Dog. He said Bad Dog had gone to get rich. If I wanted to learn more I should try talking to Ferry, who was always in the soup kitchen around noon or one o'clock, and who wore a white bandage around his neck. I found Ferry easily enough, almost as if it were a game I couldn't lose. He was a middle-aged man, slight of build, with a limp. Bad Dog, he said, had gone off to get rich. How, I asked, did he plan to do that? Volunteer, says he. Volunteer for what? I asked. Medical research, says he. After a bit of aimless conversation he dug a soiled and bent piece of heavy paper from his pocket. It seemed to be an advertisement that promised a ride to a medical facility and twenty pounds a day. "Bad dog volunteered to do this?" I asked.

'"He did. I saw him get in the van," said Ferry, nodding his head as if to reassure himself that he had actually seen it. I asked if I could have the advertisement. No, Ferry wouldn't give it to me. So I bought it from him for twenty pounds. "You got to try Sunday morning, but sometimes they aren't there," he said. "Sunday

morning, west side of Russell Square. But some days they don't
come."

'I slept rough that night, for I wanted to look the part, to be
convincingly scruffy if the van appeared as promised. I walked early
to Russell Square. The advertisement said nine a.m. I lingered. Saw
a few others lingering. At a little after nine o'clock a silver van
appeared. It stopped at the corner of the square. I sauntered towards
it. So did another man. The van door opened and the driver looked
at me, smiling. A short happy fellow. "Good morning, sir," said he.

'"Good morning – is this the right van?" I asked.

'He squinted, took my measure. "I'd say it is," said he. And as
I climbed aboard he said, "Medical?"

'"Yes," I said.

'"See your ticket, mate?"

'I took out the advertisement, handed it to him. "This is all I
have."

'"Good enough," says he.

'I sat down in the third seat. Soon the other man came on board.
And, just as we were about to leave, a third. The driver looked at
his watch, said, "That's it, then," and we were away.

'During the long drive neither I nor the other two passengers
spoke, and the cheery driver only spoke a few times. After a few
hours we stopped at a roadside restaurant and the driver gave us
each eight pounds to buy what food we liked. When we resumed
our journey he told us we were headed to Cornwall. I occupied my
time by observing my silent fellow travellers. I was surprised to
observe that the man named Dan had been a missionary in China,
a mercenary in Sudan and a banker in London. He was about sixty.
The other man, Ben, was in his fifties. He had suffered polio as a
child, seemed to have fleas, and quite obviously had been a concert
pianist before turning to drink and slowly falling to street level. I
wondered why he had turned to drink, but I could not find the
answer by simply looking at him.

'We arrived in Port Paul in the afternoon, drove immediately
to the edge of the moor along small roads. We travelled to the
hospital by an indirect route seemingly devised to confuse us and
prevent us from knowing exactly where we were. The hospital
was impressive, a hybrid building made of an ancient monastery
and a modern building that looked as if it had been designed by
Picasso and by a slightly inebriated aeronautical engineer. Three

very large men in white garb escorted us into the facility. They all were very genial in a pressing sort of way, and all were foreign. One was a Dutchman named Fritz, one a German, one probably Hungarian. I decided to go along with their programme, whatever it was. They took me to a small office where a rather icy, blonde female with exceedingly bright blue eyes took information from me. I gave my name as Cedric Coombes. She asked how long I had been homeless; I told her four or five years. She asked what work I had done; I said I remembered nothing of my past life previous to the day I found myself unconscious on the street near the Wellington Monument. This answer seemed to please the woman. When she asked if I had had any illnesses, I mentioned frostbite.'

'Holmes,' I cried. 'You are irrepressible!'

'One of the burly chaps, the German, then escorted me to a very nice private room with en-suite facilities, in the old monastery section of the building. He showed me a well-stocked cabinet where the shaving equipment, soap, combs, and so on were kept, and he suggested I take a shower. I did so. He said he would collect my clothes and have them laundered. I undressed and handed the clothes out to him, keeping my wallet and personal belongings, which I hid behind the extra tissue rolls on a high shelf. While the clothes were being laundered he said I was to wear the pyjamas and the robe hanging behind the door. I emerged from the shower and was surprised to see he had taken not only my clothes but my shoes. A pair of paper slippers was all that he had left for me. I wanted to walk down the hall and look about, but when I tried the door I found it was locked from the outside.

'Later in the evening two burly men wearing white hospital uniforms appeared at my door. They supplied me with the supper I had ordered. They also informed me that in the morning the doctor would be in to discuss the operation that was scheduled for Monday. After the operation, they told me, I would be paid two hundred pounds cash and given a train ticket back to London.'

'Good heavens, Holmes!' said I. 'You have lost me. What operation was he speaking of?'

Holmes looked back at me as he pushed through a gate and into another field. 'An operation to remove one of my kidneys – and perhaps a slice of liver.'

'For what purpose, pray tell!' I cried.

'For profit, Wilson – for profit! Haven't you guessed?'

'No, I haven't guessed,' I replied. 'You said *medical research*. Surely you didn't volunteer to be operated on!'

'And neither did anyone else. But wait a while, you will hear.'

'Carry on, Holmes!'

'A hospital that collects homeless people from London streets, buses them hundreds of miles, locks them up in a room, and promises them money if they participate in an unspecified "operation", is a facility that arouses my suspicions.'

'I should think.'

'I thought it best that I should make my escape *quam celeriter.* My door was locked from the outside, but the hinges were on the inside. After midnight I tapped the pins out of those hinges, using a shaving cream can as a tool. The door was heavy but I managed to unseat it, pull the hinged side open. And so I made my escape, taking my wallet and personal belongings with me. If I had not hidden them, I am certain they would have disappeared forever. The hospital is a labyrinthine place, and I spent a good deal of time floating down the halls like a ghost, trying to find the main office while escaping the notice of the occasional nurses and attendants who appeared in the hallways. The office was locked but I had noticed a janitor's cart parked outside a lavatory. Hanging from the cart was a big ring of keys. I snatched the keys, then returned to the main office, entered, and found my way into the inner office of a certain Dr Vladimir Cluj, who is the hospital director. My first bit of luck was discovering in his coat closet this long coat you see me wearing, together with a pair of shoes which almost fit. I would need those things for my escape – I could hardly appear in the town in bare feet wearing pyjamas.'

'I'm not sure I'd have been so fastidious about the proprieties, under the circumstances.'

'Once a Victorian, always a Victorian,' said Holmes, with a laugh. 'We are all victims and beneficiaries of our times. Having semi-properly clothed myself, I began going through Cluj's paper files. I found a small trove of information. I simply grabbed sheets and stuffed them into one of Cluj's briefcases. I next switched on the computer and began my search through various files and databases. I was very glad I have spent the past year learning the intricacies of computers, with a special emphasis on hacking into files meant to be kept secret. Oddly, none of Cluj's files were locked. No passwords, nothing. I copied as many relevant documents as I could, went online, opened my own email account, and attached the documents to emails which I then sent to myself and to Scotland Yard.'

'You might have dropped me a line, Holmes.'

'I meant to, and was about to do so when I heard stirrings in the outer office. I was forced to close up the file cabinets, close down the computer, and put Cluj's office back in order. Opening the door a crack, I saw his secretary busily working at her computer, her back to me. I walked quietly out – if she saw me, she saw only the back of Cluj's long coat. I walked boldly through the hallways. Once I heard a voice behind me say, "Working late, Dr Cluj?" And I waved a hand and walked on, and later someone said, "Good morning, Doctor." And then I was out into the night air. The sky was just turning pale at the fringes.

'I was not yet free, however. For I was on foot in a rural area utterly unfamiliar to me, and I had no doubt that if I was spotted by any of Cluj's employees they would attempt to apprehend me and bring me back. But again I was fortunate. As I hurried along the road a farmer in a little lorry stopped and asked if I needed a ride. He took me to Port Paul. It was too early for shops to be open, so I could do nothing to improve my wardrobe. I ate an early breakfast at a restaurant, then hired a taxi to take me to Mortestow, a place I had noticed mentioned repeatedly in the files of Dr Cluj. The other place often mentioned was Kittle Mill.'

Holmes and I had now reached the Mortestow road. We crossed it in three strides and went through the hedge on the far side and continued on our upward path. Shortly we saw before us a forking, for here diverged the three paths leading up to the cliffs – the path straight ahead which was the shortest, the path to the right which was the Mortestow cliff path, and the path to the left which was the Inn cliff path. 'Let us try the Mortestow path,' said Holmes, veering a little to the right.

'Sharp right, Holmes,' said I, for the path straight ahead also angled to the right slightly, and was a bit confusing. Then he saw the small sign, took the sharp right, and we were on our way up.

'When I arrived at Mortestow,' he continued, 'I bought a map of the area at the Tea and Pastry Shoppe, a crude little map but perfectly adequate, hand-drawn by Mrs Dingle who runs the shop. Guided by my map, I descended the path round hills and through fields to the River Neep, and thence to Kittle Mill. No one was there.'

'This was two days ago?'

'Yes, about noon on Monday.'

'I know three people had been there the day before.'

'I broke into all the buildings,' said Holmes. 'No sign of life.'

'Any indication statues might have been stored there?'

'Statues? No, no, you are on the wrong track, Wilson!' he cried, impatiently.

I waved my arm at him – also rather impatiently, I'm afraid. 'Carry on, Holmes! If you'd be good enough to put me on the *right* track, I'd very much appreciate it!'

Holmes's habit of holding his cards all in his hand, and laying them down only when he is ready to 'go out' and end the game, is sometimes rather irritating.

He skittered on up the path, still talking in a loud voice that seemed to be quickly absorbed by the hedge and the bright blowing distance. 'I then climbed up this path to the cliffs and investigated Swallow's Nest, about which I had already heard a great deal and . . . look there, Wilson.' He pointed ahead.

Two strange birds were sitting on the stone water trough.

'The ancients,' I said, 'would see in such a pairing an omen. But I can assure you, Holmes, that it is merely an albino jackdaw with a normal black-with-grey jackdaw. Albinos occasionally appear in all species, if I'm not mistaken.'

'I defer to your greater ornithological knowledge, Wilson.'

'My wife was a birdwatcher, Holmes, and the good woman gave me a great thick book and instructed me to keep in it a detailed record of all the birds I encountered. I was never interested in that book. When she ran off with her computer expert, I got rid of it.'

The birds flew, *jack-jack-jack*ing, and we continued up the path and on to the cliffs. Holmes in his black coat stood at the cliff's edge, and the coat was blowing in the breeze, and he stepped over and hastened into oblivion down the little path to Swallow's Nest. I followed. As Holmes opened the Dutch door and stepped into the little hut, I said, 'On Sunday, while you were being driven down to Cornwall, I saw a man dressed just as you are seemingly step over the cliff and vanish. It must have been Cluj; he must have stepped down on to this very path. But at the time I didn't know of the existence of this place. I thought I was hallucinating.'

Holmes laughed. 'My dear Wilson, please don't tell me you believed you saw a vampire flying away!'

Holmes ducked through the door and took a seat on the little bench that ran around three sides of the tiny hut. I sat down opposite Holmes. We seemed to be sitting on a sheer drop-off. 'The thought of vampires occurred to me,' I confessed. 'But only because I'd been put in the mood by that rascal Billy Baffin, and by young Jack, with all his monster drawings. Why a young man would draw monsters instead of beautiful women, I cannot fathom.'

'You wouldn't,' said Holmes.

Our shoes were nearly touching. The sea below us boiled on the black rocks.

Holmes suddenly looked pensive, rubbed his thin chin. He drew from his pocket the briar pipe made by the incomparable Mr Sedley of Hexham, clapped it betwixt his teeth. His hands fidgeted. Then he nervously grabbed the pipe out of his mouth and with the stem of it pointed out to sea. '*The Phantom* is gone. But when she stands off that point, Wilson, she is easily seen from here. Look what I have found!'

He turned quickly in the narrow space, pressed his fingers on the wooden wall at the back of the little hut, pulled open a little door to reveal a deep cupboard. The top shelf held a red flag and a white flag and a large torch. On the bottom shelf was a car battery with wires attached. He touched it. 'It powers the line of lights along the path,' said he.

'I saw no line of lights.'

'The wire is buried, the bulbs tiny as pebbles, scarcely to be seen amidst the gorse. Just over the edge, where no one will step on them.'

'For what purpose, Holmes?'

'Night walking. To keep from tumbling off the path.'

'Night walking into this nest does not appeal to me.'

'From here, my dear Wilson, Dr Cluj and his confederates signal *The Phantom*. Mobile phone traffic can be traced. But a signal made with torch or flag cannot be intercepted and recorded.'

'Just like ancient times,' said I. 'False lights and signal torches on the Cornwall coast.'

Holmes closed the cabinet door carefully, sighed, frowned, his

long fingers moving in faint fidgets on his trouser leg, getting agitated
again, obviously thinking on several channels simultaneously, only
one of which involved me. He clapped his briar pipe back between
his teeth and stared through the little doorway, gazing intently into
far distance over the rounding blue sea that had now turned misty
with evening. He reminded me of a mariner seeking landfall, and
not finding it. I had learned it is useless to question him when he
is in such a state. Brilliance has its prerogatives, no doubt.

By and by Holmes continued the tale of his escape from the
hospital.

'Narrow and hard, but I've slept in worse beds, Wilson! I found
an old wooden pew in the ruined church. I bedded myself down,
like any horse, with weeds from the churchyard. As I was gathering
weeds I saw you and the young lad looking.'

'It was you!' I cried.

'Of course!'

'But how did you recognize me in the moonlight?'

'A person's walk tells volumes – have I shown you my monograph
called *Styles of Walking as They Relate to Personality Traits and
the Identification of Criminals*?'

'That's one I have not heard of,' I said.

'I wonder if Lestrade has it amongst my stored things at the
Yard?'

'Do get on with the story, Holmes.'

'In short, when I saw two figures appearing on the path, I fled
away into the gloom of the churchyard and found a bush to hide
behind. Through its greenery I watched as you and the lad contem-
plated coming after me. It was quite like a miniature play, Wilson.
You hesitated, came towards me a few steps. The lad began to follow
you, almost tiptoeing.'

'But why, in heaven's name, since you knew it was I, did you
not hail me!'

'I thought it best to pursue my own researches here in Mortestow
for a while longer.'

'And you went to the length of starting fires . . . oh, the Philpot
Igniter, I presume!'

'Yes, I pulled the pin on a Philpot Igniter and dropped it into the
dried weeds I had gathered for my pew bed. I had laid the weeds
on the grave slab. I hoped to distract you, perhaps even frighten
you.'

'I wasn't frightened until the Bible burst into flames!' I said.

'Superstition undid you, then!' laughed Holmes. 'As it has undone so many!'

'Mustn't gloat, Holmes.'

'When you had gone I finished bedding my stall. All I had for comfort were a heap of weeds and this stolen coat . . .' He paused, laughed.

'You must have been cold at night,' said I, 'with only a coat.'

Holmes seemed momentarily, uncharacteristically, lost. He had vanished utterly. The sea boiled and receded from the black rocks far below us – came boiling in and faded backwards. It all felt a bit surreal. At last he said, as if far away, 'I remember Wiggins once saying to me, "There's nothing warmer than a stolen coat, Mr Holmes."'

'Wiggins?'

'Willie Wiggins, Baker Street Irregulars, the one who helped me escape London in nineteen fourteen, when I was on my way to meet the Czar and . . .'

'Ah, yes.'

'But the coat comment was when he was young, only a lad, in the days before he mended his ways and went to work for me. I can see him standing with his head earnestly cocked, insolent, brash, fourteen years old. Willie and I go back a long way.'

'You do, you do. And he dead these last forty years or so, no doubt.'

'Willie died in nineteen thirty-four – I looked it up on the Internet.'

'A strange life you've led, Holmes.'

'At all events, I wrapped myself in this long black stolen coat and, wearing nothing else but my pyjamas, lay down on the narrow pew where once choristers sang happily to God.'

'But where did you get the clothes you now have on?' I asked.

'Yesterday morning I awoke early, with the birds,' he continued. 'They chirped me awake. In the greying dawn I walked up to Mortestow and took breakfast at the Tea Shoppe. There I met a kindly resident who, realizing I had been sleeping rough, offered to take me in, and offered me a bed for the night. I accepted. And this kind soul lent me these clothes.'

'Thank goodness you had a bed last night!' said I.

'A very fine feather bed, Wilson. I owe my benefactor a debt for the kindness I was shown – and I believe I may be able to pay that debt before I leave Mortestow. Time will tell. After breakfast I walked to Flint Cove. The tide was out, and there I met a strange little fellow called Davy Deeps who was cleaning the beach. He informed me of several interesting things – he told me, for instance, of a staircase in the old mine shaft beneath Mouse Hole Cottage.'

'That explains many things,' I said.

'They tried mining in this part of Cornwall, mostly unsuccessfully. The abandoned mine shaft and mine buildings were bought in the twenties by a man from New York, who had the cottage – Mouse Hole Cottage – built from the old stone of the mine works. He evidently vacationed there till the Second World War. Five years ago the property was purchased by a European company, according to my informant – who was, in fact, the kind soul who gave me a bed to sleep in. And when the property was sold, people here wondered why anyone wanted it. I wondered too . . . so I broke into the building – subtly, of course.'

'But of course,' said I.

'From the back room a circular staircase of new cement descends to beach level where a door, that locks from the inside, leads out to the north side of Flint Cove, and to a small jetty nearby. A sign on the outside of the door warns of *Danger, Mine Works.*'

'Yes, I've seen it,' I said.

'As Davy Deeps was telling me about the stairs, suddenly he pointed out to sea and said, "There she be!" He pointed at a craft just arriving, settling into the sea a half-mile off. Knowing what I knew from having read the files in Dr Cluj's office, I knew it would anchor there. I asked Davy if he might be able to take me out to see *The Phantom*. He was happy to do so, and soon we were jiggling along in his small boat, the outboard motor whining and groaning with each passing roller. The hydrofoil we set our course for was a sleek craft, maybe eighty feet long. On deck a man was sweeping. As we drew near I stood up and waved, the man waved back. Davy took me right up to the craft and when I was in the shadow of the hull I kept my face to the water and climbed up the ladder, and I was aboard before anyone realized I was not Dr Cluj – you will remember I was wearing his coat.'

'And what did you find?'

'The gentleman on deck, having made the error of allowing me aboard, was inclined to make the further error of believing me when I told him Dr Cluj had sent me to look over the craft and propose certain modifications that might improve its use for transporting patients. A certain amount of bullying and bluster on my part was required, but apparently simple Davy had ferried Cluj to the vessel on an earlier occasion, and this seemed to carry weight. The craft, Wilson, is fitted with a number of beds in the cabin, all very comfortable. Also twenty airline-type seats, with seat belts. A good galley, a small restaurant section. *The Phantom* is a very fast hydrofoil, with turbine engines. I asked what speed she could make, and he told me more than seventy knots. Somebody has spent a great deal of money on this operation, Wilson. And well they could afford it, for a most profitable operation it is.'

'And wherein lies its profit, Holmes?'

'In body parts.'

'Body parts?'

'What is more important to every man, woman and child in the world than their own bodies? Then can you imagine, Wilson, how important replacement body parts have become! In my day replacement body parts, as such, were worthless, for no one knew how to replace one man's *bad* body part with someone else's *good* one. There was, of course, a demand for bodies, cadavers to be cut up for purposes of study by the surgeons. I myself, as a student in chemistry at St Bart's, used the cadavers in the dissecting room to enhance my knowledge. My old friend, Watson, after we had gotten to know each other, confessed to me that he had been rather shocked when young Stamford, in describing me as a prospective room-mate, had told him I beat corpses with a stick to determine how far bruising could be induced after death. But it was a perfectly legitimate thing to do, presuming the corpses were legitimately obtained – and, I must say, I sometimes wondered whether our corpse supply was entirely legitimate. There were, as I am sure you have read, *resurrection men* who dug up freshly buried corpses in graveyards and delivered them to surgeons who did not ask too many questions. A nasty business. And there were cases where people were murdered for their bodies, which the murderer then sold to the surgeons. I myself brought one such murderer to justice in solving the case of the disappearance of Stuart Livingston – you may remember having read about it.'

'No, I never read it. Watson didn't write it up.'

Holmes frowned, nodded. 'No, I guess maybe he didn't.'

'I am sure he didn't,' said I.

'But now the surgeons can replace hearts, kidneys, livers. There is a worldwide trade in body parts, Wilson! And much of that trade is black market, illegitimate – and, of course, certain doctors, hospitals, look the other way in order, as they see it, to save lives. But the flow of illegitimate organs is always from the poor to the rich. Very profitable trade it is, too! Buy a kidney from a poor man for a few thousand pounds and sell it to a rich dying man for a hundred thousand.'

'I've heard rumour of such things,' I said.

'Ah!' cried Holmes. 'It is the sort of thing the world likes to regard as a mere rumour – more comfortable that way! Lives are being saved, after all . . . at the expense of – well, let us not inquire too closely!'

'Come now, Holmes!'

'Read on the web,' said he, 'what Nancy Scheper-Hughes says is truly going on in the shadowy world of organ trading! She is an anthropologist at Berkeley, and co-founder of Organs Watch.'

'I trust your judgement, Holmes.'

'You flatter Dr Vladimir Cluj in imagining him a vampire, my dear Wilson.'

'I wasn't serious.'

'Vampires suck merely blood. Dr Vladimir Cluj of the Carpathian Mountains – yes, he is from Transylvania, as it happens – sucks whole organs right out of his victims' bodies and sells them all over Europe. Kidneys, hearts, livers, slices of liver. He is part of a world-wide network of organizations which traffic in organs. The organs are transported in little cases like ice chests, with many sophisticated features to keep the organs fresh. *The Phantom* carries organs to a point near the Scilly Islands where she rendezvous with a helicopter that flies the organs to the continent. Or else, on rare occasions, she carries rich clients in need of an organ transplant, together with their retinue of doctors and attendants, to Flint Cove, where they are ferried ashore in a lighter, landed on a dark beach, and carried by van to the hospital. Most often, though, the clients simply fly to England, enter the country legally, and come to this place by private ambulance.'

Holmes went on to tell me of the countries where trafficking was most intense – Romania, Russia, he had a whole list. Israelis, he said, seldom donated their organs, and as a result had to buy them abroad, which explained why I had seen so many rabbis at the hospital. Donors were most often sought in poor countries, where individuals were so poor they could easily be imposed upon to give up an organ – a kidney or a slice of liver – for cash. But the Cornwall operation had been begun to cater to the rich; those who felt safer in a country like England. Dr Cluj had been put in charge, and although in many respects the operation had been a success, in the past few years – judging by the correspondence Holmes had read on Cluj's computer – Cluj had begun to fall short of his profit goals. Letters of reprimand and threat had been sent to him from his bosses in the Ukraine. It was at this point, according to what Holmes could determine, that Cluj instituted practices that made his hospital more profitable, but made it also much more vulnerable to discovery. He had begun the practice of finding people on the street – people unlikely to be missed – and using them to turn a profit. He had bought Mouse Hole Cottage. He had hired a hydrofoil to ferry patients into the country illegally – hitherto, every patient at his hospital to receive a transplant had come into the country perfectly legally. All of these deviations from policy angered the men in the Ukraine. Cluj, in short, had become a problem to his bosses in Europe. They were now investigating him. Holmes had found a letter from a certain boss which warned Cluj that he had 'ventured into outright murder, which is not to be tolerated' even in a criminal organization.

Holmes suddenly struck a match. It flared in the gloom of our hut, revealing his familiar aquiline profile, the briar pipe clenched in his teeth – and it struck me suddenly that he looked as he must have looked a hundred and twenty years ago, before the Great War which he had ventured to try to halt, before the glacier, before the resuscitation, before all his long improbable journey from the Jungfrau in 1914 to St Bart's Hospital in 2004 in a single cold leap. The old Holmes. The new. The same. 'But I hope you aren't going to light that pipe, are you?' I said.

'No, no! I wouldn't dare,' said Holmes, leaning forward. 'Dr Coleman would disown me. No, no, I am just looking . . . ah, here it is. I found these the other day, and I put them out of sight under this bench. But since then I have learned what they mean, and I must have a care to preserve them.' He held out a palm full of small objects that winked in the match-light: tiny silver crosses.

'To ward off the vampire, I presume?' said I. 'You might also try garlic.'

'To ward off black lies,' murmured Holmes.

I awaited his explanation. But he said no more. Well, Holmes enjoys making little mysteries which he intends to illuminate at a later date. No use asking him. I would let him enjoy my mystification.

As he had described Cluj's operation I had grown increasingly uneasy, for I kept expecting him to outline a course of action to rescue Bertie – an action that I thought surely was needed instantly. Finally I asked him outright, 'What are we going to do about Bertie – surely he is in great danger, is he not?'

'If he is still at this Penlaven place you mentioned, at the edge of the moor, he is safe for now,' said Holmes.

'But no!' I gasped. 'He was taken away by Cluj and his men two days ago, on Monday. I described the event to you in an email – you said you had read the material I had sent. You said you read it on Cluj's computer, when you were . . .'

'But I didn't read *that* one!' said Holmes.

Perched high above the sea on a sheer cliff, in the growing dark of Swallow's hut, my brain flew in circles trying to sort out the various supposed sightings of Cluj – white and black figures in graveyards, people vanishing over cliffs. I felt slightly confused. It had, in fact, been *Holmes* I had seen on Monday evening in the churchyard, not Cluj! So obviously he could not have seen my message about the abduction of Bertie Branford (whom I had thought at the time to be Kirk Branford). I had not sent that message till after I had seen Holmes in the graveyard.

'Bertie is no longer at Penlaven,' I said. 'He was taken away in a van by Cluj and two men.'

'Then he is in grave danger,' said Holmes softly. 'We must act very swiftly.'

We sat long moments in the growing dark, in silence. The distant sound of the sea rose to us from below, and wind moaned softly round the corners of the hut. The blue of the sea had faded to black, winking with whitecaps. The sky still held a faint streak of light along the far horizon. To our left, in the southwest, the crescent moon hung. Darkness had not yet completely fallen. But soon we would be in the blackness of stars. I was glad of the little lights now barely visible in the gorse, faintly outlining the path upward to the safety of the cliff behind us.

'We'd better go,' said I.

'Yes,' said Holmes. 'And quickly.'

# FOURTEEN

## Imprisoned

We descended the dark path to the Admiral Hawke Inn and there Holmes ate a late supper. Afterward he borrowed my mobile and stood gazing out the porthole window as he phoned Lestrade in London and made arrangements for tomorrow.

Just at that moment Billy Baffin came into the room. He glanced at Holmes and, with a look of horror on his face, he cried, 'Do you dare come back, wretch!' Billy staggered drunkenly towards the beam on which hung the cutlass. He had just reached up for the weapon when I grabbed him.

'Begad!' cried Billy. 'I'll cut him again!'

'You'll not cut anyone!' said I, pushing him back into his chair rather ruthlessly. 'It is not the same man – look closely.'

'Then they must be brothers,' cried Billy, wiping his hand over his eyes.

'Welcome aboard!' cried Ensign Squeers.

I sat down with Holmes and he told me his plan for the morning. I thought the plan sounded chancy. 'And if we fail?' said I.

'The police swarm in,' said Holmes. 'But I prefer to avoid the heavy-handed approach, if possible. Crockery often gets broken. Better the delicate manoeuvre, if it will work.'

'Then let us try,' said I.

Holmes slept that night in room number three, next to mine. We were up early next morning and I took the dogs for a short walk and waited for Holmes by the car. When Holmes came stalking towards us from the inn, his Dr Cluj coat blew in the wind, and his face was half obscured by a slouch hat he had obtained from Mrs Blankenship, and the dogs, as he drew near, cowered and growled. But Holmes, ever the diplomat when required to be, made peace with them by offering each several pieces of bacon that he had stuffed in his pocket for this very purpose. And yet still they were wary. I attributed their chariness to the smell of Cluj on his coat – something I could not discern, of course, but which to them must have been as obvious as the moon. Eventually the dogs joyously leapt into my car.

We approached the Cornwall Hospital for Sailors from the north, following the road that runs between the hospital on the left and the old monastery church and graveyard on the right. According to plan, we did not go around to the main parking lot in front of the new wing of the hospital, but instead I turned right into the churchyard and parked in the shadow of an old oak. Leaving the dogs in the car, we got out into the creaking dawn. Scarcely had we done so when someone called, 'Ay, Doctor! Morning to you!'

In the grey light a figure emerged from a doorway on the side of the church. He had a spade in his hand. Holmes waved and turned away. I walked over to the man. 'Do you mind if I park there a little while?'

'Not at all,' said he, 'if you are with the doctor!'

'You are the sexton?'

'I am.'

'Much work?'

'Not here.'

'Healthy congregation, I suppose.'

'Oh, nay,' said he. 'They are dying fast, and not many left now in the old church. But the graveyard is full.'

'Then what do you do?'

'Bury them elsewhere. Our people have purchased plots in other places. Many a grave I've dug here, but now I dig no more deep than to plant a tulip or a rosebush.'

I walked back to the car, put Doolittle on a leash and, leaving Sir Launcelot in the car, Doolittle and I hurried to catch up with Holmes, who had already crossed the road to the grounds of the hospital. As we neared the front door Holmes stooped, picked up Doolittle, and put him under his coat. We walked swiftly into the front entrance. There were two people at the reception desk. Holmes stormed on past the desk without stopping, and I came up and said to the receptionist – over the head of the two people who stood there – 'He told me to follow him!'

With a confused look in her eyes, she nodded yes.

I hurried after Holmes.

We worked our way through the building, looking into each open door, pausing by each closed door. Doolittle's head was out of the cloak. He eagerly sniffed each door, as if he knew perfectly well what we sought in this quest. At room 204 he got excited, gave a little *yip*. Holmes opened the door and looked in. He entered, motioned to me, and I followed him in, closed the door behind me.

Bertie Branford lay dozing in the hospital bed with an IV in his arm. Holmes leaned close, spoke his name – whereupon Doolittle leapt out of Holmes's arms and on to the bed and began licking the man's face.

Holmes eyed the IV. 'I wish old Watson were here to tell me if this is safe,' he said, and then he tore off the first piece of tape that secured the IV.

'Safer than leaving him,' I said.

At that moment came a faint rattle at the door. Holmes grabbed the dog off the bed and hid him under his coat, and continued leaning over the bed. The door opened. A round-faced nurse appeared, a sweet-looking old woman. I frowned at her, shook my head, and said, 'Please come back later – the doctor is busy.'

'Oh, yes,' said she, and she backed discreetly out of the room.

Holmes took out the IV. Slowly, Bertie Branford came drowsily awake. We waited a very long ten minutes. We sat him on the edge of the bed, then urged him to get to his feet. We waited until he was able to stand. He was a bit wobbly.

'Must make the move,' said Holmes. 'Get his clothes, Wilson!'

I grabbed his clothes out of the closet near the bed. A moment later, we pressed out into the hallway, Holmes sweeping ahead holding the dog under his cloak, me hurrying behind as fast as I could with Bertie in his hospital robe leaning on my shoulder. Once I heard a voice behind me, 'Good morning, Doctor!' But Holmes strode on without acknowledging except by a slight raising of his right hand.

We took the elevator down and we found the side entrance that Holmes had used in his own escape. A moment later we were out the door and on to the grass. Bertie had been gaining more and more strength as we went. We crossed the road into the churchyard. Unfortunately, Sir Launcelot began to bark as we neared the car. Morning was blooming prettily as we helped Bertie into the back seat.

I drove quickly out on to the road and headed north.

'That was quite easy,' said I.

'Surprisingly easy,' said Holmes. 'I must say I am rather pleased at how well we managed it.'

'You fit the part, Holmes. You have a certain cold-blooded charm that fits the common conception of what a vampire should be.'

'My god, Wilson!' he cried. 'Honesty is a virtue – but there are limits!' He began to laugh.

Bertie Branford leaned forward and put his head between us. 'Thank you for the rescue,' said he, with laboured slowness. 'Much appreciated.'

'Our pleasure,' said I.

Bertie leaned back. In my rearview mirror I could see he looked a little dazed. 'I say, who are you two gentlemen? And what are you doing with my dog?'

'I am James Wilson.'

'And I am Sherlock Holmes.'

'You say . . . what do you say your name is, sir?'

'Sherlock Holmes.'

'How very odd,' he said, rubbing his eyes. 'Why, then, I must be Alexander the Great!'

'According to my calculation,' said Holmes, 'you are merely Albert the Grateful.'

He laughed. 'Oh, yes, you are quite right, I *am* grateful. But, I say, tell me the truth: are you Sherlock Holmes – like the great detective of yore?'

'Very like him,' said Holmes.

'But I thought he was *dead*!' cried Bertie.

'So did I,' said Holmes. 'But they proved me wrong.'

'I mean,' slurred Bertie, 'I thought he was alive, but years ago. A hundred years, maybe. That's what I thought.'

'That's what most people thought – for he certainly seemed alive. If he wasn't, he had a lot of people fooled,' said Holmes.

'Good heavens, Holmes, don't toy with him,' I said, for I could see in the mirror that Bertie was looking ill.

'My medicines have confused me, and made me woozy,' said Bertie.

'Were you really on the Athens-to-Santorini ferry when it capsized?' I asked.

'And it was a very long swim, I can tell you,' said Bertie. 'I swallowed sea water.'

A moment later Bertie's head lolled over and he had fallen asleep. His little dog licked his face, but Bertie was oblivious.

When we reached the inn we put Bertie to bed in room four, to recover from whatever it was that the Cluj medical team had filled his veins with.

# FIFTEEN
## The Statues Again

The ground floor of the Admiral Hawke Inn was all hearths and dark beams and benches in nooks and gleaming mugs and glasses floating over the bar. And on this Thursday late afternoon it was strangely quiet. Like a room of wax figures at Madame Tussaud's. Nothing moving. Sherlock Holmes sat on a hard-backed bench near the front hearth. He was reading a book. Youthful Bertie Branford sat on a cushioned bench in the alcove near the other hearth. Bertie's head was tilted back and his mouth slightly open, as if he'd just run a race and was exhausted. On the opposite side of the nook, beneath the porthole window, sat the bulky and motionless figure of Billy Baffin, staring straight ahead, his thick hand encircling a full glass of unsipped beer. I gazed at this motionless tableaux from a corner wooden chair, my legs stretched out.

Suddenly into this stillness Ilsa appeared behind the bar, singing. What a lovely thing she was to look at, and to hear. She was serving alone today, for Jack and his mother were at the hospital with Mr Blankenship.

Holmes turned a page.

I ventured, 'What are you reading, Holmes?'

He held up a small volume which I recognized as James Swallow's poems, *Street Song*.

'I'm on to another mystery, Wilson, and this little book may contain a clue. You will remember that the first time you saw me I was seeking clues in books.'

'You were actually cooking the books, as I recall, on a kitchen stove in order to extract DNA from their pages, by some arcane chemical method of your own devising . . . or was it an alchemical method?'

He laughed. 'You cannot help being a bit sarcastic, Wilson, whenever you mention that episode. I noticed the same faintly disparaging tone, or at least comic tone, when you described it in that first volume in which you began presenting my modern career. But, I confess, *The Strange Return of Sherlock Holmes* was, on the whole, a fair and restrained presentation. You didn't try to sensationalize anything.'

'The tale was so sensational in itself that I didn't need to. The facts were sufficient.'

'I often told my old friend Dr Watson to stick just to the bare facts,' mused Holmes. 'He had a penchant for the dramatic.'

'I must tell you, Holmes, that I have often thought you were a bit unfair to Dr Watson – in your criticisms of his manner of writing, that is.'

'Unfair?'

'Yes.'

'Surely not!'

'I am afraid you were, my friend.'

'I only said that instead of presenting the chain of logical reasoning that led to my solutions – which was the essence of my method and my success – Watson often rearranged things so that surprise and drama were enhanced, and the logical process somewhat obscured.'

'My dear Holmes! If Watson had been writing merely a treatise on logic he would, no doubt, have done well to emphasize the logical process. But he was writing a tale of your life, the essence of which was not mere logic, mere arranging of facts but, more than that, the slightly patrician style in which you approached people and problems, and the seemingly magical ease with which you turned darkness into light, transformed heaps of contradictory facts in to an incriminating pattern. No one is interested in seeing a boxer practising and sweating and lifting weights day after day. People want to be there on the day of the fight and see the knock-out punch. It's what the world cares about and it is perfectly normal. Drama, colour, theatre. You yourself, Holmes, if you will admit it, have a penchant for the dramatic.'

He shrugged – an admission.

'Always dressing up in costumes, playing roles. Not to mention that you often withhold information even from me – evidently so that while everyone else is sitting around the table feeling baffled as they gaze at their hands full of confused facts, you can spread your cards on the table in one dramatic swoop, make a grand slam, and go out.'

'Touché!' Holmes held up the book, keeping his place with an inserted finger. 'You read any of these?'

'Rather good, some of them.'

'I thought so too . . .' He opened the book and was about to read something when a slight commotion was heard in the hallway.

Patrick, the Irish wolfhound, entered the room. Sir Launcelot rose to greet the big beast. Doolittle lay quietly watching from beneath his table.

'Here, now, Patrick!' said Sara Timmons-Swallow as she entered the bar. She snapped her fingers and tried to get the dog to his usual place. But Patrick was full of joy at seeing Holmes, and rushed to him, nuzzled his shirt collar and trousers, then his boots, very excitedly – sliding his front feet down in the oddest position to get low enough to sniff Holmes's toes. At last he retreated, looking a bit humbled by Sara's chastising, and with a sigh he slid down to the floor in his usual place.

'Welcome aboard!' cried Ensign Squeers, and with a fluffle and a squawk he began jumping up and down on his perch. I heard someone opening the front door, and the bird seemed overjoyed to greet the newcomer . . .

Lestrade walked in!

'Good morning, Chief Inspector,' said I. 'What magic is this! I am not used to seeing you anywhere but London.'

He smiled his reserved smile. 'Good afternoon, Wilson . . . Holmes.'

'Shall we sit here, in the nook?' Holmes motioned us.

Bertie Branford still showed no sign of revival. He had slept for two hours in the room upstairs, then insisted he wanted to get up, so we had helped him downstairs. But he had fallen asleep again almost instantly.

Dilly Daffin sat slouched in the corner beneath the porthole in one of his quiet, almost trance-like moods.

'We are assembling the men,' said Lestrade.

'Excellent!' said Holmes. 'I am very glad you came down to take charge of the operation, Lestrade.'

'We are set to move at eight this evening. Cluj customarily works until nine or so, and we don't want to disturb the running of the hospital any more than necessary – so we are avoiding the daytime, when hospital operations are in full flow.'

Somewhere *Rule Brittania!* struck up . . . Lestrade pulled out his phone, answered it, then pushed the speakerphone button. He said, 'Start again, Nigel. Holmes is here.' He held the phone so we could all hear, and he said to Holmes, 'It's the man who worked with you at Cheddington, Nigel Lyme.'

'*Holmes?*' said the voice of Nigel Lyme. '*I'm afraid he can't be of much help to us, if he's in Cornwall. The thefts are moving north.*'

'Let us see if he can be of some help, nonetheless,' said Lestrade, in a faintly acerbic tone.

'*Of course, sir, by all means.*'

'Tell us what has happened.'

'*We learned only this morning, sir, that a Greek marble panel is missing from a private collection near Nottingham, presumed stolen. A window was jimmied and opened without setting off the alarm. I can't tell you much about the artwork itself. Other than that it is Greek, a carving of a* frenzied maenad *– if that's how it's pronounced. They faxed us a picture.*'

'Other details?'

'*Not at the moment, sir. We just learned about this. You instructed me to report such thefts immediately.*'

'Please keep us informed.'

'*Most certainly, sir. I have decided to go up there myself. I'm on my way.*'

Lestrade snapped the phone closed. 'My heavens, will this never end?'

Holmes sat frozen a long instant, pressing the side of his index finger across his closed lips. 'How very odd,' said he.

Lestrade knew better than to ask. So did I.

Several minutes passed. Holmes was lost in some other world. Lestrade and I ordered beers.

'The link!' cried Holmes, springing from his bench and bumping into the table as he did so. Staggering slightly, Holmes paced into the next room, turned, and held up his finger in the air as if warning us: 'The dog doesn't swim, and Bertie paid with a fifty-pound note.'

'Wine and cheese for all my women!' cried Ensign Squeers.

Holmes took the smokeless briar pipe out of his mouth and waved it. 'The link is the Grand Union Canal!'

'I haven't the least notion what you are talking about,' said Lestrade.

'Have you a road atlas in your car, Wilson?' Holmes gave me one of his startled looks.

I hurried outside and came back with my atlas, and I laid it on the table. Holmes leaned over it and peered through his magnifying glass, and with a pen he began marking the route of the Grand Union Canal from London northwards, flipping pages. The canal was a very faint and insignificant feature amidst all the boldly drawn highways, but Holmes made it bold and plain with his felt-tipped pen. 'It is just as I remembered!' he cried at last.

'What is the significance of the canal?' asked Lestrade.

'You will recall, my dear Lestrade, that the stolen ambulance used in the Chelsea robbery was abandoned on Blomfield Road.'

'That is true.'

'The Grand Union Canal runs alongside Blomfield Road, and always there are numerous canal boats moored along the bank. The gate to the moorings is locked at night, but the iron fence is a low one and easily surmounted.'

'True,' said Lestrade.

'The second robbery took place at Hemel Hempstead, within a mile of the canal. The third took place near Cheddington, again close to the Grand Union. Look here, gentlemen!' He flipped a page or two. 'See how the Grand Union Canal links with the Trent Navigation, which leads to the Fossdyke Navigation – see here – which proceeds right through the centre of the city of Lincoln . . . then it becomes the Witham Navigation –' He tapped his finger on the map – 'which flows through Boston, and thence by a sea lock out to the Wash, and to the North Sea beyond.'

'Nearly every town in England is near a canal of some sort,' said I. 'And the Grand Union is the most extensive canal.'

'He's right, Holmes,' said Lestrade. 'It does seem rather a leap.'

'But there is the matter of Doolittle, the non-swimming dog,' said Holmes.

Lestrade shook his head. 'I don't follow.'

'And then the matter of the fifty-pound note,' said Holmes.

'A dog who can't swim and a fifty-pound note,' said Lestrade.

'Doolittle's track led to the edge of the canal, then vanished at water's edge. Sir Launcelot picked up the scent again on the far side of the canal, but an eighth of a mile or so north. If Doolittle didn't swim there, he was carried – possibly under someone's arm. But that seems unlikely. But let us imagine a canal boat took both man and dog aboard, and that it then cruised up the canal a little distance . . . before setting them both ashore on the other side. That would explain everything.'

'Why would Bertie have gotten on a canal boat?' asked Lestrade.

Holmes flipped his hand through the air. 'Bertie was contacted by whoever is behind these robberies. He agreed to supply his father's Cycladic idol for a sum of cash. The exchange of statue for cash was made on the canal boat, and the statue was paid for in large bills. Bertie was set ashore with his dog and money, and he walked to the train station, paid for his ticket with a fifty-pound note, then travelled here to Cornwall.'

'And why did he travel here, Holmes?' said Lestrade. 'He had his money, he—'

'To buy his friends out of their trouble!' said Holmes. 'Out of their obligation to be operated on by Dr Cluj – to provide them sufficient cash so they'd agree not to go through with what he had come to believe was a very dangerous operation.'

'Exactly, Mr Holmes,' said a voice in the corner.

It was Bertie Branford. He was struggling to sit up straight.

'Ah, Mr Branford,' said Holmes.

'Good morning, lad,' grunted Billy. 'You look like you've been lying in the bilge.'

'I feel it, Billy,' said Bertie.

'Have a drink on me! Come here, wench!'

'I never drink till noon, Billy, you know that,' groaned Bertie. 'But thank you.'

'Never have I seen a lad so fastidious as Bertie Branford!' cried Billy, looking towards Holmes, then winking at me and Lestrade. 'Begad –' he pounded the table – 'it will be the death of him!'

'I never drink until noon,' repeated Bertie.

'It is almost noon,' observed Holmes coolly. 'Live a little.'

'A beer then,' said Bertie. He sat up and rubbed the back of his neck. 'I lost track of time.'

'Time is a local illusion,' said Billy. 'I hope.' He waved an arm at Ilsa.

'Billy and I rescued each other,' said Bertie. 'We are the best of mates.'

'That we are,' said Billy Baffin.

Billy stood up and took the beer off Ilsa's tray. He presented it to Bertie.

'How did you save each other?' asked Holmes.

'It's a long tale,' said Bertie.

'It's a long afternoon,' said Holmes.

Billy laughed. 'Tell him, Bertie.'

'I presume,' said Holmes, 'it started when you needed money, and met a silver van in Russell Square.'

'Exactly, Mr Holmes,' said Bertie, 'and what a dreadful day that was. Eight of us in that van came down here from London – six men plus Shakira and her child. We were told there would be a test done on us, perfectly safe, and that after the test we would be paid two hundred pounds. They took us to the hospital that first evening, and gave us supper, and separate rooms, and the next morning they gave us blood tests and physical exams, and that evening they drove us to Kittle Mill settlement and we were all very pleased with our comfortable lodgings there, in two lovely cottages with big bedrooms. After having been on the street, sleeping in doorways, we found Kittle Mill akin to heaven itself. Many of us felt we were in no hurry to leave – it was paradise; meals brought in a van every day, clean towels . . .

'They took Vinny for his procedure the very next day. Vinny was an old gentleman, very timid, very polite, very sick. I think they took him first because they feared he would otherwise die on them before they could operate. And die he evidently did, Mr Holmes – at all events, we never saw him again. They kept reminding us we would soon have our procedures and be off with our two hundred pounds in our pockets, plus a train ticket back to London. So they told us. But it didn't work out that way. Next to go was Alf, a desperate drunk who was a true gentleman despite his affliction. They came for him in a van. Alf was all smiles and many a fond farewell we wished him, for we had become a bit of a family by then. But by now, more because of the manner of the van drivers than anything else, I had become somewhat suspicious of our situation, and doubtful. I had become rather close to Shakira, and I worried about her. I had heard of a place up the river, an upscale bed and breakfast guesthouse called Penlaven. I told

Shakira that she and her little boy, Biki, might be in danger and I said that I had a way to get money, and I convinced her I could keep her safe. We left early in the morning and walked up the river path till we saw the huge old medieval house called Penlaven. I presented my plea to the woman of the house, Carolyn Hart, who was most understanding. She agreed to house Shakira and Biki for a week, on the understanding that I would return with payment at the end of that time. Next morning I made my way on foot to Mortestow and took the bus towards Port Paul, but I got off at the crossroads leading to the Cornwall Hospital for Sailors. I intended to find out what had happened to Vinny and Alf. The woman at the front desk could give me no information. She insisted that neither of them had been to this hospital. I therefore insisted on being shown to the director of the hospital. I made such a fuss that to quieten me they showed me into the office of Dr Cluj. Cluj was very civil, if a little odd. He gave me a lot of what an old American friend of mine would call double-talk, intimating that I would surely understand the need for secrecy in experiments such as these. He then assured me that I could be the next subject in the experiment, that I would undergo my "procedure" the following morning. He pushed a button and two large assistants appeared. Dr Cluj then informed me of the need to monitor my functions for a few hours before the test was performed. One of his burly assistants produced the medical collar that, he claimed, would do this. But the collar further inflamed my suspicions. Something about it seemed phony, and implausible. I'd never heard of a medical collar. I said that I had changed my mind and did not want to participate in the trials. Cluj's attitude changed when I said this. The atmosphere became distinctly threatening. "We have already paid you twenty pounds, my dear sir, and brought you down from London. We cannot allow you to back out now. Surely that would be unfair!" I began to realize I was trapped. I intended to give a good account of myself, but I had the gloomy feeling that the two big assistants would do me damage. I was feeling quite desperate . . . and just at that moment Billy Baffin burst into the room, and Cluj said, with a patrician softness, "What are you doing here, Baffin?"

'"I have come to quit!" cried Billy.'

'And so I had,' said Billy.

'Billy had never seen me in his life, but he saw what the

situation was,' said Bertie. 'He warned me not to put the collar on if I valued my life. For a moment it appeared that the two large assistants in white were about to try to subdue both Billy and me, but Billy quite masterfully held up a finger in warning and said, "Careful, Cluj! I am a man who knows your operation. A word to the local constable and . . . Phhhft. No Cluj." And then Billy drew a long knife. The enforcers backed away. Cluj gave no commands. Billy cut the cord of the parrot that tied it to its perch, and the bird hopped on to Billy's shoulder. In short, we got out of there. The one big assistant was Austrian, I think. The other was also a foreigner. Billy had been making a salary as captain of *The Phantom*, and he still had money. He had come in a cab and the cab was waiting. He asked me where I would like to go. I said Mortestow. He gave the command and the driver took us here. When Billy saw the inn, and was free at last of his duties, he thought he might like to have a drink or three.'

'Drink was always my weakness,' said Billy.

'Wine and cheese for all my women!' cried Ensign Squeers.

'Women!' said Billy, glancing at the bird. 'I have been led astray a time or two, but that was years ago!' He sighed. 'Long years.'

Bertie took a big drink from his mug, and set it on the table near him. 'I knew now that I must steal my father's statue, trade it for cash, and set my comrades free. I borrowed some money from Billy – though by then he was so drunk I'm not sure he understood what he was doing when he gave it to me.'

'I well understood!' cried Billy. 'And glad I was to give it!'

'I sent an email from this very inn, using Mrs Blankenship's computer, to a gentleman who had made me an offer some months earlier, at the British Museum, and who had given me his card. He called me back here on the house phone, said he was surprised to hear from me. He said that I had luckily called at a very convenient date. He told me that if I delivered the statue at a precise time on a precise day, I would be paid thirty thousand pounds cash for my trouble. That date was exactly a week hence. I took buses and trains till I reached Cheddington. For several days I stayed in town in a small bed and breakfast, letting the date approach. The night before the appointed day I went late to my father's house. Knowing where the key was hidden, it was no trouble to get in. And fortunately it was my parents' bridge night.

I took the statue from its shelf. To my great surprise I then heard a dog coming, growling – and then Doolittle leapt at me, wagging and moaning. He was so overjoyed that I could not resist when he yipped and led me to the pantry, as he had done so often of old. There I found Black Forest gateau. I took two pieces and went with Doolittle to the gazebo where we shared our treat as we had done in the old days, when he was but a pup and I still happy. But I knew I must leave quickly, before my parents returned. I said goodbye to Doolittle and set out for town. But Doolittle followed. I put him back in the house and hurried on my way – but then he came up behind me again. I had forgotten about the doggy door on the other side of the house. At that moment I saw lights from a car approaching up the drive. I had no choice but to hurry away across the fields carrying a Cycladic statue wrapped in a blue sheet I had snatched from the clothesline. Doolittle was close upon my heels. I kept hoping he would turn back, but he didn't.

'I slept the night in a hedgerow, which was quite pleasant after years of sleeping on city sidewalks. At the appointed time, six in the morning, I was standing on the east side of the canal fifty feet north of lock number thirty-two. A black canal boat of unusual design was moored not far away. *Proteus* was written in blue letters on her stern, and it made me think of Wordsworth's poem, the one ending with *Great God! I'd rather be / A Pagan suckled in a creed outworn; / So might I, standing on this pleasant lea, / Have glimpses that would make me less forlorn; / Have sight of Proteus rising from the sea; / Or hear old Triton blow his wreathèd horn.* Those lines were running through my mind and simultaneously I was wondering if that black canal boat could have anything to do with whoever was to meet me. Scarcely had I thought the thought than a man appeared on the front deck. He stood a moment, gazing towards me. Finally he waved his arm. I made my way over the rough ground and went aboard. Doolittle leapt after me. The man was rather compact and energetic looking, barrel-chested, with blond hair pasted to his brow. Perhaps thirty-five years old. He looked genial. I was wary. He wore a very long knife in a sheath on his belt. I handed him the statue. He unwrapped it and looked at it briefly, then handed me a big envelope. I counted the money while he waited pleasantly. "All well?" he asked. I told him yes. "Out you go, then," said he, "and mind you don't touch the side of the hull – she's just been painted and you will have a black hand."

'I hadn't noticed that while we talked we had been moving. We now glided to the west bank, where the towpath ran. I picked up Doolittle and a moment later was ashore, and the long black boat was gliding away to the north. In jumping I had, unfortunately, touched the hull despite the man's warning, and my hand was black. I thought I'd have a deuce of a time cleaning up, but when I swished my hand in the canal the black came off readily. The boat was long, a seventy-footer, I think.

'I walked to the train station, bought a ticket, and was off to Cornwall with Doolittle. We arrived the same night, and I stayed with Billy. Two of our party were gone, Vinny and Alf. That left five plus the child. I divided my money into five parts and gave Billy his six thousand pounds that morning. I then set out for Kittle Mill. When I arrived there I found that collars had been put on Sinjin, Winston and Harvey. They said they did not want their money, wished me to keep it until they could get free. I determined to go up to Penlaven and give Shakira her share of the money and urge her to leave for London. This I did. But she refused to go without me, and I had still to free my three friends at Kittle Mill. The next day I rented a car from a local garage – paid the man five hundred pounds cash as deposit – and drove back to Penlaven, parked it. Shakira knew how to drive and I urged her to leave immediately for London, and to go to my sister's place in Primrose Hill. For the child's sake, I said. But she felt safe now, and would not leave without me. The next day, Sunday, I tried to disconnect the invisible electric fence, for I knew the connection must be somewhere in the graveyard. I had seen men in there earlier, rigging up the connections. I had no luck. The next morning I was ill, a raging fever, I stayed in bed all day, and that was my downfall. In the evening Cluj came for me at Penlaven. How he found out I was there I do not know. I told Shakira to slip out the side door, get the car, and drive for London. I hope she did.'

'I saw her drive away,' I said, 'though where she went I do not know, but she turned north. I was watching your lodgings when Cluj and his men came for you. I almost imagined you went willingly.'

'I dared not resist too much, so long as they did not push into the rooms. I wanted to give her a chance to escape. As long as they were moving away from where she was, I was happy. And I suppose, gentlemen, you know more of the rest than I do. I was very happy to feel myself being carried away from that dreadful hospital room. And here I am, almost like magic, back at the old Admiral Hawke. And amongst friends!' He raised his mug. 'Here, here!'

'A handsome lad, ain't he!' cried Billy.

Holmes was eager. 'But can you tell us, Mr Branford, the name of the man who offered you thirty thousand pounds for your father's statue?'

'Not his name, Mr Holmes. But I can tell you how I met him. Rather odd, that. I was at the British Museum. I often went there to get out of the cold or the rain, or to feel a little less like a street person – or just for entertainment, for the British Museum is a free education. On this particular day I was peering into a glass case containing a marble statue of a woman, from the Cycladic islands, created in two thousand five hundred BC or so, and as I stood looking at it I sensed another gentleman at my shoulder, likewise looking intently at the same statue. We got to talking, and each of us was a bit surprised that the other knew so much about Cycladic art. We seemed to be kindred spirits. I mentioned that my father owned such a statue, and the gentleman was surprised at this, and he asked my father's name, and soon he asked whether I thought my father might be willing to sell the statue. I had the impression he recognized my father's name. I said my father never sold anything, just collected. "If ever he should change his mind," said the gentleman, "you may tell him I would be quite willing to pay a hundred thousand pounds cash for it, presuming it is genuine. And I've heard your father's name, so I am sure it is genuine." This bizarre statement startled me. He handed me his card, which I slipped into my pocket without really looking at it. I asked him, by way of changing the subject, what else he had been looking at today, for he struck me as a man of wide yet deep interests, and I thought I might learn something if I could keep him talking. I had nowhere to go but the street. Conversation was welcome. He answered that he had been looking at the Elgin Marbles and wondering if they were secure. I laughed and said it seemed doubtful anyone could steal them. He nodded thoughtfully and said, "Yes, it would be difficult."

'I was astonished. I asked him if he seriously believed anything short of an army could wrest the Elgin Marbles from the British Museum. "Well, you know," he said, "theft is an art in itself."

'He said this in such a way that it impressed me – impressed me favourably, strange to say. And I began to believe he knew a way, knew how the Elgin Marbles might be stolen.'

'Zeus!' interrupted Holmes, startling all of us.

Even Ensign Squeers looked startled.

Bertie paused, abashed, uncertain.

'You don't suppose . . . But do go on, do go on!' said Holmes eagerly.

'Well, anyway,' said Bertie, 'my new friend expressed how much he had enjoyed our conversation, but he said that he must be going. He then grasped my hand with his two hands and said, "My dear fellow, would you do me a favour?"

'"Of course," I said, "if I can" – feeling myself locked in his warm grasp.

'"Then please –" and here he quickly slipped something into my hand – "please be good enough to take this and to invest it for me in the best way you can."

'He released me, said, "Bon chance, mon ami!" and hurried away. I looked in my palm and saw that he had given me two fifty-pound notes! Already he was vanishing in the crowd, far down the long hallway.'

'May I tell you what this gentleman looked like?' said Holmes.

'Why, I don't know,' said Bertie slyly. 'Do you think you are up to it?'

'I suspect he was about sixty, about your height, a little over six feet,' said Holmes, 'greying hair neatly combed, very blue eyes, slight accent, resonant and soothing voice, elegant manner, well dressed – probably in grey or blue – and small ears.'

'I don't know about the small ears,' said Bertie, 'but all else you said is perfectly correct. He wore a blue jacket, grey slacks, grey sweater, expensive Italian shoes. His voice was remarkable. He might have been an actor.'

'You evidently kept the card he gave you?'

'Slipped it into one of the pockets in my cargo pants I always wore, and forgot about it. Yet the minute I decided to steal the statue, I knew where it was.'

'May I see it?' asked Holmes.

Bertie fumbled, found it, handed it across.

Holmes held the card so both Lestrade and I could see it. It was black with an email address printed in gold across the front. Nothing more. Holmes flipped it over to reveal Greek words in gold on a black field. 'It appears,' said Holmes, 'to be a quotation from Aeschylus.'

Holmes stared at the card, tilted it, finally handed it back to Bertie. 'But the hundred thousand pounds had shrunk to thirty thousand.'

'He said that the price on stolen goods was naturally less than what could be realized on the auction market. I was quite happy with thirty.'

Holmes again stood up, agitated.

'You think it is Lindblad, don't you,' said Lestrade.

'I fear it,' said Holmes.

'You don't . . .' Lestrade frowned. 'You don't think the Elgin Marbles could be in danger. Do you?'

Holmes shrugged, shook his head. 'One or two are small enough to move.'

Ensign Squeers began crying 'Welcome aboard!' as more people came into the bar.

Holmes found no space for his customary pacing. He leaned against the mantel, took the unlit briar pipe out of his mouth and gestured with it, a little wildly. 'Let us go back, then, Lestrade, to the vanishing Greek statues. The Artemisium Aphrodite, a very large and heavy statue, was stolen in Chelsea, then evidently driven in a hospital van to Blomfield road, where the van was abandoned. Why there? I suggest the answer is that it was because the Grand Union Canal runs along Blomfield road. I suggest the statue was put on to a hospital bed and wheeled to a boat moored on the canal next to the road. The macabre elements of the crime – the headless macaw dripping blood as it hung upside down from its perch, and the missing Persian cat, are easily explained. When the bird began making a fuss that might have awakened the neighbours late at night, Wylie Blunt slashed the creature's head off with his long knife. The head dropped to the floor, the cat snatched it, and the cat, carrying the macaw head, made his exit when the thieves made theirs.'

'Quite possible,' said Lestrade.

'The canal, Lestrade!'

'So you say,' said Lestrade, calmly.

'The link in these crimes is the Grand Union Canal – where in days of old the goods and trade of dear old England flowed! For how are these men to get a huge statue out of the country? Through what seaport or airport? That is the question they must ponder. The *Proteus* glides north along the old Grand Union Canal, puttering up locks and down locks, under bridges, through tunnels, making way amidst holidaymakers in rental canal boats who are seeing the green country at a leisurely pace – but our thieves have chosen the canal not for leisure but for leaving, leaving merry England by a quiet seaside lock.'

'It's a theory,' said Lestrade.

'No more, I admit,' cried Holmes. 'But let us see how my theory might fit the facts. Near Hemel Hempstead they moored the boat, according to my theory, walked a quarter mile, laid long ladders against the high fence of Philip Corey's compound, climbed over and entered his grounds at midnight. They entered the pavilion and there, among the numerous marble statues, they identified the most valuable; which suggests there was, amongst the thieves, an art expert who not only recognized the statue but knew also where and how the genuine Greek head should be separated from the replica torso upon which Corey had mounted it. Now, let us consider the dead man, the headless nude. He was a big man.'

'Very large.'

'But not,' said Holmes, 'particularly muscular, am I correct?'

'Flabby,' said Lestrade.

'So not a man, one might suppose, who was accustomed to climbing fences and lifting statues. We may conclude, therefore, that he was there for another reason – for his expertise in art.'

'Possibly.'

'We might also suppose, because of the nitroglycerine capsule clutched in his hand, that he died of a heart attack.'

'That is what the coroner concluded,' said Lestrade.

'Did you read the Herodotus passage I suggested?' asked Holmes.

'I am sure your suggestion was brilliant, Holmes – but I am afraid I haven't had the time. Sorry. Perhaps you might capsulize the tale for me. The short version.'

'The tale of Rhampsinitus,' cried Holmes, 'is the tale of a crime that took place several thousand years ago – a crime re-enacted, my dear Lestrade, last week in Hemel Hempstead. Herodotus tells of two brothers in Egypt who had learned from their father how to enter the King's treasury by moving a secret stone in the wall. These brothers entered the treasury numerous times, and stole gold whenever they needed it, but by and by Rhampsinitus began to notice that gold was sinking in his coffers. The doors were locked, the gold was sinking. It was impossible! Finally the King thought of a way to solve this mystery. He set a mantrap in the treasury. The next night the two brothers entered to steal gold, as usual. But one was caught in the trap, and both of them working together could not get him out. The trapped brother said to his brother, "I am as good as dead, for the King will execute me when he finds me. Therefore, kill me now, cut off my head, and take it away – for otherwise the King will know who has done this and will kill you also." The brother was reluctant, but was finally convinced. He cut off his trapped brother's head and took it away. And the King was frustrated again.'

Holmes stopped talking.

Two fingers of Lestrade's right hand were drumming lightly on the arm of his chair. 'And you are suggesting the thieves cut off their own man's head in order to hide his identity?'

'If we learn the identity of the headless corpse,' said Holmes, 'we are very likely to learn for certain the identity of the mastermind behind these crimes – and a quick and ruthless mind it is! When their art expert died on the job, the other thieves could not possibly get his corpse over the high fence. So they stripped off the corpse's clothing, cut off its head, and carried both head and clothing up the ladders, over the fence, and probably back to the canal. Drag the canal, Lestrade, and you may well find a head . . . and some very large trousers.'

'We shall try that,' said Lestrade. 'We have checked missing persons in Europe, and a man missing from France for a few days fits the general description of the corpse. We have learned from his wife that he did have heart problems.'

'Ah,' said Holmes. 'And what else do we know of this missing man!'

Lestrade pulled out his electronic device, brought up a screen. He gazed at it, spoke quietly, squinting as he read: 'Conrad Duvall, art dealer, once worked for Sotheby's, now has several art galleries, one in Bath, one in Stockholm, one in Nice.'

'Stockholm!' said Holmes. 'This tends to confirm my theory.'

'His wife is Swedish,' said Lestrade. 'He lives in Stockholm usually, though they are living now in Nice. We don't know whether Duvall is our corpse, but we are checking DNA.'

'It is surely as I feared!' said Holmes. He nervously stepped away from the mantel, made a little circle round a table and came back again. 'The Elgin Marbles may be in more danger than I thought possible.'

'Have a seat, mate!' roared Billy.

Holmes stared at him, smiled. 'Am I unbalancing you?'

'You are making the deck tilt, sir. You are giving old Billy the heebie-jeebies – all this darting and strolling about!' He downed the last of his beer and pounded the table. 'Innkeeper! More wine!'

'Right away, Billy,' sang Ilsa. 'But you are drinking beer, no?'

'Hay for the horses!' cried Ensign Squeers.

'When will you know the result of the DNA testing?' asked Holmes.

Lestrade shrugged. 'Maybe we know already. Let me check, Holmes – maybe something has come through.' Lestrade slipped his phone out of his pocket, deftly as a card shark. He tried to call, tried again. Nothing. No service.

'Reception is sometimes bad in the bar. Walk outside on to the lawn and try,' said I. 'You may have better luck.'

Lestrade vanished out the side door.

'And you, Billy Baffin!' cried Holmes, turning on him suddenly. 'A fine parrot you have!'

Billy froze with beer mug halfway to lip. He raised his eyebrow, dramatically. 'He is the house parrot, is Ensign Squeers.'

'But surely he is yours – the bird is attentive to your every quiver. If he were human I'd say he was in love with you.'

'I hadn't noticed,' said Billy.

'Hah!' laughed Ilsa, as she set down another beer. 'Men never notice who really loves them!' She patted Billy on the head.

'Careful, lass!' cried Billy. 'I am old, I am broken – but I am a man, after all!'

She laughed, darted behind the bar.

'I am dangerous to women,' said Billy.

'The bird talks in your voice when he talks sailor talk,' said Holmes.

'Clever bird,' said Billy. 'He is a salt.'

'And in the voice of Dr Cluj when speaking of scalpels.'

'He is a bird of the world,' said Billy. 'He suits his tongue to his company, and so makes friends of all men.'

'I put it to you, Billy,' said Holmes, 'that you have worked with Dr Cluj, and that you lent him your parrot.'

'He is a bird of the world, but aboard so swift and small a ship my poor Ensign was dazed, amazed, and crazed. So Cluj took her, kept her in his office.'

'You were captain of *The Phantom*.'

'Aye. Captain Baffin, that was me.'

'Tell us the tale, Billy,' said Holmes. ''Tis easily told.'

'Ay, that it is.' Billy nodded big, took a swig, set down the mug. Sniffed. 'Cluj found me on the streets of Southampton – his men, they did, his minions, sir! And they offered me to be tested, my poor body, for medical research, for which I would be paid . . . thirty pounds, it was. I agreed, sir! For I had no money at all but what I could beg, you see. I was broken down by time and events. But then Cluj learned I had been captain of a Condor Ferry, and he said he wanted a man like me! I agreed, sir! For it seemed my fortune had changed as swiftly as wind. But later, when the bodies began going overboard, I realized the worst. I am a man of many a drink and many an error, but no accomplice to murder am I!'

'So you quit working for Cluj,' said Holmes.

'I am not a timid man!' cried Billy. 'I'll not be trifled with!'

'And how long were you living on the street, Billy?' said I.

Billy looked up, his big face was tilted and full of pleading. He spread his big hands. 'It is so easy to fall, sir! I was captain of a large ferry, I knew the sea, I knew the ways of ships. But one tiny error I made as we docked in a storm, and a man was killed, and they said liquor was involved – boards of inquiry, lawyers . . . they let me go.' He waved his hand, took a sip of beer, and set the mug down. 'How easy it is to fall, gentlemen! One minute a commander on deck, the next a wreck in a public puddle. Cluj found us, me and poor Ensign Squeers, queer and ruffled in the streets of Southampton. I should have left poor Squeers in St Malo, where I bought him from a baker's wife! *Boulangerie Pascal*. But he's all right now, is my birdie. A true sea-bird is Ensign Squeers. He used to voyage with me on the big ferry.'

'It seems evident,' said Holmes, 'that Cluj kept Squeers, among other places, in an operating room.'

'Cluj is a strange one,' said Billy. 'He is the master, and all the rest his minions.'

'Scalpel! Scapel!' cried Ensign Squeers, and he hopped and fluffled.

Lestrade returned.

Holmes watched him, hawk-like, intent, smiling faintly as he leaned against the fireplace once more, pipe in teeth. 'It appears you've learned something,' said he.

Lestrade nodded. 'They've matched the DNA to his brother. The dead man was indeed the art dealer, Conrad Duvall.'

'An art expert was required in these burglaries,' mused Holmes. 'Considering the trouble they have taken to obscure his identity, it is likely he is prominently connected with someone in the world of crime – and in view of the fact that Lars Lindblad is a known collector of Greek art, you might . . .'

'Duvall is Lindblad's brother-in-law,' said Lestrade. 'They just told me. I asked them to look for a connection, after I learned of your suspicions several days ago.'

Holmes snatched his pipe from his mouth. 'Then we have little time! We must move quickly or those pieces of art will be out of the country.'

'I just spoke with Nigel Lyme,' said Lestrade. 'I described the black canal boat *Proteus*, told him to look for it on the inland waterway from Lincoln to Boston.'

'That is precisely what must be done,' said Holmes. 'Excellent, Lestrade! One presumes they will take the boat through the sea lock at Boston and out into the Wash, there to shift its cargo to a sea-going craft, or to an amphibious aircraft that will spirit the spoils away to Lindblad's private collection in Sweden – or wherever he keeps it. Considering Lindblad's penchant for flying, the latter seems the likeliest scenario.'

'If our first encounter with him is any guide,' said I, 'Lindblad can be counted on for a final surprise or two . . .' I was recalling how Lindblad, in the affair of the stolen Shakespeare Letter, had made all of us look rather foolish by escaping with such ease – and such panache.

Holmes nodded faintly towards me, his eyes squinting as if focused on some distant possibility. Then he turned to Lestrade. 'My dear Lestrade,' he cried, 'call Nigel Lyme back. Tell him he must check every boat on the canal that is over sixty feet long – of whatever colour, whatever name!'

Lestrade looked surprised, waiting for explanation . . .

'The boat, after all, is named *Proteus*,' said Holmes. 'He may plan to transform it, give it a new look.'

'Then surely he would not give the game away by naming it *Proteus*,' said I. 'I think you are being a bit fanciful, Holmes.'

'You have lost me, gentlemen,' said Lestrade.

'Proteus was a Greek sea god,' said Holmes.

'His main claim to fame,' said I, 'was that he was able to change his shape whenever anyone tried to catch him – transform himself into a lion, a porpoise, an eagle, a bear, and so on.'

'Then I'm afraid I agree with Holmes,' said the chief inspector. 'Naming his boat after a Greek god to taunt us before turning it into a – what, a helicopter? – would be precisely the sort of stunt Lindblad would pull. I am convinced that he devises his crimes nowadays less for booty than for the pleasure of the game, a game which he has come to find so boring – after winning it for forty years – that he now spots us points every time he plays, just to make it interesting.'

'You are undoubtedly correct,' said Holmes.

Lestrade looked intent, disturbed. 'He amuses himself by taking enormous chances, then making fools of the police. I sometimes think he actually wants to get caught. Who but Lindblad would imagine that there is even the remotest possibility of being able to steal the Elgin Marbles off the wall of the British Museum?'

Holmes laughed.

'I confess I find nothing funny in the man,' said Lestrade. 'He has humiliated Scotland Yard too many times for me to appreciate the light side of his existence.'

'Then we must try to redress your injury!' cried Holmes. 'I owe a great deal to Scotland Yard.'

'I am astonished to hear you say so,' said Lestrade. 'We do try.'

'On many a case I have solved,' said Holmes, waving his thin hand as if wafting smoke away from his head, 'I have thought that the boys from the Yard might well have solved it on their own . . .'

'Good of you to say so.'

'. . . eventually, if they had put a few more men on the case.'

'Holmes, Holmes! I suspected your graciousness could not last!' Lestrade smiled and shook his head.

'But what a debt I owe the Yard!' cried Holmes. 'What could be more exhilarating than the double thrill I have so often experienced, of defeating a criminal at his own game while simultaneously out-sleuthing the world's best police force!'

'I will take your compliment and ignore the rest,' said Lestrade.

'All narrow boats on the canal that are sixty feet or longer must be regarded with suspicion,' said Holmes. 'Regardless of name or colour – but especially long boats that have blue hulls and names written in black.'

Lestrade stared at him. So did I. Neither of us asked.

'But I'm afraid there is a flaw to your theory, Holmes. No narrow boat could long survive in the North Sea.'

'No ordinary narrow boat,' agreed Holmes. 'But one built by Lindblad, called the *Proteus* . . . who can tell? *There are more things in heaven and earth, Horatio . . .*'

Holmes was feeling in a dramatic mood.

'We will check blue boats in particular. And black.'

At that moment the phone behind the bar sprinkled the air with jangle. Ilsa answered with her usual cheery lilt, but her voice quickly fell, and she sighed. 'Oh!'

She hung up and came round to our table. 'That was Mrs Blankenship, calling from the hospital. They recommend an operation for poor Mr B – first thing in the morning.'

'What!' cried Billy.

'A bypass operation round his heart,' said Ilsa.

'Egad!' cried Billy. 'If he has an operation at Cluj's hospital, he'll come out with fewer parts than when he went in!'

'He'd better go to another hospital,' said Holmes.

I walked to the bar and had a word with the distraught Ilsa. 'Call her back, Ilsa. Tell her that she must put off the operation, and schedule it at the hospital in Port Paul or Bodmin. Will you do that?'

'Yes,' she said, looking at me rather uncertainly.

'It is important,' I said.

'Yes, I will. Right away,' she said.

'Man overboard!' cried Ensign Squeers.

'I never heard him say that before,' said Ilsa.

'Clever bird,' said Billy, raising an eyebrow.

'At this moment,' said Lestrade, 'we have men assembling who will surround the hospital to make certain Cluj and his assistants cannot escape before the witching hour when we arrest them. Shall we go, gentlemen – and be in on the finale of this little mystery?'

'By all means,' said Holmes.

'You may need me,' said Billy. 'I'm a fightin' man, I am.' He rose from his table, unsteadily.

'You stay here, Billy, and guard the fort,' said Holmes. 'In case Cluj comes here.'

'Ay, I'm ready for him,' cried Billy. 'I'll drive a wooden stake through his merciless heart!'

'Then let us go, gentlemen,' said Lestrade. 'Time and tide wait for no man.'

# SIXTEEN
## The Vampire Flies

In the basement of the old Town Hall of Port Paul we met the officers who would raid the hospital. They were all drinking coffee, strapping on gear and being very calm. At a little after seven in the evening we set off in force for the old Cornwall Hospital for Sailors. According to plan, I drove round to the main entrance of the new wing and let Holmes off. He walked briskly towards the glassy doors, looking a bit incongruous in his white safari jacket and white flat cap, a cap of the sort one wears while driving a sports car. He vanished inside amidst reflections. He would sit in the waiting room until Lestrade's men entered, and then would lead them to the offices of Dr Cluj.

After letting him off I drove into the churchyard across from the monastery section of the hospital. A van from a power company was parked in the shadow of the church, and I wondered if it might be a surveillance vehicle in disguise, part of Lestrade's plan. The strange light of dusk had descended on the churchyard. All was silence except the whistle of a songbird somewhere nearby in the gloom, and the distant *caw*ing of a crow. I closed the door of my car softly, put my hand in my pocket, made sure I had my mobile phone. Holmes was to call me when the arrest of Cluj was complete.

A sudden sound of musical wind surprised me, soft music. An organ. By and by the music stopped. A few people began coming out of the church – a man in a wheelchair, a young woman pushing him, an old woman with a cane. A cleric in black appeared in the doorway, a very big man. He watched benignly as another man, a skinny redheaded fellow, came out of the church.

I was startled by a footstep behind me, and I turned to see the sexton. He held a pruning knife in his hand.

'Small funeral,' said he.

A hearse appeared, glided round to the far side of the church, out of sight.

'Who died?'

'The old outlive all their friends . . . and very few are left to see them off,' said he, shrugging.

'At least you have no digging duties,' I said.

He laughed softly. 'I've hung up me shovel, mate. Didn't expect to see you back again so soon.' He gave me a quizzical eye, beneath a bushy grey brow.

'Lost my address book – may have dropped out of my pocket when I was reading gravestones. Thought I'd have a look.'

'Getting a bit dark.' He walked away slowly. 'Good luck.'

I went amidst the graves and pretended to look at the ground.

After a time I wandered back to my car. By then the utility company van had vanished. My friend the sexton had also vanished. Ten more minutes passed, and then the call came. I drove round to the front of the hospital, and Holmes came from one direction and Lestrade from another, and they both were rather breathless as they got in.

'Did you get the files you needed?' asked Holmes.

'Everything,' said Lestrade.

'And what about Cluj?' I said.

'Gone, along with the associates,' said Lestrade.

'Gone!' I cried.

'We think he got suspicious when Mrs Blankenship cancelled her husband's operation. No doubt he imagined the hand of Billy Baffin in that decision, feared Billy had been talking. Drive north, Wilson. I expect we will find them all at the first roadblock. My men have stopped a utility van with six people in it.'

'There was a utility van at the church a half-hour ago,' I said.

'No doubt that is the one,' said Lestrade.

We drove north along the narrow road. By and by we saw, through deepening dusk and evening mist, lights of parked police cars ahead, and the blurred form of the van between them. The roadblock.

Several people were in the custody of the police, handcuffed. I recognized the big priest with the flat nose, the skinny redheaded man. And there were two large men speaking to each other in German – perhaps they were the two big assistants that Bertie had encountered before Billy rescued him. But no sign of the repulsive Cluj.

'Have any other vehicles been through here?' asked Lestrade.

'A Rover with an elderly man driving, no passengers,' said the sergeant. 'And a hearse. The driver was the sexton at St Ursula's church, just down the road. He was carrying two coffins for burial at Minehead.'

'Two?' said Holmes.

'Two young people killed in a car accident, evidently,' said the sergeant.

We got back into my car and slid away in the dusk. 'The sexton told me that an old person had died,' I said.

Lestrade pulled out his phone, punched buttons. 'I'll alert law enforcement to stop the hearse if he is travelling on the A39.'

We slowed to a stop at the first crossroads. 'If I'm not mistaken, a right turn here will bring us to the A39 in a few miles,' I said.

'Go left,' said Holmes. 'Drive for Mortestow.'

We careened through dark and twisting lanes, headlights dizzily sweeping side to side, hedge to hedge. At the Mortestow Road I turned north.

'Turn on to the Flint Cove Road,' said Holmes. 'Just ahead.'

A few moments later we were in the Flint Cove parking lot, gazing out at the starlit sea.

'There it is,' said Holmes. '*The Phantom.*'

The white shape of the craft was faintly visible, flickering into view and out as the rollers passed beneath it.

'Quick, to the cliffs through the farm fields, Wilson!' said Holmes. 'They may have gone there to signal the ship to send in a skiff.'

'Surely they would simply telephone the boat,' said Lestrade.

'No,' said Holmes. 'To send a boat in, *The Phantom* must first receive light signals from the Swallow's Nest. Nothing else is valid. I have read the protocols on Cluj's computer. No mobile phone calls will bring him in. Mobile phone traffic can be monitored. They are very cautious men.'

We drove back on to the main road towards Mortestow, and north. Just beyond the Admiral Hawke Inn I stopped at a farm gate. Holmes and Lestrade jumped out to open it. I drove through, they jumped back in, we ascended a dirt track through fields, rising towards the cliffs. Bemused sheep appeared. Sheep and turf and stones in the flare of our headlamps. Then a sudden scene presented itself, like a tableaux, frozen: two coffins on the ground behind a hearse, the sexton leaning over the first coffin.

'We seem to have arrived in time,' said Holmes.

The sexton pulled off the coffin lid. Cluj arose from it, wearing his black coat. Cluj and company seemed oblivious to our headlamps shining on them, as if perhaps they imagined we were one of their own vehicles, the utility van. Cluj, looking gallant and gaunt, stooped over the second coffin, lifted the lid. A beautiful woman rose from the coffin, dressed in a white dress, silvery high-heeled shoes.

'The chilly blonde from the hospital,' said Holmes.

I recognized her also, had seen her at the nursing station desk. I recognized the sheen of her shoulder-length hair, the impatient toss of her head as she stepped from the coffin on to the field.

Only as we drew up within a few yards of the three actors in this little scene did they seem to become aware of us. Cluj whirled, gave us a frightful look. The girl glanced at us angrily. The sexton frowned a ferocious frown.

We leapt from the car and ran – I quite easily grabbed the high-heeled floozy, while Lestrade collared the clumsy sexton. But the lean and nimble Dr Cluj darted away and Holmes pursued his fleeing figure up the track towards the cliffs. Lestrade quickly cuffed the girl to the sexton and the sexton to the door handle of the hearse. I ran up the track. Ahead I could see the bobbing figure of Holmes in his white Safari jacket, and much further ahead I could occasionally glimpse the strange figure of Dr Cluj, his black coat floating, his arms seeming to stab the air as he ran, as if attempting to fly like a bat. (Holmes, when he sees this draft of our adventure, will no doubt remark that such observations as I have just made only deflect attention from the simple facts of the tale, and are misguided attempts by me to make the moment more laden with mystery than it was, and to colour my tale with hints of the supernatural. I can only say that I have recorded, to the best of my ability, my exact thoughts and observations as I ran up that track. There is a psychological component to events that, even if untrue, is true. If my vision was distorted, it is because I am inside the world which I am trying to analyze from the outside, and this can never be done. Not even in retrospect. The world is not entirely susceptible to quantitative analysis.)

As I ran up that track, my rowing and rugby days at Eton seemed to surge out of the past to inspire me, for I had been an athlete of some ability when young. I sprinted hard and gained on Holmes – which surprised me – and soon I was shoulder to shoulder with him. Cluj fairly flew over the gate that barred the track from the free land of the cliff tops. Holmes and I reached the chained gate, climbed over it. Scarcely had we done so when a strange, terrific and almost unbelievable scene unfolded before us.

Cluj ran upward and upward on the grassy black slope in starlight, upward over the swelling ground towards the edge of the cliff, running and running and seeming scarcely to move. Whereupon suddenly from our right a huge hound materialized out of fairyland gloom, soaring along the ridge, outlined against stars . . . Cluj, suddenly aware of the beast, veered left and seemed to lurch ahead.

The scene, so stark and strange, was almost comic, like an illustration from a children's book. Here was the grotesque Dr Cluj hurrying with his coat floating out behind him, here the furious hound behind him and gaining with every bound, here Sherlock Holmes just ahead of me running hard, his cheek and nose and distinctive profile etched against star-sprinkled sky.

We reached the top of the ridge and could see the cliff's edge and the sea below. Holmes stumbled, I grabbed him, and we stopped to get breath. As we paused there on the heights we witnessed a scene so bizarre, so fantastic, that even now I have difficulty believing it really occurred. With the hound perhaps thirty yards from him, Cluj came to a sudden stop at the cliff's edge, paused, spread his arms, gave a hop . . . and vanished.

'Good God!' I cried.

'He has made an error!' said Holmes.

That seemed to me obvious – but I was soon to learn that it wasn't so obvious.

The hound cruised to a halt and looked curiously over the cliff edge, then backed away from the drop-off and sniffed the grass. He sniffed his way cautiously to the cliff's edge again, looked into the void, then backed away as if utterly bewildered.

A figure emerged over the top of the rise to our right – a woman.

The great hound bounded towards her, for it was Sara Timmons-Swallow, the widow of the Reverend. I was about to step forward and hail her, but Holmes reached out and restrained me with a touch. She passed by unaware of us. Her step was steady, the dog joyfully trotted at her heels. She turned her steps away from the path and walked to the edge of the cliff at the very place Cluj had vanished.

'Did she see what just happened?' I said softly.

'She saw nothing,' he replied. 'She is standing there for another reason.'

We gazed at her in silence.

She seemed to be communing with the vasty globe of stars overhead, her head tilted back, gazing upward into the galaxy.

'What is she doing, Holmes?'

'That is where her husband stepped over the edge – and the two girls after him. Death Drop, they call it.' Despite the starlight shadows on his face I could see his frowning brow. 'Ah, there she goes.'

She retreated from the cliff edge, proceeded along the cliff path, then turned left on to the path that led down along the fields to the Admiral Hawke Inn. She passed through the swing gate and vanished.

'Come,' said Holmes eagerly, and he hurried away into the dark, seeming to sniff the air like Patrick the wolfhound. I followed him to the spot where the woman had been standing. I looked over the edge and saw naked black rocks extending a goodly distance out into the sea, for the tide was out.

'Scarcely a breath of wind,' said Holmes. 'Look here, Wilson. Notice this white stone on which we are standing.'

It was simply a slab of slightly undulating rock, quite level with the grass all round it, a white and rather slippery-looking rock, as if worn by the sea.

'Come over here, and take note of something else, Wilson.'

I walked to where he stood.

He pointed over the edge. 'What do you see?'

'The Venus Pool I think it is called.'

'And what else?'

'Stars reflected,' I said. 'Hallucinatory, isn't it. Which is the mirror and which is me, in such starlit darkness?'

'Come!' He strode away to the north till we reached Swallow's Nest.

'Now look under your feet!' he cried.

'Similar white stone,' I said.

'Precisely, Wilson! And what do you see when you look over the edge?'

'The path down to the hut,' I said, 'marked by those tiny lights.'

A dark figure approached us. 'Gentlemen,' said Lestrade, 'where is Cluj?'

'He's flown,' said Holmes.

'Flown!' cried Lestrade.

'To the rocks below,' said Holmes, 'a hundred yards back, at Death Drop.'

'Can you see him?' asked Lestrade, peering over the edge.

'No chance,' said Holmes. 'You won't be able to recover the body easily till morning.'

'And you'd better do it before the tide comes in,' I said. 'For if the body washes out with the tide, you may never find it.'

'And then,' said Holmes, 'the people in this superstitious village are likely to claim he was a vampire after all, and flew back to Transylvania.'

Lestrade laughed – nervously, I thought.

We walked back to Death Drop and we stood there with sheer air beneath our feet and the sky overhead filled with a million stars, and for a moment I felt a bit floatingly, as if none of this were real, as if we were on a huge stage in a theatre somewhere, and all the shadowy insubstantial earth but a fantasy.

'Any word of statues found on a canal boat?' asked Holmes.

'Nothing, I'm afraid,' said Lestrade.

We turned and climbed over the gate and walked down the dark field, and eventually reached the hearse where our two shivering prisoners were shackled to the door.

# SEVENTEEN
## Ensign Squeers Speaks His Mind

A green streak flashed out the door of the Admiral Hawke Inn and sailed across the garden and landed on the shoulder of Sherlock Holmes, who was standing with Lestrade.

Holmes flinched as Ensign Squeers said, 'Hello!' in his ear.

Lestrade stepped back in surprise and was bumped by a fat tourist, one of many who had just begun streaming off the noon bus and hurrying towards the picnic tables. Lestrade straightened himself up and said, 'No, Holmes, we could not find the body. It simply was not there.'

Squeers ruffled and fluffled and looked perfectly in command.

'You searched the area by the Venus Pool?' asked Holmes.

'Our men went out in a boat as the sun came up, landed on the beach, searched amongst all the rocks and looked into the pool itself. Nothing. The body was gone. We searched a quarter mile up and down the beach.'

Young Jack set food before two people at a nearby picnic table and, turning to us, said brightly, 'Cluj was a vampire and he flew back to Transylvania, that's all!'

'As good a theory as any,' I said.

'Unless he flew up into our rafters!' Jack laughed, and tossed his head towards the roof of the old Admiral Hawke Inn – and for a moment I could picture the freakish Cluj hunkering in the gloom beneath that roof. 'Maybe you should draw that fantasy, Jack,' I said. 'Vampire in the Rafters.'

'Maybe I will,' he said, and hurried away.

'You are sure he went over the cliff?' asked Lestrade.

Holmes nodded. 'Quite sure. Any word from Nigel Lyme about the *Proteus*?'

'They have found a number of seventy-footers, but none suspicious in any way,' said Lestrade. 'Most are tied up, haven't moved in days. We've checked the registrations on all of them but found nothing amiss. They all check out perfectly. No *Proteus*. No boat anything like the *Proteus* anywhere on the waterway from Cheddington to Boston – blue, black or any other colour.'

Holmes frowned.

Sara Timmons-Swallow appeared beside us. 'I almost forgot,' she said, looking up at Holmes. 'You left your penknife on the bedside table.' She handed it to him.

'Ah! Thank you,' said Holmes.

'Then it was you, Mrs Swallow,' said I. 'God bless you, madam, for taking in this bedraggled fellow of ours, and saving him from sleeping another cold night amid the tombs!'

'I've slept in colder spots,' said Holmes.

'For decades,' said Lestrade.

'The warmth of your welcome, my dear lady,' said Holmes, 'and the luxury of your guest room, were a true joy after hard nights spent in London streets and a graveyard.'

Dr Livesey strolled near. 'I am curious, Mr Holmes – how many cases do you have in hand at a given moment?'

'Four at this moment,' said Holmes.

'You startle me,' said Lestrade. 'What are the other two?'

'Mysteries flock to him like geese to ponds,' said I.

'I hope to soon conclude,' said Holmes, 'the adventure of the Bob Tawp deception, the matter of the stolen Greek statues, the mystery of the missing street people, and the case of the slandering of Reverend Swallow.'

'He deceived us all!' said a big woman who suddenly appeared at Holmes's shoulder. She had been struggling to shoulder her way through our group, trying to get to the cupcake table. Now she paused to intrude on our conversation.

'He deceived no one,' said Holmes. 'You deceived yourself, my dear lady.'

Dr Livesey looked surprised. 'Have you discovered new facts concerning his death, Mr Holmes?'

'One new fact. But the truth was always there to see, in the character of the man himself. Anyone who has read his poems, listened to his life, heard his sermons, should have solved the mystery instantly.'

'Rubbish!' said the fat woman.

Holmes smiled at her, distantly, and looked away at Dr Livesey. 'Swallow,' said Holmes, 'was not only a minister but a poet who wanted his young flock to understand the whole realm of religious thought and feeling. He knew that they had all decided that the Bible was their own doorway into the spiritual realm, so he gave them Bibles, and he wrote in their Bibles *"This is your chosen path to God, though there are others. Let us journey towards higher ground and make the leap of faith together."* That is a simple statement, written in the Bible for people for whom the Bible was a sacred book. It was obviously a message of spiritual encouragement, nothing more, nothing less. Only in retrospect, after the terrible accident of that night, can those words be read as something diabolical, as the forecast of a madman – and then only by people who are neither very charitable nor very intelligent.'

'Accident, Mr Holmes!' said the fat woman with scorn. 'He knew the cliff well, and he led them off of it.'

Sara Timmons-Swallow put her hand to her mouth, and looked about to cry.

'You are speaking, Madam, utter rubbish,' said Holmes.

Attracted by the intensity of our conversation, a number of people had gravitated towards us and now stood on the periphery of our little group, drinks in hand, listening curiously and with increasing interest to the monologue of Sherlock Holmes. Bertie Branford sat on a bench nearby, sipping tea.

'At Kittle Mill, which was then owned by the parish,' said Holmes, 'Swallow met with his young catechism class, gave them their Bibles, and then led them singing up the path towards Mortestow and the cliffs. Everyone here who knows the three cliff paths well – the Admiral Hawke Inn path, the middle path, and the Mortestow path – knows that where these three paths meet, in a staggered fashion, near the crossing of the road, there can be a bit of confusion as to which fork one is on, and particularly this is so in the dark of a starlit night. It is more particularly so, one supposes, when one is marching with others and singing songs. What we do know is the Reverend Swallow *thought* he was on the Mortestow path. We know this because he warned the young people not to stumble on the stone water trough – warned them in a song, inserting his warning into the song itself – a trick which so impressed one of the young men that he has been repeating the story for years. In fact, however, the group were *not* on the Mortestow path, but on the middle path, feeling very high with the religious exaltation of the moment, and also, it must be said, at least in the case of the Reverend, high on marijuana.'

Sara Timmons-Swallow nodded faintly.

'The ecstatic Reverend Jim Swallow simply did not realize, in the darkness of a starry night, where he was. I have walked those paths; their similarity is striking. In the dark, I dare say, anyone could become confused.'

Several men nodded assent.

'Swallow passed through the gate on to the high cliff grass, turned left, came to a white stone slab embedded in the turf, and assumed it was the stone above his own hut – but, in fact, it was a nearly identical stone by what is now called Death Drop. Jim Swallow believed he was above his own hut. And that is where he *would* have been had he come up the Mortestow path, as he thought he had. Now, remember: his wife had placed little lit candles on the path down to his hut, and when he looked over, he saw those candles.'

'But the candles weren't there,' said someone.

'Only stars,' said Holmes.

'Stars?' said Livesey.

'Reflected in the Venus Pool, Dr Livesey. The tide was out, the Venus Pool catchment was full of water. Stars were sprinkled over the still surface of the pool like tiny candles in the gorse. In the midst of his religious ecstasy and song, Reverend Swallow glimpsed those starry reflections in the Venus Pool, knew them for the candles he expected, and so he stepped over the edge – full of faith – on to the path that was not there.'

'I saw stars in the pool last night,' said Lestrade.

'And then there is the matter of the five silver crosses,' said Holmes. 'Reverend Swallow, according to the tale, had promised each of the young people a parting gift, which he said he would give them at the hut. I found those gifts in the same place I found the signal torch and signal flags of Dr Cluj – in an artfully disguised cabinet at the back of the hut. I doubt that many people know of that cabinet, with its trick door. Cluj found it, I found it. Perhaps others have found it over the years. But the gifts had fallen below the bottom shelf, into the dirt at the back of the hut. It is my habit to investigate minutely, and with excruciating care. I used my pocket torch and found those gifts. I have them here.'

Holmes opened his slender hand to reveal five small silver crosses.

'On the front of each cross is the name of one of the five young people,' said Holmes, 'and on the back of each are the words *From Rev. Swallow.*'

Sara Timmons-Swallow was touching her eyes with a handkerchief. 'Thank you, Mr Holmes,' she said.

He put them into her palm.

Billy Baffin whistled to Ensign Squeers, who flapped off of Holmes's shoulder and on to Billy's own – where, if truth be told, the bird looked more comfortable.

Davy Deeps sauntered up, smiling, with his hand in his pocket.

'Cluj,' said Holmes, 'made the same sort of mistake Reverend Swallow made, and on the same sort of night: the tide out, a moonless sky filled with stars. Cluj was distracted not by religious ecstasy and marijuana, but by a wolfhound bounding towards him out of darkness. He ran, found himself on a white stone slab, looked over the edge, thought he saw the tiny lights he'd rigged to mark the path to the Swallow's Nest. So he stepped over the edge, intending to hurry into the hut to find safety from the dog. Instead, he plunged to his death on the rocks below.'

'If he is dead,' said Lestrade, 'where is the body?'

'Five fathoms deep!' cried Ensign Squeers.

'The bird is right,' said Holmes, 'and we have in our midst the very man who can prove he is right.' He looked suddenly at Davy Deeps. 'Would you show us what you have in your pocket, Mr Deeps?'

Davy Deeps, finding himself the centre of attention, was abashed. His empty blue eyes registered fright, confusion. He drew his hand from his pocket and held out a large ruby ring.

'I took it,' said Davy, 'cleaning the beach.'

'You took it from somebody's finger?' asked Dr Livesey.

'From his pocket,' said Davy.

'And what did you do with the man, Davy?' asked Dr Livesey.

'Towed him out and sunk him with a stone,' said Davy.

'The bird is smarter than I am!' said Billy.

'But we have asked you not to do that, Davy,' said Dr Livesey.

'Mr Blankenship paid me,' said Davy.

'But he didn't mean *people*,' said Livesey.

Davy nodded, seemed to agree.

'Would you care,' said I, 'to disclose your method, my dear Holmes – for the edification of posterity and present company?'

Holmes said, 'I knew that Cluj, of course, could fly – from the cliff tops down to the rocks . . . but I also knew that he could not do it twice. And I knew that Davy Deeps preferred to do his beach searching before the sun rose, for he told me so. I knew also that children who have found new treasures can scarcely keep from assuring themselves of their good fortune. So when I saw Davy touching his pocket so frequently in the past hour, it was not a large leap to think he may have found a treasure during his early beach-combing. I had no idea what it was, but I thought it very likely that Davy must have been on the beach this morning, and found some-thing, and it was not a large leap of imagination to think that he might also have found the body of Dr Cluj.'

'He was doing no more than Cornish men have always done,' said Billy. 'Scavenging a wreck!'

'And what,' I asked, 'of the other two mysteries, Holmes – the matter of the stolen Greek statues, and the curious case of Bob Tawp – can you wrap those up before lunch?'

'I'm afraid those two must await our return to London,' said Holmes.

Ensign Squeers gave a squawk, a flap, leapt from Billy's shoulder, made a swooping circle over the crowd – causing several people to duck and several to gasp – and he landed again on Billy.

'You'll lose that bird,' said Livesey. 'He'll fly away one of these times!'

'Nay!' said Billy. 'Ensign Squeers will never desert his captain, not he. Too many years we've been mates, through storms and doldrums and the monster-plagued deep.'

'Best tether him to his perch, Billy,' insisted Livesey. 'He fright-ened some ladies.'

'Merdes! Merdes!' shouted Ensign Squeers, in a voice I had never heard before.

'What!' cried Billy. 'I bought him from a Frenchman, but I never heard him speak French before this very moment.'

'Je t'aime!' cried Ensign Squeers, and he began to lift his wings and bob his head. 'Je t'aime!'

'Begad, I love you, too!' cried Billy, and he laughed so loud and laughed so long that the ladies fell quiet, and shrank. 'This calls for a drink!' cried Billy, and he staggered towards the bar.

# EIGHTEEN
## Proteus Performs

B leak light barely sketched our sitting room. Rain pattered on the panes. The shape of Sherlock Holmes was outlined against the grey window where he stood in his typical pose, sports coat rumpled, hands in pockets, gazing at the laptop computer on the high table. He turned as I emerged from the kitchen, and he said, 'So we learn there's been another robbery, Wilson. This one near Nottingham. A marble panel, Greek, high relief, picturing a frenzied maenad swirling a knife over her head, holding half a goat in her left hand. It was stolen from a private home. But how does Lindblad – and surely it is Lindblad – know of these pieces, so obscure, in country houses and city houses here and there about England, and all near the Grand Union Canal?'

'I have done some online research, that might be of interest to you,' I said. 'There is a group called the Greek Art Society of England, and they publish a newsletter, in which members discuss the art they own.'

'Ahh!' cried Holmes.

I handed him a slip of paper with the society's Web address printed on it.

'That is the second piece of good news I've received today,' said Holmes.

'And what was the first?'

'This morning I received an email from Lestrade informing me that the owner of a boatyard near Cheddington not only remembered seeing the *Proteus*, but thought it so unusual a craft that he took a picture of it. Lestrade is to send me the picture shortly. That may confirm my suspicions.'

'You think a seventy-foot narrow boat might elude us by turning into . . . what? A bat?'

'Consider, Wilson. The man behind these thefts is almost certainly Lars Lindblad, a man who has eluded every police force in the world for the last forty years – in Europe, the Middle East, South

America – the most notorious international criminal of the age, a man who now uses crime not merely for profit but for fun, as a sport, as a way to amuse and to challenge himself. He constructs his crimes not merely to succeed, but to surprise. You will recall that he is a musician, art collector, inventor – in short, he is possessed by a creative impulse which he indulges at every turn. You will also recall that in our last encounter he escaped in an open cockpit biplane of his own design, which transformed itself in mid flight into . . .'

'How could I forget. But what could a canal boat convert itself into, pray tell? A submarine?'

His computer began to beep.

'We might soon have our answer!' He darted to the table. 'The photograph has come through – and a note . . . Lestrade wants to meet us at The Golden Dog in an hour."

Holmes printed the picture and laid it on the table. It revealed a long, black narrow boat, with the word *Proteus* painted in blue on the side. It appeared to me to be merely a canal boat like many another.

'The superstructure is strange, is it not?' said Holmes.

'Boxy, if that's what you mean.'

'Boxy and black. But we know the blacking will wash off and beneath is another colour, perhaps blue. We should be looking for a blue-hulled boat with an entirely different cabin. The boat appears uncommonly tall. Barely fits the tunnels, I expect. Take off the outer shell and we will find something very different beneath it – a holiday cruiser, perhaps, with hanging flower pots, and with a new name and registry on the side.'

'Worth a try, Holmes.'

'We will have him!' said Holmes. 'Lestrade has arranged to have the Grand Union Canal blocked from Crick Tunnel in the south to the Fossdyke Canal in the north. At six o'clock tomorrow morning a boat will be sunk at the north end of the Crick tunnel, and the Torksey lock at the entrance to the Fossdyke will be closed for engineering works. The *Proteus* will be trapped between the two.'

'Not quite, Holmes. The *Proteus* could continue north on the River Trent, past the Fossdyke Navigation and up to the Humber – and so sail down the Humber past Hull, and out to the North Sea.'

'I have thought of that,' said he. 'But the confluence of the Trent and the Humber will be watched. No boat will be allowed to pass without inspection. I am going to be there myself in case any troubles about search warrants are encountered, in which case I will take matters into my own hands.'

'You plan to board the craft illegally, Holmes?'

'Will you accompany me, Wilson?'

'In for a penny, in for a pound,' said I.

'Excellent!'

Scarcely were we out on the street and walking briskly towards Baker Street when Holmes whipped out his mobile and called Lestrade. 'My dear Lestrade,' said he, 'would you be good enough to meet us in half an hour at The Golden Dog? . . . of course it is important . . . no, no, I prefer you *in the flesh*, dear fellow. We'll wait.'

'You mystify me, Holmes,' said I. 'I thought you said Lestrade had invited *us* to The Golden Dog.'

'Strange things are afoot, Wilson!'

We arrived at The Golden Dog and took a table by the old leaded window. By and by Lestrade floated in, like flotsam on a wave of young men in blazers, seeming suddenly very small and old. He slid into the cushioned bench by our table and said, 'Why are we meeting here, Holmes?'

'I like a place where people get dressed up,' said Holmes.

'You didn't dress terribly fashionably in the old days,' said Lestrade. 'Wearing a deerstalker.'

'You never actually wore that hat, did you Holmes?' I said.

'A few times,' said Holmes. 'I preferred a bowler. But there was a case – I can't recall if Watson wrote it up – when a deerstalker cap was required. And it happened that Sidney Paget, Watson's illustrator, was with us that day, and he saw me prowling through the hedges of Hampshire in my deerstalker.'

'And the rest is history,' said Lestrade. 'False history, as it happens.'

'Not entirely false,' said Holmes. 'When Lamar Klegg shot the original hat off my head, I bought another and wore it a few times on country walks.'

'Shot it off your head!' said I.

'Holmes,' sighed Lestrade, 'has lived an exciting life.'

'Twice,' said I.

'I sometimes think once was quite enough,' said Holmes.

'I sometimes think once is one too many,' said Lestrade.

'Tell me, Lestrade,' said I, 'will you actually sink a boat in the Crick tunnel?'

'Sink a boat?'

'To block the canal,' I said.

Lestrade looked at me queerly. 'What has Holmes been telling you?'

'Just a passing thought,' said Holmes. 'The main point is that you must now set your men in search of two thirty-five-foot boats travelling fast on the Grand Union Canal, possibly travelling at night. If you find such boats – boats whirling up locks and down, moving with an urgency seldom seen amongst the leisurely canal-boating fraternity – stop those boats. Particularly any boat with a blue hull.'

'I have lost you, Holmes,' said Lestrade.

Holmes brought out the photo of the *Proteus*. 'My belief is that this boat has now been split into two boats. Perceive the peculiar symmetry of the craft,' said Holmes.

'I don't perceive it,' I said.

'Nor I,' said Lestrade.

'Two wind turbines for electricity, one at each end of the craft – why two?'

'I haven't the foggiest,' said Lestrade.

'Note also how the windows are arranged, three towards the front, an odd gap, then three more windows – and a large windowless stretch between them. Look closely at that middle section, where there are no windows. It seems to be made of different material than the rest of the boat.'

'I couldn't tell,' said Lestrade.

'Nor could I,' said I.

Holmes took out his pen and, using the wine menu as a straight edge, drew a line on the photograph, a line that divided the narrow boat exactly in half. He tapped the picture. 'Imagine cutting the boat in two. Imagine we are looking at two linked boats, one in front, one behind.'

'Then the back half would have a flat prow,' I said.

'Unless it has a pointed prow that docks into the back of the front boat.'

'Anything could be engineered,' said Lestrade. 'That we concede.'

'The middle section looks like it might be removable. It might be a sheet metal section covering the rear deck of the boat in front, the front deck of the boat behind.'

'Anything *might* be,' said Lestrade.

'Remove the sheet metal,' cried Holmes, 'then unlink the docking mechanism that joins front and back sections – and, voila! Two boats.'

'What happened to your theory that they removed the superstructure to reveal another cabin beneath?' I asked.

'That was just deceptive talk,' said Holmes. 'This is more likely.'

'Two boats in one does seem the sort of mad scheme that would appeal to Lindblad,' said Lestrade.

'Remember to watch the canals at night, all hours. Seldom do boats move at night, Lestrade – but these will. Relentlessly.'

'It shall be done, my friend,' said Lestrade, rising from the table. 'You are strange, Holmes, and sometimes a bit trying. And yet I suppose – though I am loathe to admit it – I would have done anything you asked; even sunk a boat in the Crick tunnel.'

Holmes gazed up at him, almost tenderly – tenderly for someone like Holmes, that is. Well, let us call it a gaze of surprise. 'That won't be necessary,' he said.

As we rode in a taxi back to Dorset Square, Holmes's familiar profile – aquiline nose, pipe, cap – was very still and brooding against the sliding backdrop of London streets. What he was thinking I could not guess. When we returned to our flat he walked into the sitting room and looked out the windows at the square, and he said in a loud voice, almost shouting, 'They very likely have turned the *Proteus* into a seventy-foot coal boat, Wilson – and buried the statues under the coal.'

'What!'

'Typical ploy. Many a smuggler has done it – contraband under heaps of legal cargo.'

'But, I thought you just said that most likely they would—'

'Please, Wilson!' he cried. 'Don't subvert me with your nonsense!'

'Subvert you!' I said.

'I am thinking of cosmic possibilities,' said Holmes, and he waved his hand grandly.

'I was merely trying—'

'Don't try quite so hard,' hissed Holmes. He made an extravagant face at me, which puzzled me utterly.

He began pacing. He stalked to the wingtip chair by the fireplace, whirled, and said, 'One thing worries me, Wilson.'

'What's that?' I replied, scarcely daring to say anything for fear of setting him off.

'At Boston Grand Sluice the River Witham becomes tidal, leading down through Boston and into the Wash. But the locks accommodate boats only fifty feet long . . . so how will the *Proteus* get through?'

'But Holmes!' I cried. 'You've already explained that when you suggested—'

He shushed me. 'But Lestrade will block the canal at both ends tomorrow, and then we shall see!'

I went to bed feeling puzzled, and very concerned about my friend's mental state. Long ago I had worried whether the resuscitation process employed by Dr Coleman might have been flawed – as so many stem-cell experiments on animals have been flawed in the past – and I wondered whether Holmes's mental powers and whole being might be subject to sudden decay. Now these old fears were revived. As I fell into the arms of Morpheus I heard Holmes playing his violin in the front room, carving the most soulful Italian melodies out of thick air.

# NINETEEN
## Aphrodite Flees England

Holmes and I had been invited by Cecelia Branford to visit her in her flat on Primrose Hill for a Sunday séance with tea and biscuits. She wanted to thank Holmes for taking on her father's case. But Holmes was in a cogitation frenzy, not in a congenial frame of mind, refused to go. He begged me to go in his stead, and to offer his apologies.

When I arrived, a brightsome, slender, dark-haired woman of thirty-something greeted me effusively and introduced herself as Cecelia. She gushed me into her sitting room, which was decorated like a gypsy's lair. Tarot cards were splashed on one table, a Ouija board lay on another, the traditional crystal ball rested majestically on yet another. A big painting above the sofa depicted a spirit wisping upward out of a dead body in what appeared to be a graveyard. A white cat lay luxuriously on the high back of a cushioned chair. A black cat slunk out of sight behind a curtain. Then a bell rang and in came Alice Branford, big and blonde, a bit wrinkled about the eyes, a handsome and plucky woman. We three soon sat down by the Ouija board and Cecelia switched off the lamp. The room was lit only by a faint streak of light that leaked under the drapes. Cecelia solemnly pronounced that she would attempt to contact her brother, Bertie. She began swaying in the gloom, her pretty face a pale blur on the darkness. After a time she cried, in a searchingly sweet voice, 'Bertie? . . . are you there, Bertie?'

Silence.

'Can you hear me, Bertie?' she pleaded, brightly.

Silence.

'Are you here, Bertie?' she asked.

'Yes, I am here,' said Bertie.

'You are very clear, Bertie. Speak to me!'

'Of course, I'll speak to you,' said Bertie. 'I've missed you very much.' He leaned down and touched her shoulder.

Cecelia gasped, looked up at him. Then she threw the switch, and the lights came up. 'Why, it's a miracle!' cried Cecelia. 'I didn't know I had so much power!'

'You don't,' said Bertie. 'It's really me.'

'That's what I mean!' she said, and she leapt to her feet and hugged him.

Alice, who had arranged this meeting, was full of buxom laughter.

For the next several hours we sipped tea, ate sweet biscuits, and listened to the strange adventures of Bertie Branford. His sisters kept probing him with question after question. Bertie cheerfully obliged their curiosity. He told them how he had often wanted to make himself known to them, tell them he was alive, but kept putting it off because he wanted to return to the family as a success, not as a street person. He said he had applied to get back into nursing school, and that Shakira was intending to go to nursing school also.

'Then you are in love!' said Cecelia. 'Daniel Ma told me you were alive, but I did not know whether to believe it.'

'Why didn't you believe it?' he asked.

'I didn't dare,' she said.

'Remember what I said, little brother,' said Alice. 'You, Shakira and Biki may stay at my flat indefinitely, if necessary.'

'When will you go see our parents?' asked Cecelia.

'Unless Mr Holmes retrieves the statue I stole, never,' said Bertie.

'Don't be silly!' cried Alice. 'Father is not so mad as to value a statue above the lives of the people you saved.'

Bertie's handsome face clouded. A blond lock drooped over his right eye. 'I only wish I could have saved Sinjin Chitterlie and Derek Winston.'

'Would you like to talk to them?'

'I don't think I want to talk to them now,' said Bertie. 'They're dead.'

'We could try,' she said.

'Oh, let the poor fellows rest,' said Alice. 'The world is filled with so much chatter that conversation from the grave seems quite unnecessary.'

Bertie laughed.

I took my leave and walked west through Regent's Park. I gazed up at the bland sky-hazy London sun, drifting behind feathery clouds. The world was very green with May, people strolling, ducks making wide Vs in smooth water. I was struck by what a sweetly pleasant and civilized place Old London is – so different from the blowy, gloomy, mysterious coast of Cornwall with its raw rain, dark nights, claustrophobic hedges, bleak moorland, empty cliffs and peace-shattering sea.

I crossed Baker Street, passed by the Sherlock Holmes Museum that had so surprised Holmes when he first arrived in the twenty-first century. A few minutes later I reached our digs in Dorset Square. Holmes looked up from his book and said, 'Is the poor woman still talking to shadows.'

'Doing her best to explain the mysteries of the world – just as you are.'

'Quite so,' said he, laying the book aside. 'I fear that in my old age I'm getting impatient.'

I laughed out loud. '*Getting* impatient!'

He seemed in a mood. Uncharacteristically quiet. Contemplative.

'Cecelia Branford is far from alone, you know, Holmes. Many people believe in the afterlife – and therefore in the possibility of communicating with ghosts.'

'People will believe in anything they cannot prove!' said he, and he sprang to his feet.

The old Holmes, I thought!

'All round us, Wilson, are crowds of seemingly sane people who populate the night skies with ghosts, angels, vampires, demons – spirits of every description.'

'It's called "religion", Holmes. You may have read about it.'

He began to pace nervously. Several times he phoned Lestrade but was unable to reach him. After supper I took Sir Launcelot out for a walk. When I returned Holmes was gone. I went to bed.

The following morning gloomy shreds and tatters filled the ragged sky, and rain was pattering on the panes. I poached eggs, popped down toast, and we ate in silence. Holmes was far away, brow furrowed in a frown. He was making notes in his moleskin notebook. I have learned to mind my own thoughts on such occasions. I cleared the dishes. Lancy was watching me with such forlorn eyes that I gave him a biscuit. Just at that moment the bell rang and Holmes, to my surprise, broke out of his brown study and darted instantly to the door. Nigel Lyme appeared. Scotland Yard was certainly going out of their way to accommodate Holmes, sending officers to our flat on a Monday morning simply because Sherlock Holmes preferred face-to-face meetings of the sort he had been accustomed to in the old days. But Holmes, having opened the door, now began behaving a bit oddly. 'Inspector Lyme!' said he.

'I have a report,' said Lyme.

'Ah, excellent!' cried Holmes. 'But come – let us have a bit of fresh air . . . I am anxious to hear what you have learned. Come along, Wilson, you will be interested, I think!'

'It is raining out, sir,' said Lyme.

'What could be more appropriate than rain in London on a Monday morn,' said Holmes, taking Lyme by the arm, easing him out into the hallway – a gesture which startled me, for I had never seen, or imagined, Holmes pressing another person in so rude and familiar a manner. We all descended to the street where Holmes produced his key and let us through the iron gate into the rainy garden. The gazebo in the middle was barely visible, blurry in grey mist. We walked to it. I stood under the overhang and Holmes and Lyme sat down on the faintly damp board bench. They both looked very straight and stiff, like schoolboys being disciplined.

'On Saturday night, Mr Holmes, we sent a helicopter over the length of the waterway you instructed us to search. Did this several times. We detected several boats moving late at night, but most were just changing position by a few hundred yards, to tie up at more suitable moorings. Only one was moving purposively. I thought we might be on to something, thought that you might have been right, for the crew were cranking this craft through locks one after the other and running their boat a little above the four-mile-per-hour limit. They did this for hours on end. It struck all of us as odd, and we followed the craft by road, and at various bridges we waited and saw it passing under. Yesterday very early, in the bare light of morning, I walked along the towpath and approached the boat at a lock. The old woman at the tiller was just throwing the old man a rope. The old gentleman towed the boat into position, and as they locked through Torksey Lock into the Fossdyke navigation I watched them closely, and I saw nothing suspicious. The old man was struggling with the lock so I helped him crank. The old woman appeared on the deck and invited me in for breakfast, urged me. I told her I had eaten. She must have been seventy-five if she was a day. Pancakes, she said. With lingonberries.'

'What's this?' said Holmes, startled. 'Lingonberries?'

'I asked why they had been travelling all night,' said Lyme. 'The old man explained that mechanical difficulties with the rudder had delayed them in Leicester. They needed to be at Lincoln by noon, for they were to be picked up there by their grandson who would drive them to a wedding in York.'

'Please describe the boat,' said Holmes. 'I presume it had a blue hull, and that its name was printed in black.'

'Blue hull, yellow cabin, flower basket hanging by the rear deck full of blue and yellow flowers, very trim and well kept, thirty-five or forty feet long, I should guess.'

'Did it have a wind generator on top.'

'No, I . . . yes, I believe it did, actually.'

'Did you check, since then, to see if the boat is at Lincoln? Blue and yellow should make it distinctive.'

'I can do that,' said Lyme, and he pulled out his phone and made a call.

'And the name of the boat?'

'As you say, the name was painted in black, and the name was *Minos.*'

Holmes turned pale. I had never seen such a reaction in him. He stood up, walked clear round the gazebo, anticlockwise, and appeared coming from the other direction. 'I fear you may have made an error, Inspector Lyme.'

Lyme stood up. 'I doubt it, sir. I will phone you when they find

the boat at Lincoln. Do you wish us to do anything more than just
. . . find it?'

'No, no,' said Holmes. 'If you find it, all is well.'

Inspector Lyme took his leave. His strong shoulders faded away
in the green gloom of the garden; he went out the gate.

'You suspect that boat was the one we are after?' I asked.

'I am almost certain of it.'

'And why?'

'If the boat began at Nottingham, it was moving for at least
eleven hours on the canal at night, and had at least three more
hours of travel before it would reach Lincoln. That isn't a journey
that people in their seventies would be likely to make. Ergo, they
weren't old people. And does a seventy-five-year-old woman heave
a rope . . . or does she hand it gently ashore? Lyme says she
threw it.'

'A younger person in disguise?'

'Almost surely. And then, of course, the lingonberries.'

'Swedish pancakes.'

'You are in excellent form today, Wilson. And the boat was yellow
and blue.'

'Swedish colours.'

'Correct. And one final point: the boat was named *Minos*.'

'I see no connection there, Holmes. The king of Crete was neither
Swedish nor Greek.'

'But Daedalus the Athenian spent most of his life in Crete, under
the patronage and protection of Minos. And Lars Lindblad is exceedingly interested in Daedalus.'

'What, if I may ask, makes you think so?'

We were walking through light rain.

'Ah, that is a tale for another day,' said he, and he opened the
gate, and we went out, and suddenly the rain came down heavily,
slashing through the thick canopy of the trees.

I went to my club for the day. When I returned to Dorset Square
it was very late and I was very tired. I could see our lit window.
The light must have been just right, and I must have stood in just
the right shadow, for I saw on our white curtain the familiar
silhouette of Holmes in profile, and he seemed to be talking to
someone. He was standing frozen, his hand out, as if gesturing
towards a late-night visitor in the room. I thought it lucky no
modern Colonel Moran was lurking with airgun in hand. Odd

things like that occurred to me from time to time – as if Holmes
were not really quite in this century, not really quite substantial
in my life (as I knew very well he *was*) but was still inhabiting,
in some magical way, the fogs and byways of Edwardian London.
When I opened the door of our flat he was real enough. I smelled
his tobacco. He never smoked it but he kept a little pile of it on the
mantel just so he could have a waft of that old, now-forbidden
pleasure. A bit messy, but it pleased him. He had, however, no visitor.
His mobile phone was on the coffee table. It was his habit to set the
phone on that table, turn on the speaker phone, and talk to the little
device as if it were a person, gesturing, pacing, and so on.

'So who were you talking to?' I asked. 'Lestrade?'

Holmes nodded, paced to the fireplace. He leaned against the
mantel, looking very casual, intense, debonair, aristocratic. He
struck a match, pretended to light his pipe, threw the burnt match
into the grate. Suddenly – as if giving up on that little charade – he
grabbed the bowl of his briar pipe and clacked it out of his teeth
and slipped it deftly into the soft wool of his pocket. 'Another
robbery has taken place, Wilson. A small Aphrodite, taken from a
house in Lincoln.'

'And what of the canal cruiser, the one . . .'

Holmes made another of his frantic and incomprehensible
gestures, put his fingers over his lips, took my arm, motioned me
towards his bedroom. I followed him into his room and he closed
the door.

On his low dresser were beakers of chemicals, sheaves of papers,
and a chunk of Stilton on a plate. I felt a bit awkward. I said, 'I
was about to ask, Holmes, whether there has been any sign of that
yellow and blue canal cruiser.'

'Vanished. Not to be found in the canal from Torksey Lock to
Boston Grand Sluice. Lestrade sent a helicopter over the top of the
waterway, and a motorboat through it. Nothing.'

'Maybe it's just out of sight, concealed in a boatyard dry dock,
like the time – remember – you were looking for a boat in the
Thames, a steam launch . . .'

'The *Aurora*.' He laughed. 'The Jonathan Small case.'

'*The Sign of the Four*, as Watson called it.'

'We caught the *Aurora*, but that was years ago. I fear the *Minos*
is out in the Wash long since, and its cargo picked up by now by
some speedy ship, or possibly a seaplane.'

'A canal narrow boat would not survive in the Wash, Holmes. Particularly with the rough weather they have been having up there.'

'An ordinary narrow boat wouldn't survive the sea. But I suspect this one isn't ordinary,' said Holmes.

'And what of the twin to the *Minos*. What is your guess?'

'My guess is that the second boat is long gone . . . I fear we have lost the game, set and match, Wilson . . . and yet . . .' He frowned.

'And yet?'

'We are playing against a bold adversary. If his boldness turns to folly, and he tries another theft of Greek art, why, we will have him, Wilson – for now we know what we are looking for!'

'Goodnight, Holmes.'

'Goodnight.'

He opened the door and let me out of his bedroom.

I turned to him. 'Tell me, Holmes. What is this all about?'

He put his finger over his lips.

I went to bed. Perhaps I had eaten and drunk a bit too much at the club, for that night I dreamt of walking to Baker Street Station and although my watch said eight in the morning, the moon and stars were out. A pretty girl sold me a chocolate éclair. I tucked it into my pocket. People were coming out of the wrong tunnel so I knew I had taken a wrong turning, but I couldn't go back against the flow of the crowd. The narrow boat slid into the station and I was thrust aboard by the crowd. We cruised quite swiftly through tunnels with a curved ceiling of old stone, and I realized these were the sewers of Paris. A skinny old lady wearing a wig and a Greek fisherman's cap told me to get off at the next stop, which was Cité. I got off and was surprised that the walls were covered with graffiti, strange monsters – stranger than the fountain at Place St Michel – and words in Greek. I looked overhead and saw a real bat nearly as large as a man. He was hanging upside down, his feet tangled in an old electrical wire. He winked at me and opened and closed his jaws. A moment later I stepped out of the Earl's Court Underground station. Across the street, seven men in orange overalls stood by a tall iron fence, their backs to me. They were painting the fence black. One turned and pointed at me with his brush – his face was the face of Vladimir Cluj. I walked away quickly, not wanting to look like I was afraid . . . then I woke up.

# TWENTY
## The Daedalus Discs

Tuesday morning was gloomy. But in the afternoon the sky cleared and I met my fiancée on the tennis court and we played three good sets and then I returned to the flat in Dorset Square to change my clothes, intending to meet her for dinner. But as I opened the door – bursting with the happy news that I had won a set from Rachel, for once – I saw Lestrade and Lyme sitting with Holmes. Holmes gasped, and leapt from his chair. 'My heavens, they surely did not take all of them!'

'I am afraid they did,' said Lestrade. 'The Daedalus Discs are gone, together with the stone casket. The casket alone must have weighed a ton.'

'Be good enough to tell me the details, my dear Lestrade – omit nothing,' said Holmes.

'The Leeds Institute for Ancient Languages is open Tuesday to Friday,' said Lestrade. 'Sir Marbry locked up Friday evening and only discovered his loss this morning when he came to work. This means the discs were taken sometime between five o'clock Friday and eight o'clock this morning.'

'Three and a half days,' mused Holmes.

'The front door was demolished,' said Lestrade, 'but the thieves superficially repaired and painted it so the damage wasn't noticed till this morning when the clerk arrived to open up.'

'It was very well planned,' said Inspector Lyme.

'We believe we know how it was accomplished,' said Lestrade, 'for there were small tracks visible on the floor of the institute, and in the nearby canal we found a midget tractor with a front-end loader. It had been driven into the canal where it sank out of sight. A canal boat hit it, which is how it was discovered. The real mystery is how they disarmed the alarm system.'

'Only a few people knew about the discs,' mused Holmes. 'They were a closely guarded secret.'

'Not so closely as you thought,' said Lestrade.

'It seems impossible,' said Holmes, 'that four hundred and eight discs in a stone coffin could be carried on a tractor loader through the streets of Leeds without anyone noticing!'

'I'm afraid we have not yet found any witnesses,' said Lestrade. 'Yet the coffin and all the discs are vanished. That is all we can say for sure.'

Inspector Lyme looked earnestly at Holmes. 'You seem to know a great deal about these discs, Mr Holmes – how did you know there were four hundred and eight?'

'It was I who decoded them,' he replied.

For a moment Lestrade, Lyme and I were struck dumb, frozen in our chairs.

'Decoded, you say,' said Lestrade softly.

I had no idea whether Holmes was referring to something he'd done last month or in 1898. 'A little explanation would not go amiss, Holmes,' said I.

'I suppose it cannot hurt to tell you now,' said he, 'though I have been sworn to secrecy.' He walked to the fireplace, turned, faced us. Yet still he paused, as if deciding.

'It is a police matter now, Mr Holmes,' said Lyme.

'Quite so, quite so,' said Holmes. 'I must go back a little, to that memorable year two thousand and four, the year when both I and Daedalus of Athens were brought back to life – I having been dead for ninety years, he for three thousand five hundred; I having been found frozen intact in a glacier in Switzerland, and he – or at least his words – having been found pressed into clay discs in a coffin in Sicily.'

'Pardon me, sir,' said Lyme. 'Who is Daedalus?'

Holmes's jaw dropped an inch, and he seemed to reel as if stunned by a blow from behind. But he gallantly recovered himself, made a gracious gesture with his hand, as if to wipe away his startlement, and he said, 'I shall get to that momentarily, Inspector Lyme, never fear. At all events, a certain English gentleman of my recent acquaintance – an archaeologist specializing in Cretan culture – acquired the discs in a most curious manner. He has a Sicilian brother-in-law who one day phoned him from Agrigento to tell him that sewer workers, while digging a trench in the nearby little town of Sant'Angelo Muxaro, had unearthed a heavy block of stone that turned out to be not a block but a stone container that held many neatly stacked discs that were covered on both sides with markings that appeared to be writing. The discs in their lovely carved coffin subsequently appeared in England and were stored in a ground floor room of the Leeds Institute for Ancient Languages. I cannot say whether they were brought here legally, or not. I am a detective, not an international lawyer. But I suspect that their legal status, like that of the Elgin Marbles, could be a matter of debate . . . and *would* be a matter hotly debated if the Italian authorities knew of the existence of the discs.'

Lestrade had leaned back in his chair, and his eyebrows had taken on a curious arch. 'But how did you get involved, Holmes?'

'That is a mystery that has baffled me these last few years,' Holmes replied. 'One morning when I was recovering in St Bart's Hospital, after Dr Coleman's intricate manipulations of my cells, I received a letter. Its appearance surprised the nurse who delivered it, surprised Dr Coleman, surprised me. Who would be writing me a letter? Only the hospital staff knew of Dr Coleman's project, and only Dr Coleman and a very few of his associates knew my true identity. Yet here came a letter addressed to "S.H., aka Cedric Coombes". Nothing at all subtle about it. The letter was from Sir Marbry Nabs, director of the Leeds Institute for Ancient Languages. He said he had in hand a cryptology project that might interest me. He asked if he could visit me. Several days later he did visit, and he told me the story I have told you. I asked how he had heard my name, and he replied that a rival of his – a man who had wanted the discs badly enough to offer a huge sum for them – had, when he learned Nabs wouldn't sell, been gracious enough to give him the inside information that Sherlock Holmes was being resuscitated, and to suggest that I might be the man who could crack the code.

'I agreed to try. Sir Marbry soon supplied me with large photographs of each disc, and in my hospital room I set to work. He gave me two of the actual clay discs as samples to help me in my work. Each pottery disc was about a half-inch thick, surprisingly light, well fired, and had a hard reddish surface. Both sides of each disc were covered with symbols neatly aligned between straight rule-lines pressed into the clay. It took me but a week to realize, with astonishment, that this script appeared to be quite similar to Linear B, an early script associated with the island of Crete. In deciphering the script I have had the great advantage, unavailable to most scholars on errands like mine, of having a vast amount of related and clearly imprinted script to work from, nearly all of it relating to matters already well known through the writings of the ancients – namely, the story of Daedalus. I also had the advantage of knowing that Linear B was early Greek. This was shown in nineteen fifty-two when Michael Ventris, a British amateur, deciphered the Linear B script. I naturally began by assuming that what I might be looking at was an early form of Greek. When I realized, after several weeks of work, that I was reading the autobiography of Daedalus, the evidence in favour of this being a form of Greek was suddenly not merely probable, but overwhelming. Certain that Greek was the language before me, I pressed ahead and never looked back. I should add that the script of the Daedalus Discs is a greatly expanded and amplified version of Linear B. Linear B was used exclusively for matters of inventory and bookkeeping. It was, in effect, a script for business, not literature. And the autobiography of Daedalus is nothing if not literary, in the treatment of its subject matter, in its range of feeling and complexity of thought.'

'So you've translated the autobiography of Daedalus?' I said.

'No, I merely cracked the code, my dear Wilson! Someone else then took up the task of translating the whole work . . . I simply provided the key.'

'But there was no such person as Daedalus,' said Lestrade quietly. 'It was myth. That's what I learned in school.'

Holmes looked as if someone had slapped him. He lurched to his feet and became very animated, almost breathless. 'Before eighteen fifty, gentlemen, nearly everyone assumed that the tales told by the ancient poets were just that, tales. But then, in the last half of the nineteenth century, the great Schliemann came on the scene. This German son of a baker believed passionately in the truth of Homer, and he proved Homer's truth first by discovering Troy, then Mycenae. Today no scholar doubts that Homer's *Odyssey* and *Iliad* are, if not documentary history, at least based on historical events. Troy did exist, was besieged, was burnt, and Agamemnon did return to Mycenae on the Greek mainland, the city of much gold where Schliemann found not only the ancient palace but graves with bodies of kings whose faces were covered by gold masks. Most scholars now believe all this occurred in the thirteenth or fourteenth century BC.'

'But what has this to do with Daedalus?' asked Lyme.

'Ah,' said Holmes. 'Another old tale, frequently mentioned by ancient writers, was in many ways even more fantastical and implausible than the Homeric tale of a war between Greeks and Trojans. This one had to do with the island of Crete where the legendary King Minos ruled (according to Homer) in over ninety cities. Numerous poets and historians tell how Minos exacted tributes of live children from Athens, flung the children into a labyrinth where a bull-headed monster was imprisoned, and there made them serve the monster's pleasure. The labyrinth had been built for Minos by Daedalus, an Athenian artist, inventor and architect who seemed to be the Leonardo da Vinci of the Bronze Age, both in versatility and in genius. Daedalus had been exiled from Athens and spent many years in Crete where eventually he helped the Athenian hero Theseus enter the labyrinth to slay the Minotaur, and then Daedalus helped Theseus run off with the king's own daughter, Ariadne. The angry Minos imprisoned Daedalus and his son Icarus in the labyrinth, but Daedalus and Icarus escaped by flying off in contraptions of his own devising. This was the famous flight during which Icarus fell into the sea and drowned. But Daedalus flew on and escaped to Sicily. If anything seemed like fantasy, this tale did. Then, in nineteen eleven, Sir Arthur Evans began to dig in Crete. I remember reading about the dig in The Times – Watson pointed out the article to me at breakfast one morning. Anyway, Evans uncovered at Knossos a vast and labyrinthine palace. On its walls were painted many bulls, including scenes of athletes leaping into the air and doing somersaults over the backs of charging bulls. Again, archaeology began to confirm what poetry had long proclaimed. The Daedalus Discs are but another in a long series of archaeological discoveries tending to confirm what our folktales told us. And it is a tragic and terrible thing, gentlemen, if they are lost.'

'Did you read the whole story of this Daedalus, then?' asked Lyme.

'Parts only. Most intriguing. It is being translated by an American, a woman called Sabrina R. Brryms. I've read a few of her chapters – very fluently translated. The opening paragraph is quite good. Daedalus of Athens was a very modern man, though he lived in fifteen hundred BC, and she caught that modern note right at the outset. But there is something odd about the whole thing.'

'Odd?'

'Sabrina R. Brryms is an anagram of Sir Marbry Nabs.'

'Anagram?'

'Rearrange the letters and Sir Marbry Nabs can be turned into Sabrina R. Brryms, and also into other names. And I can't but wonder if one of those other names – to be found in those same letters – would reveal the identity of the true translator. But why should there be such a secret? I don't know.'

'To come back to the point,' said Lestrade, 'we may yet prevent this crime. The discs and some of the other booty may still be in the canal system, in the other half of the *Proteus*. Shouldn't be too hard to find. We know the length, probably the colour. We'll inspect every boat of that length in all directions from Leeds – west towards the Irish Sea and, what is much closer, east along the Aire and Calder Navigation towards the Humber, and Hull, and the North Sea.'

Holmes frowned. 'If the theft took place several days ago, the boat will likely be long gone into the North Sea. Yet already they have lingered in this country much longer than I should have imagined they would have dared. And if the theft was Sunday or Monday, then . . .'

'A huge storm has been raging up north since yesterday,' said Lestrade. 'The Humber is boiling with waves several feet high. The port is closed.'

At that instant the door chime reverberated. Holmes pushed the button without inquiring as to the visitor. A few moments later came a knock. I opened the door and was surprised as a redheaded man brushed swaggeringly by me with scarcely a glance in my direction, and said, 'So, Mr Holmes . . .'

I recognized him instantly as the angry Bob Tawp. He wore pale-blue jeans, a blue shirt, scuffed Clark's shoes. He had a shiny Bluetooth device in his ear peeking out from amidst his flaming and mussed red hair. 'Mr Holmes,' cried he, approaching the great detective boldly, raising his arm as if hailing a taxi in our sitting room. 'I have news.'

'I suspected you might,' said Holmes.

Bob Tawp, seeing the two detectives, laughed. 'Well, it looks like it's Old Home Week. How go the wars, Inspector?'

'Good afternoon, Bob,' said Lestrade. 'Haven't seen you in a while.'

'I'm not sorry for that,' said Bob.

'Staying out of trouble?' asked Lestrade.

'Not willingly,' said Bob, and he gave Lyme a sarcastic look. 'Who is this ramrod – have I seen you before?'

'I don't think so,' said Nigel Lyme.

Tawp shrugged. 'I have a message for you, Mr Holmes. It is from a gentleman of your acquaintance.' He took a piece of paper from his hip pocket and unfolded it, and handed it to Holmes.

'A Web address?' said Holmes.

'Click on it, Mr Holmes, and you will see the magic man.' Tawp tapped his Bluetooth. 'He talks to me like God.'

Holmes went to his desk in the corner of the room, sat down and typed in the address on his computer. Lestrade, Lyme and I gathered round, looking down over his shoulders. On the screen appeared a gentleman I instantly recognized. I had met him only months earlier, in a Scottish castle, in connection with Holmes's investigation of the missing Shakespeare letter – an investigation which (as I have chronicled in a volume called *Sherlock Holmes and the Shakespeare Letter*) nearly cost us both our lives. It was Lars Lindblad, the man who looked like anything but an international criminal. Lindblad, handsome and relaxed and genial, smiled at us. Lars Lindblad, international criminal, *bon vivant*, man of many parts, smiled at us as the camera moved in. 'Good afternoon, Mr Holmes, Mr Wilson. So good to talk to you again.'

Elegant, restrained, subtly flashy, he wore a royal-blue v-neck sweater with a tiny gold gull embroidered over the left breast, and beneath that a pink and blue striped shirt. His blond hair, streaked with grey, seemed to echo the tone of his grey corduroy trousers. 'Welcome to my Grotto of Art, gentlemen,' said he, and he strolled by a large statue of a beautiful woman, which I recognized as the Artemesium Aphrodite stolen in the London robbery. 'I thought you gentlemen might like to see a boat of my own design, which I hope you will find intriguing.'

Instantly a long black narrow boat appeared. It was moored by a canal bank. The camera moved in on the *Proteus*. A series of short images revealed the *Proteus* being hosed down, mopped (by hands with invisible owners). Its blackness drained away, and suddenly it was a long boat with a blue hull and yellow cabin. Next we saw disembodied hands removing sheet metal from the middle of the boat, hands pulling levers . . . whereupon the seventy-foot boat split into two boats that slowly floated away from each other. A close-up showed the word *Minos* on the one boat, and another close-up showed *Midas* on the other. The scene shifted. The *Minos* was moored at canal side. Along the towpath a man approached.

'Good heavens!' said Nigel Lyme, who was standing beside me.

It was none other than Nigel Lyme strolling along that towpath. From the camera angle, it appeared that the videographer was in another boat, one perhaps moored ahead of the *Minos* by the bank. An old woman appeared on the front deck of the *Minos*. She invited Nigel Lyme to come aboard for breakfast. Her voice was soft. 'You look weary, officer – would you like some tea. We have a pot just fresh.'

Nigel Lyme refused the old lady's offer, shook his head. He smiled, he gestured grandly, impatiently, and he said sternly but politely, 'Thank you, madam.' And he passed briskly on down the canal, along the towpath.

Whereupon the old woman took off her wig and waved at the camera, and straightened up into . . . Lars Lindblad.

On the screen was Lindblad again, in his Grotto of Art.

'So much for the investigative powers of the Metropolitan Police,' said he, shrugging, gesturing as though he'd just emptied a teacup on the ground. 'Had Lyme come aboard he would have found a rather handsome statue filling the interior of that boat – this one, in fact.' He walked back and pointed to the Aphrodite, and stood by her, admiring her. Then, strolling as he talked, he passed a Greek head that blurred by in the foreground as the camera panned, perhaps the one taken in the second robbery, at Hemel Hempstead. 'You may wonder, my dear Holmes – I love that quaint phrase! – I say, you may wonder, *my dear Holmes*, how I whisked these glorious Greek works to my Grotto of Art. Let me show you how.'

The scene now shifted to the choppy grey open water of the sea. The *Minos* appeared, strange outriggers extended to keep her stable in the heavy seas, another of Lindblad's engineering designs. He seemed to have an obsession with *transformation*. Holmes, I realized, was appreciating the performance. There was a faint smile on his face. The *Minos* drew up to the black side of a ship – we did not get a good look at the ship. Disembodied hands wrapped the statue of the Artemesium Aphrodite with a net. The net jerked once, tightening, and then was lifted slowly upward from the removable roof of the *Minos* and out of the picture – presumably on to the ship.

Lindblad again, strolling. 'That ship you just saw, Mr Holmes, made her way into the North Sea where it rendezvoused with my seaplane, to which the statues were transferred. They were then flown here.' Lindblad smiled. The camera panned to follow him as he wandered behind some marble statues. He was speaking of the stone coffin and the Daedalus Discs, and of the marble panel with the frenzied maenad, and as he spoke of these treasures a blur of marble slid by the lens, the camera panning to stay on his casual figure as he strolled and talked; a very cinematographic effect. Lindblad did everything with style.

'Alas,' said Lindblad, 'we were forced to sink my little inventions in the North Sea.'

Here a brief video clip played, showing one of the blue and white boats tilting and going under the sea. And then we saw the other blue and yellow craft sliding out of sight into Poseidon's realm.

Lindblad appeared again, walking now by white walls hung with paintings, amongst which I recognized a Van Gogh stolen recently in France. Also a Matisse, likewise recently in the news as stolen. And what appeared to be a Picasso. Lindblad paused at a grand piano. He stood with his hand resting on the black edge, above the white keyboard. 'I confess, my dear Holmes, I had hoped to keep my own role in all these thefts secret. I fear it may be a while before I am able to plunder England again. I see your hand in the matter of identifying my brother-in-law, Conrad Duvall. He was sent along on the mission, as I'm sure you have guessed, to identify the art worth stealing, and to make certain that no mistakes were made. Unfortunately, the poor chap chose a very inopportune moment to drop dead. He has had heart problems for some years. You will be glad to know that we carried his head out of the country, along with the lovely Greek art we acquired, and we shall bury his head in an appropriate place, on a promontory overlooking the sea, as he would have wished. If he were able to poke his head out of the ground and look, he would see the same lovely seascape he has often painted. I'll show you the spot sometime, my dear Holmes, if ever you visit me, which I certainly hope you will. To have you as an antagonist is a joy beyond my wildest imaginings. Sometimes I imagine that the frivolous gods arranged for you to emerge from that glacier merely to give zest and energy to my flagging life. It would be like them, wouldn't it – the Greek gods, I mean. So childish they are! So full of energy. I tell you, Holmes, I have toyed with the police of forty countries for forty years. It was amusing for a long while, but the game has come to bore me. I'm sure you can understand. One needs a worthy opponent. I pin my hopes on you, Holmes, to challenge me a little. To help raise me to my best game. It will take a little time, obviously, for you to become acclimated to the twenty-first century, to become as effective in this age as you were in an earlier one. But, my dear Holmes, I am counting on you!'

He sat down at the grand piano, put his hands on the keys, paused. Then took his hands off the keys, laid them on his thighs, and looked at us. 'I know you are a connoisseur, Holmes, of music, of paintings, of scientific theories. You are much like me. I regard you, in fact – and I hope you don't take offence at this – I say, I regard you as my brother in crime. You inspire. To be pursued by Sherlock Holmes – what greater thrill for any criminal!

'You really must plan to visit my Grotto of Art someday soon, my friend. I am certain you would approve of my collection – apart, of course, from the fact that it is all stolen.'

Lindblad turned to the piano once more, and began to play the lovely second movement of Beethoven's *Pathétique* sonata. As he did so, these words appeared across the screen, in a handsome script:

> *With all best wishes I am, my dear Holmes,*
> *your brother in crime,*
> *Lars Lindblad*

And the last two words wrote themselves across the screen as a signature. And then the screen faded to black. And the music faded to silence.

'Well, that's it,' said Nigel Lyme. 'We've missed it.'

'Looks that way,' said Holmes.

'But how could I have known?' asked Lyme.

'Wait a minute!' cried Lestrade, looking about the room in startlement. 'What happened to Tawp?'

Holmes gestured towards the window.

We looked where Holmes pointed . . . there was Bob Tawp, just climbing on to his red bicycle by the high black iron fence encircling the gardens. He wobbled once, gathered speed, sped away, pedalling in the vigorous but awkward manner of a workman.

'It appears that the case of the stolen Greek statues is at an end,' said Holmes, briskly. 'And we have lost the game. But no use crying over spilled milk. If you gentlemen will excuse me, a man from Shropshire just arrived at Paddington and will be here in twenty minutes to consult with me. He just texted me.'

'Consult about what, Holmes?'

'He has a horse that his wife believes is haunted.'

'The mystery of the haunted horse,' I said.

Holmes bent over the fireplace wingtip chair, took a small object from the crack in its cushion, set the object on the hardwood floor. 'Here, now, careful Wilson, don't stand on that chair – what are you doing!' he cried. 'Have a care or you'll tip it over!'

'What!' I said. I feared his strange behaviour was returning.

Holmes stomped on the little object with his heel, smashing it.

'Now, Lestrade,' said Holmes, trembling with excitement, 'let us for once be quick and do the right thing. The first boat is gone, but the second is almost surely in the Humber, waiting out the storm so that its ancient cargo may be loaded on to a ship.'

'But you said it was gone – you *saw* it is gone!' said Nigel Lyme.

'Let us be quick, gentlemen,' cried Holmes. 'Time's a'flying and so, very soon, will be the Cycladic idol, the frenzied maenad and the Daedalus Discs. But at the moment they are still within our grasp, somewhere in the stormy waters of the Humber. There you will find a blue and yellow craft called the *Pasiphaë*. Detain it and you will have saved at least something from Lindblad's clutches.'

Holmes refused further explanation. He demanded immediate action. 'If the storm abates before your men find the *Pasiphaë*, the statues are lost!' he cried. 'It may already be too late.'

Lestrade and Lyme hurried away on their mission.

# TWENTY-ONE
## Frenzy on the High Sea

To: HellmeshCrooks@QuillNet.com, AfghanWilson@QuillNet.com
From: Lestrade@met.police.uk

Success, gentlemen. All turned out as Holmes predicted. Craft spotted making out from shore towards a ship in storm. I joined the police launch. A lurching voyage over big waves brought us near to wallowing *Pasiphaë*, but she rose out of swollen seas like a rocket, spinning spray like an angel. In prosaic terms, a hydrofoil. Your god friend, Proteus himself, could not have done better . . . or maybe he could have, for you told me he always escaped. *Pasiphaë* did not. Our helicopter soon brought the craft to bay. We boarded her, found stolen goods, arrested the two-man crew, both members of Lindblad's notorious Falköping Seven, his inner circle.

Daedalus Discs are intact. Ditto Cycladic statue and marble high relief of Miss Maenad.

I am off to Brighton for two days. I don't like Brighton but wife does. I think only because she likes Graham Greene. Nigel Lyme has handed in his resignation. Poor fellow takes life too seriously.

*Lestrade*

# TWENTY-TWO
## Monster Art

Sherlock Holmes sat imperturbably reading a book as the June night grew wilder. Rain was coming down in black sheets, battering our windows, seeming to explode with new force moment by moment. Horrific winged monsters peered out of a sheaf of ink drawings that lay fanned on the coffee table. I was about to ask Holmes if he wanted a cup of tea, when there came a knock at the door. I opened it to find Chief Detective Inspector Lestrade standing there in a dripping rain slicker. 'Good evening, Lestrade,' said I, and I helped him out of his slicker and hung it, dripping, on the coat tree. 'What brings you out in such a storm!'

Lestrade leaned forward from the ankles, stiffly, as he niftily tugged the front hems of his blue blazer, straightening it. 'Curiosity, Wilson.'

'Curiosity.'

'Yes, for some weeks I've patiently waited. I can stand it no longer.'

I ushered Lestrade into the room.

Holmes had vanished.

A giant bat stood by the storm-lashed windows, wings outspread, as if about to dive out into the storm. A flash of lightning lit him up.

Lestrade gave a start . . . shook his head. 'Really, Holmes – do act your age!'

Holmes whirled towards us, and the black coat lifted on air. 'I cannot act my age!' he cried, flourishing his right arm. 'To act like a pile of dust is beyond my thespian talents!' Here he swept off Cluj's coat and tossed it on to the sofa where it landed like a large dead crow. He motioned us towards chairs, rather grandly.

'You are the quirkiest man in England,' said Lestrade, and he sat down.

'I sometimes think so myself,' said Holmes.

Lestrade leaned, with a faintly astonished and horrified look of curiosity, and picked up several of the ink drawings, gingerly. 'What's this?'

'Young Jack Blankenship drew them,' said I. 'You remember Jack?'

'Certainly,' said Lestrade. 'Strange lad, wasn't he.'

'A bit – his father died last week, by the way.'

'Ah, sorry to hear it,' said Lestrade. 'His widow has her work ahead of her, poor lady – running that inn on her own.'

'Billy Baffin,' I said, 'has promised to help Mrs Blankenship manage the inn. Billy has sworn he will stay away from drink and "become respectable".'

'A strange turn of events,' said Lestrade.

'Holmes is helping young Jack get into art school here in London.'

'Is he!' said Lestrade.

'Holmes has enthusiastically taken the lad under his wing.'

Holmes laughed. 'Lad ought to go to art school, if that's what he fancies. I merely tried to direct him to the right people.'

'You also sat for him while he did your portrait,' said I. 'You are seldom so patient.'

'Patience is seldom a virtue,' said Holmes.

'You are a hard man, Holmes!' laughed Lestrade.

'I am beginning to think so myself,' said Holmes.

I walked over to the dining-room table and picked up the portrait that Jack had drawn of Holmes: Holmes stood by the fireplace with an aristocratic casualness, yet his gaze was electric with energy, as if he were about to dart off after a rabbit. 'If I write up this little Cluj and Cornwall adventure of ours,' I said, 'I may ask Jack Blankenship if he will do some ink drawings as illustrations.'

'I am sure he would be flattered,' said Holmes. 'But I wonder at the wisdom of your plan, dear Wilson. Dr Watson used illustrations, but in a different era. Nowadays illustrations seem out of fashion except in children's books.'

'I don't follow fashion, Holmes! I *set* fashion,' said I.

Lestrade laughed.

A new burst of thunder rattled the window, a rush of black rain hit the panes, and the lights dimmed momentarily. Sir Launcelot decided he'd had enough. He got up and hurried away to the bedroom – no doubt intending to seek silence under the bed, as he often did during storms.

'You chose a strange night for a visit, Lestrade,' mused Holmes.

'I can quell my curiosity no longer,' said Lestrade. 'I have waited long enough. Now you really must tell me.'

'Of course,' said Holmes. 'I am at your service.'

'How did you know that the second boat was not named *Midas* but *Pasiphaë*, was not black but blue and yellow with the name painted in black, and was in the Humber on its way to a stormy rendezvous? I confess, Holmes, everyone has been correct for a hundred and thirty years    you are brilliant.'

'Not terribly brilliant,' said Holmes. 'You forget that Lindblad has eluded me again. Not to put too fine a point on it . . . he has won again.'

'Just a minute!' said I. 'Not quite *won*.'

'Good of you to take that point of view,' said Holmes. 'But facts are facts.'

'Quite so, let us stick to the facts and take an accounting,' said I. 'It is true the *Minos* escaped you, and took with it the Artemisium Aphrodite, the head of Apollo, and the small Aphrodite stolen recently from Lincoln. That's three points for Lindblad. But saved were Branford's Cycladic statue, the high relief marble panel with the frenzied maenad, and – most important of all – the Daedalus Discs. That's three points for Holmes. The *Pasiphaë* was taken from Lindblad, so subtract a point from his total, and the final score is Holmes 3, Lindblad 2.'

'To return to the purpose of my visit on this rainy night,' said Lestrade, 'what I should like to know, if I may be privileged, are the simple deductions . . .'

'Yes, yes, of course,' said Holmes. 'My deductions were simplicity itself. But to explain fully I must go back a little, to the day that Bob Tawp first turned up here in this room. I knew immediately that he was lying to me, of course – that he wasn't sick with Parkinson's disease but was a schizophrenic, that he hadn't come from Ireland, that his name wasn't Barrymore, and so on. Naturally, I was disinclined to take the case of so blatant a liar. Yet I was curious what he was after. I was just pondering whether I ought to take the case in order to find out his true purposes, when I saw him put a bug in that easy chair by the fireplace.' Holmes pointed. 'This suggested that the whole so-called murder case in Ireland was bogus, that Tawp had come to me at least in part for the purpose of bugging my flat, and that he was working for someone – someone who was very likely controlling him by talking to him through the Bluetooth phone in his ear.

'What puzzled me most was the question of who would want to bug my flat. I decided to leave the bug in place, in hopes of finding out. There are many tricks a man may play on someone who is listening to his every word but does not know that his supposed victim *knows* he is being bugged. For instance, I might say I'm going out to such and such a place alone, then hide myself in a spot where I could watch the watcher who came to do to me whatever it was he intended to do. Or, I might speak as if I were leaving the flat, in order to give the listener opportunity to break in, if that is what he intended – and then not leave it at all. My plan was to play my eavesdropper like a trout, and see if I could land him.

'But then you turned up, Lestrade, and put me on to the case of the vanishing statues. Within two days I was out of this flat and living on the streets of London, and soon I was in Cornwall.'

'Maybe I *will* write up the Cornwall adventure,' I said. 'It has elements that will appeal to a wide public.'

'If you do,' said Holmes, 'kindly omit all your speculations about the supernatural – that's the sort of thing that really ought not be allowed into a record of reason, deduction, discipline, and all the higher mental powers of man.'

Lestrade laughed.

'Carry on, Holmes!' said I.

'On a Saturday, Lestrade, you sent me a picture of the *Proteus*. It struck me then that perhaps Lars Lindblad was the one who had bugged this flat. So in this flat I offered one speculation as to how the *Proteus* would change. In the pub, where I insisted on meeting you, I gave my true theory, that the long black boat might have been transformed into two boats of another colour.'

'So that,' I said, 'was why you were acting so strangely, and saying such contradictory things. I'm relieved.'

'You thought I was having a relapse?' mused Holmes.

'I feared it,' I admitted.

'Back in our flat I then said, as I had earlier said in the flat, that you, Lestrade, would block the canal at the Crick Tunnel with a sunken boat, and also at the Torksey Lock with a closure for engineering works – and that we would then investigate every boat between those two points. I hoped this ploy would send at least one of the boats scurrying towards the sea – and so it did.

'The rest is simple enough. On Tuesday you came and told me of the theft of the Daedalus Discs. By then Lindblad had already for several days had his first boat back in . . . back in Sweden or wherever he is. But the storm had prevented him taking off the other boat, so he put together a video to deceive us. And he sent Bob Tawp to make sure we watched it.

'The video was artfully but not flawlessly done. We were shown a clip of the *Minos* drawing close to the sea-going vessel, and being unloaded, but we never really saw the *Midas*. We were shown a picture of the *Minos* being scuttled, and the name was plain on the hull as she went down, and then Lindblad announced that the *Midas* was being pictured sinking . . . but it was the same clip, with the letters $n$

and *o* in *Minos* blurred electronically so that they might have been *d* and *a*. What we really saw was two views of the same boat going down. And it struck me as very clever to claim the second boat was the *Midas*, but not very convincing. What did the king of Phrygia have to do with the King of Crete? Nothing. They lived in different times. The only connection was the similarity of the names. It seemed to me that the second boat would likely be named after Minos's wife, Pasiphaë.

'As Lindblad strolled about his Grotto of Art we saw plainly enough the Artemisium Aphrodite taken from Chelsea, and the head of Apollo taken from Hemel Hempstead, and the small Aphrodite taken from Lincoln the other day. But we never saw the Cycladic statue taken from Cheddington, nor the marble panel with the frenzied maenad taken from Nottingham, nor the casket containing the Daedalus Discs. Lindblad *spoke* of these works, and as he spoke certain blurry marble images glided by the camera lens, but all we could see were blurs that might have been any pieces of marble. Lindblad strove to give us the impression we had just seen something we had not seen.

'All this led me to believe that while the *Minos* and its cargo were gone, the other craft, carrying the Cycladic statue and the frenzied maenad and the Daedalus Discs, was still in the Humber, trapped by the storm. When I told you the game was over and that we had lost, that was solely for the benefit of Lindblad, who was surely listening to us on the bug. I then pretended Wilson was clumsily knocking over the chair, whereupon I stomped on the electronic device.'

'Ah,' murmured Lestrade. 'And then we were free to make our plans.'

'Quite so,' said Holmes. 'To make our plans without alerting Lindblad – who doubtless would have moved the stuff off the boat if he had guessed we were continuing the search.'

'One other thing, Holmes – the colour of the boats. How did you know they were blue and yellow.'

Holmes shrugged. 'An artful guess, Lestrade. We knew the *Proteus* was covered with a chemical mixture of blacking that would easily wash off. We knew also that the name *Proteus* was written in blue. It seemed logical that the blue name was made of the colour beneath, so that when the blacking was washed off the name would disappear. Likewise, it seemed likely that the blacking obscured the painted black name of the new boat. It was the way I would have done it, that is all. Wash off the blacking and the name in blue would vanish into the general blue beneath, while the painted black names *Minos* and *Pasiphaë*, obscured at first by the blacking, now would appear. Quite simple. And if the hull was blue, would not a Swede paint the rest of his boat yellow?'

'Well, the storm has abated,' said Lestrade, rising from his chair. 'I'd best be going. Ah, little fellow, here's one more,' and he leant to give Sir Launcelot (who was gently touching his leg) a special treat.

Holmes darted from his chair and grabbed the black Cluj coat, and he handed it to Lestrade. 'Take this along, Lestrade. Perhaps you can put it in the Scotland Yard Museum of Crime, if there is such a thing.'

Lestrade laughed. 'The police have no use for it, Holmes.'

'Do take it away anyway, Lestrade – give it to charity. It oppresses me.'

'Why, Holmes,' said I, 'surely you haven't become superstitious in your old age!'

'That coat has the reek of death about it,' said Holmes, frowning. 'I can almost imagine it is a coat from Hell.'

I was astounded. I said, 'I can't believe my ears, Holmes! To hear you talk that way . . . the man who not a month ago was lecturing me on the silliness of people who see the world in terms of evil spirits, goblins, devils and so forth.'

'Take it away, Lestrade!' cried Holmes, shuddering and waving an arm. 'Leave it on a park bench. I have a terrible premonition that it may at any moment burst into flame.'

Lestrade took the coat, shaking his head. 'I can't imagine what has come over you, my good fellow, but—'

'Look out, Lestrade!' I cried.

Smoke had begun leaking from the pocket of the coat.

In an instant the whole side of the garment was flaring with flames.

Lestrade had the presence of mind to fling the coat into the fireplace, where it began to burn rosily.

'I don't suppose,' said Lestrade, 'you want to give us an explanation for that little episode, Holmes?' Lestrade shook his head in disgust, brushed himself off, straightened his blazer. He took his slicker from off the coat rack.

'A little proof that ancient technology and ancient talent, whether that of Daedalus or that of Professor Quigley Philpot-Smalls, is not to be despised by later ages,' said Holmes.

'We are hardly the despising sorts,' said Lestrade.

'Of course not,' said Holmes. 'And now, gentlemen, since I have been deprived of my cocaine by Scotland Yard, and deprived of my tobacco by Dr Coleman, little is left but liquor, food and music. I am feeling in an expansive mood! I will pay! Shall we step out and have a drink and a bite at the Criterion Bar? Afterward, if we are lucky, we may acquire tickets for a symphony concert at South Bank – better still, let us find a jazz club to while away the evening.'

'I am pleasantly surprised at your broad tastes in music, Holmes!' said Lestrade.

'I missed the Jazz Age. I am trying to catch up.'

I looked at Lestrade. 'I missed the Jazz Age too, come to think.'

'Me too,' said Lestrade.

'Then it's agreed,' said Holmes, and he grabbed his raincoat.